The DIRTY Divorce 2

A NOVEL BY
MISS KP

Life Changing Books in conjunction with Power Play Media
Published by Life Changing Books
P.O. Box 423 Brandywine, MD 20613

Library of Congress Cataloging-in-Publication Data;

www.lifechangingbooks.net
13 Digit: 978-1934230770
10 Digit: 1-934230774

Dedication

To my mother, Ms. Lita Gray. Thanks for raising me to be an independent strong woman. I appreciate you.

Acknowledgements

This has been quite a journey and truly a blessing. I would like to first thank God for giving me the opportunity to live out my dream to be a writer. To my daughter, Kameron, I'm proud to have you as my child and I love you dearly. To my best friend Rodney (Lil Rodney and Jordyn), thanks for your patience during this process. I love you for that and much more. Many thanks again to my mother, Lita Gray (EB). I love and appreciate you for the person that you've raised me to be. Much love to my father, Willis Poole. To my sister, Mia (Brent & Sydni), this year has been challenging and your support has been a blessing. Many thanks to my sister and brother Jawaun, and Cornell (Javone). Family means everything to me and I'm thankful to have you in my life. Ivornette, Lafondra, Tonya, Dione, Tiesha, and Tori love you guys!

To my extended family Arnita (Kevin), Big Rodney (Darlene), Eve, and Jaron, thanks for accepting me with open arms. Much love to the West clan- Delonte, Dmitri (Christine), Danielle, Aunt Delphine, Ava, Lil Wayne, Lil Alton (Candace), and Alan (Tia).

Friends come and go, but the real one's stay true. Many thanks my true friends that are always there through it all without passing judgment and being real- Toya, Toni, Pam, Samantha, Shana, Peta Gaye, Endiah, Tiffany, Tanya, and Jermaine. John "Whitey" thanks for believing in me. Frank, my Godbrother Detrick (Renee & Jalyn), Dab, and Mike Walker thanks for being a friend. To my Mt. Pleasant family- Julette, Pam, Rayshawn, Janell, Shelvy, Snookie, Deon, Mimi, Tarik, Kenyatta, Bernard, Donnie, Farad, Perry, Berry, and Jodie. Danielle and Lonnie thanks for your support. Carla (CCB) your mentorship has truly been a blessing. Karla P., Caroline, Carla L., Deb, Stephany P. and Stephanie C. Thanks for believing in me. Mr. Abdullah, thank you for your support through some difficult times in my life.

To Leslie Allen, the best editor in the world and Tressa Smallwood, the best publisher ever. Thanks for your support and believing in me. I appreciate you both so much. Much love to Tasha and Kellie.

To my LCB crew, Tonya Ridley (Money Maker), Jackie D. (Love Heist), VegasClarke (Snitch), J. Tremble (My Man Her Son), Danette Majette (Good Girl Gone Bad). C.J. Hudson (Chedda Boyz), Capone (Marked), Tiphani Montgomery (The Mistress Series...oh, congrats on the baby), and anyone else I missed...it feels good to be on a great team. Thanks to my test readers, Cheryl, Tonya, and Aschandria.

Many thanks to my readers and all of the bookstores who have supported The Dirty Divorce Part 1. Thank you in advance for your support going forward. Quita and Shawn (Literary Joint) thanks for making my first book signing a huge success. Sistas in Sync and Books and Babes book clubs, thanks for inviting me to the book club meetings. I enjoyed you guys.

I apologize in advance to anyone that I may have forgotten. I'm thanking you now. Who would've thought, two books in a matter of one year... now that's God's work. Thanks again to my readers. Your postive feedback was inspiring.

Much luv and hugz!
Miss KP

www.misskp.com
www.twitter.com/misskpdc
www.facebook.com/misskpdc

Chapter One
LISA

"Oh my God!" I screamed while squeezing my son Juan's hand…nails and all.

My contractions were less than two minutes apart and I knew that my baby would be coming any minute. I wasn't even eight months yet but obviously my baby boy could no longer wait. I tried so hard to leave the drugs alone, but I guess that last line put me straight into early labor. Continuous nightmares of Carlos' death kept me awake almost every night, so my occasional sniffs here and there had obviously taken it's toll on my unborn seed.

"Please give me something. This shit hurts!" I yelled.

"Sorry, Mrs. Sanchez, it's too late for an epidural. You're already ten centimeters. We don't even have time to take you to a normal delivery room. You're gonna need to be strong. The worst of it is almost over," the emergency room doctor informed me. I could barely understand what he was saying through his thick Arabian accent.

"Yes, please try and calm down. You're gonna need your energy to push," the nurse added.

"Fuck calming down. You come do this shit since you think it's so easy," I shot back as another contraction quickly approached.

The nurse and I had been on bad terms since I arrived

twenty-five minutes ago. I snapped on her each time she asked me one of those dumb-ass hospital questions. I then became furious once the questions turned to my prenatal care. Her interrogation was irritating, especially when she gave me a, *I think you're lying* look. It was almost as if she could read my mind…like she was calling me out on all my bullshit.

A single tear ran down my left cheek as I thought about what I'd put my baby through over these past few months. Monthly doctor visits had become nonexistent and I couldn't even remember the last time I took a prenatal vitamin or ate something healthy. I hadn't even had a sonogram. Even though I loved my baby, I guess the fact that I still hadn't gotten over Carlos' death had clouded my judgment. Now, God was punishing me. I guess I deserved it.

"Okay, here's another one. Juan, I need you to hold your mom's leg all the way back, come on push Lisa!" the nurse ordered.

"Bitch I am pushing, aighhhh. This shit hurts!" I cried.

"Ma, come on! Push 2-3-4-5-6-7-8-9-10!" Juan yelled, while struggling to hold his phone.

"Put that fucking phone down. Who are you trying to call?" I screamed. Seeing how calm he was, it looked as if he'd been through this shit before.

"The baby's head is almost crowning. Only a couple more pushes. You can do it," the doctor said with assurance as he studied the monitor for another contraction.

I was glad his ass was confident because it felt like I was going to die. Never did I recall labor being this brutal. With Juan it also didn't go this fast. I must've gone from zero to ten centimeters in less than an hour. It felt as if I was being punished by the Creator himself. The feeling of sharp pins and needles rushed through my stomach and extreme pressure lived between my legs. For some reason, I felt like the baby was determined to rip my insides apart. I just wanted it all to be over. I would've given anything to stop the excruciating pain.

I looked over at Juan. "Please help me."

"Come on, Ma, focus," Juan replied.

"Okay, here's another contraction, come on push, Lisa. Let's go 4-5-6-7-8-9-10," the doctor coached.

Holding my breath, I began to push with all my strength until my vagina started burning. "Aighhhh it hurts!"

"Mrs. Sanchez, don't stop pushing. Every time you stop, the baby goes back into the birth canal," the doctor informed.

"Get it out!" I screamed.

I started to sweat profusely as my body shook uncontrollably. "Can you just cut it out? It hurts so bad, please can you put something in my I.V? Juan make them help me!" I begged.

"Mrs. Sanchez, your baby's heart rate is starting to decline. We need you to deliver ASAP. To give you anything at this point can put the baby at even more risk. We have to deliver with as few complications as possible," the doctor informed.

"Okay, here's another one. Let's make this one count Lisa. This is it. Push!" the nurse yelled.

The nurse was right. I wanted my baby to be okay, so I had to make this last push count. Not to mention, no matter what, I couldn't lose the only thing I had left of Carlos. Right before holding my breath again, I said a quick prayer to myself. *"Father God in the name of Jesus, I come to you with a humble heart. I promise you if my baby survives this, I will be the best mother I can be. I promise to leave the drugs alone, God, just please let my baby be okay. Oh, and please God let it be a boy too. In your name I pray…Aighhhhhh!"*

It felt as if I was pushing him through a ring of fire. "Oh, my God!" I yelled one final time before the doctor finally pulled him out. The instant relief of pain consumed my entire body as I tried to control my rapid breathing. Watching the doctor suction out his nose and mouth, I placed my hand over my chest waiting for him to tell me the big news. He had a head full of hair, just like Carlos.

"It's a girl!" the doctor announced as he cut the umbilical cord.

I immediately freaked out. Not only because *he* was a

she, but also because there was no cry. Even when the doctor handed her off to the nurse, she still didn't make a sound.

"Why isn't my baby crying, what's wrong with my baby?" I yelled. Finally after a few seconds, I heard a slight whimper. "What's wrong with her?" I asked again. "Is she okay?"

The nurse never said a word as she quickly cleaned her off and whisked her out of the room. Even Juan looked concerned as he stared at the closing door.

"Where did she take my baby? I need to see her. Juan did you get to see her? Who does she look like?"

"Ma, everything happened so fast I don't know," Juan replied.

"Mrs. Sanchez, your baby doesn't appear to be breathing very well, so the nurse is gonna take her to the Neonatal Intensive Care Unit or better known as the NICU. Don't worry, everything will be fine," the doctor tried to convince.

"What do you mean don't worry? I'm her mother. I'm supposed to worry!" I looked at Juan. "Go see if you can find out what's going on. I need to know!"

After placing his phone in his pocket, Juan kissed my forehead, and rushed out of the room. As the doctor began to deliver the placenta, all I could do was think about my newborn child. Okay, maybe my priorities were a little fucked up, but I really needed my baby to give me that piece of Carlos that I'd been missing. Just to hold her for one minute would help soothe the emptiness and pain I'd been feeling for the past seven months. Even though I wanted to have his first boy, at least now I had his baby girl. I had something to hold on to.

I knew I had turned into a person that my son was no longer proud of, but I also knew that I needed this baby to get my life back on track. Flashing back just a few hours when my labor began, I was in my bedroom trying to escape my problems. Snorting the last line, I promised myself that this was it. It was the last time that I'd planned to indulge in the poison. As I laid back on the bed, sudden sharp suddenly pains came over me followed by a flush of water between my legs. Juan's facial expression was priceless once he ran into my room and took a glimpse at the tray of powder that fell to the floor. Taking his focus off the obvious, Juan wasted no time getting me to the hospital and even held my hand the entire ride in the car. Not only did his words of encouragement keep me calm, but he saved my daughter's life. For that...I had to return to the old Lisa.

After the doctor informed me that I didn't have to be stitched up and left the room, I took a glance by the door as an image of Carlos appeared. Either I was tripping or his spirit entered the room to assure me that our baby girl would be okay. Then it dawned on me, I had the perfect name. In honor of Carlos, I would name her Carlie. A combination of Carlos and me, that's exactly what she was. Saying another prayer to myself, I asked God for forgiveness and prayed that despite the drug usage, my daughter would have a clean bill of health. Just as I was about to burst into tears, the nurse I didn't care for entered the room.

"Mrs. Sanchez, we're ready to move you to your room now."

"How's my baby?" When the nurse didn't answer, my heart rate immediately started to increase. "How's my baby?" I repeated.

"Please lower your voice."

"Then answer me."

"Your daughter suffered some trauma during labor and we want to get you in a more comfortable environment to ask you some further questions. We need you to help us evaluate the situation."

"When can I see her?"

"We need to keep her under observation for a few hours, but I don't see why we can't take you to meet her some time later today."

"Later today. No, I need to see her now!" I demanded.

"Well, Mrs. Sanchez that's not going to happen. Your

daughter is in a critical stage and we're trying to stabilize her. Nurse Thomas will be coming to transport you to your room in a few minutes."

"Whatever," I mumbled as she walked out. Moments later, Juan came back and I let him know that they were moving me to my room. Looking at my son, I could see disappointment and fear in his eyes.

"Juan, what's wrong? Did you get a chance to see her?"

"No, they wouldn't let me."

"So, where have you been?" I asked with a huge frown.

"I stepped outside to make some calls."

"Hold up. You didn't call your father, did you?"

"No. I had to take care of some business."

"Are you lying to me, Juan?"

Juan shook his head. "Ma, you need to focus on your baby and your health. I'm good."

I knew my son. When he snapped at me that normally meant something was wrong. "Are you mad at me?"

"Just disappointed. I thought after all that happened with Denie, you had changed your ways. It just hurts, that's all. I just want my little sister to be okay."

"You saved her life, thank you Juan. I know I owe you."

Juan placed his hand on my shoulder. "You don't owe me anything but to get your life back on track. I mean, I just don't know who you are anymore. What you did to Denie was enough, but come on, using while you're pregnant. That shit is just foul. You're letting Rich win. When you're reckless it just gives him one up over you. I just…"

"Juan, I'm sorry. I'm really sorry, okay. I just miss Carlos so much. I just needed to get my mind off of things to keep my sanity. I just lost focus. Now that I have Carlie…"

"Who?" Juan asked with a confused expression.

"Carlie. That's her name. Do you like it? It's my name and Carlos' put together."

"You betta hope Uncle Renzo and Marisol don't figure it out."

"Fuck Marisol. Besides, I think Uncle Renzo would be happy that I named my daughter in honor of Carlos."

"Yeah, okay. If you say so."

When Nurse Thomas finally came to take me to my room, I was relieved. Juan was my heart, but I was ready for the lecturing to end. Little did he know, he didn't have to preach to me anymore because I'd learned my lesson. I was determined to be the mother I used to be. After I got settled, Juan left and said he would check in with me later. As soon as I closed my eyes to get some much needed rest, the Arabian doctor and another woman entered my room and woke me up.

"Mrs. Sanchez, I'm sorry to wake you, but I have Ms. Gray, a social worker here at the hospital with me. We both have some questions for you."

"Social worker?" I finally looked at the name on his lab coat that read, Dr. Ahmed Saleem. "Look, Dr. Saleem I know I'm going through a divorce, but I don't need a social worker, I'm not on welfare. Y'all think because my daughter's father wasn't here that I need a social worker. Is that what y'all think about all black people?" I snapped.

Dr. Saleem looked concerned. "Mrs. Sanchez, your daughter had traces of heroin in her system. We need to try and get you the help you need so that..."

"I don't need any help from you people!" I quickly interrupted.

"Your daughter needs your help," the social worker chimed in. "Look, I'm not here to lecture you. I'm here to be a voice for your child. She needs..."

"I don't need you to tell me what my daughter needs. You don't have to worry about me or her. We'll be fine! Now, when can I see her?"

"I'll check with the doctors in the NICU to see if she's stable," Dr. Saleem answered.

"And I'll be in touch before you leave. I know you've been through a lot today, so I'll give you some time with your new baby girl," Ms. Gray followed up. "Oh, and congratulations."

"Thanks," I responded dryly.

I wanted to tell them both to get the fuck out. They didn't know the mother I used to be. I knew I could be her again. Carlos lived in Carlie, and now since we shared a child together, it gave me more power to be the mother to her that she needed. As I finally drifted off to sleep, I thought about when Rich found out that he and Carlos were brothers; a conclusion that explained their similarities in looks. Uncle Renzo was treacherous for keeping such a deep secret. I wondered if Carlos would've known they were brothers, if that would've changed anything between us. Maybe it worked in my favor that they thought they were cousins. Carlos' face became etched in my mind as I slipped into a deep sleep. I was in the middle of dreaming about us making love in a bed of beautiful red roses when I was awakened by Nurse Thomas tapping my arm.

I gave her the look of death. "This better be good."

"One of the doctors in the NICU just informed me that it's okay for you to go see your daughter. Would you like to go now?"

"Of course," I said, quickly getting a ball of energy.

After obtaining a wheelchair, Nurse Thomas helped me into the seat then quickly escorted me to the Intensive Care Unit. From there, I was handed off to a NICU nurse. As soon as I washed my hands then entered the dim and quiet specialized unit, it immediately made me depressed. Seeing all the sick babies; some inside incubators some hooked up to several monitors and ventilators brought tears to my eyes. I cursed myself for putting my baby girl through so much stress already.

"Here she is," the nurse informed me. "I can tell she's gonna be a little fighter. She's already showing signs of trying to breathe on her own."

"Is she gonna be okay?" It was hard to see her in the incubator.

"It's a little too early to tell. Plus preemies have good days and bad, but I have high hopes. The emergency room doctor said that he thinks you may have been about twenty-nine or thirty weeks along, so she definitely has some work ahead of her."

I covered my mouth with my hands as tears consumed my face.

"Don't worry. Like I said, she's gonna be a feisty little thing. Oh, by the way I'm Nurse Brooks. I'll be one of your daughter's nurses while she's here."

I looked at the thin black woman who had big eyes and a pointy nose like the *Girlfriends* actress, Tracee Ellis Ross. "Can I hold her?"

"No, it's a little too soon for that, but you can touch her," Nurse Brooks informed as she opened one of the little round doors to the incubator. "I'll leave you two alone. Let me know if you need anything," Nurse Brooks said as she pushed me closer then walked away.

I smiled at my new bundle of joy. I couldn't wait to get a closer view. I wondered if she had both me and Carlos' complexion. The anticipation of who she looked liked was killing me as I inched my face closer to the glass.

"Hi Carlie, are you going to wake up for mommy," I whispered, before gently touching her little arm.

After a few strokes, my daughter finally opened her eyes. They were too familiar, light brown, with a tiny mole under her left eye. She was the spitting image of Rich.

Chapter Two
RICH

"Hold up…so you're leaving and that nightstand is empty," Shelly snapped.

"Bitch, I've given you enough fuckin' bread in the past to get free pussy for years. You aight," I answered then pulled up my jeans.

"Muthafucka, I got bills. It's the first and my mortgage gotta be paid. You know the drill. Now, you gonna make me treat you like the rest of these niggas and make sure I get my money first before you get some."

"I ain't good for some free shit as much as I looked out for your ass? Your damn son is in private school because of me, so don't get cute."

"Nigga, I'm not trying to hear that shit. Pay me my money," Shelly said, with her hands on her wide hips.

I shook my head. "All you whores are the same. When a nigga down y'all still wanna have y'all hand out. Well, you takin' one for the homies, cuz I ain't givin' your ungrateful ass shit."

"Rich, you're a petty muthfucka. You could at least give me some money to pay my babysitter!" Shelly yelled as the hotel door slammed.

"The bitch better be lucky I fed her ass," I said lookin' at the room service tray outside the door. "Plus, we at the damn Westin." As light as my money had been lately, she was lucky I ain't take her to the Days Inn. "Damn, where's Honey when you need her. She never complained," I said, walkin' down the hall.

As bad as I missed fuckin' Honey's grade-A pussy, I couldn't trick her out of some sex like I could with Shelly. I had been fuckin' Honey for so long, I knew she counted on my money to make ends meet, so hookin' up wit' her wasn't in the plans. Besides, my dollars were valuable, so payin' for pussy wasn't an option right now.

Since Carlos got killed, I'd been avoidin' Uncle Renzo for the last couple of months which had definitely put a damper on my bread. I wasn't used to watchin' my money and budgetin', but the situation wit' my daughter Denie and my soon to be ex-wife Lisa had cost me some major cash. Every time I think back to the day my relationship wit' my daughter went downhill because of that bitch Lisa; the shit made me hate her more and more every day.

That bitch had actually made me shoot my own fuckin' daughter in the stomach, tryin' to fight her for the gun. I called myself tryin' to save her from Lisa's deranged-ass, and ended up makin' matters worse. I couldn't believe my son Juan didn't even bother to help, but I could remember like it was yesterday when the smirk on that nigga's face turned to fear when he saw his sister get shot instead of me. His reason for not helpin', I'm sure was so Lisa could finally get her revenge, but I bet he didn't realize his sister would be the one hurt in the process. Reflectin' back to that day made my fuckin' blood boil. Hatin' Lisa for makin' me kill my brother, Carlos was no comparison to how I felt about that miserable bitch now. She knew that hurtin' Denie would break me, and I couldn't believe she'd stooped to such a low.

Once the hotel valet pulled my car up and I drove off, thoughts of the drama I went through when Denie got shot continued to flood my mind. Then there was my cash flow problem. The moment Denie was shot, I immediately called up a doctor I used to deal wit', named Toyia, who worked at Washington Hospital Center's trauma unit. Not only did she rush to my side because of the dick I used to put on her, but also because she was forever grateful to me for keepin' her house out of foreclosure when her husband's gamblin' caused them some major debt.

Of course, Toyia came through. She took a leave of absence from her job which cost me $100,000 for her to care for Denie around the clock for three months. I also ended up movin' Denie back in wit' me at my mother's house, which allowed Toyia to nurse Denie back to health. Words couldn't even describe how happy I was that she was able to save my baby. I was devastated to find out that not only did my daughter suffer from a shattered pelvic bone and damage to her kidney, she also lost a life in the process. My daughter was pregnant. Not only did I nearly kill my daughter, but killed my grandchild, too. My relationship wit' Denie was already broken because I forbid her to see Nelson, but all of the recent events made things even worse. In the past I could buy her a new car, a new bag or some shoes and she would forgive me, but this was the first time that my money couldn't get me out of the deep hole Lisa had dug for me.

Every day I catered to Denie, tryin' to make up for all the pain that I'd caused her. It took months for her to regain her strength and heal, but no matter how much she'd healed on the outside, I knew it would possibly take a lifetime for her to forgive me. I even allowed her to see Nelson, thinkin' that would make her at least talk to me, but nothin' would break her silent treatment. That was the only time I heard her speak, when Nelson was around. Even though I used to love him like a son, when I learned he was fuckin' my daughter, that love turned to hate. However, I had to put all those ill feelings to the side. I owed them both since I was responsible for the loss of their child.

As I drove toward my house, I started thinkin' about the big fight we'd had the day before. I didn't even know how to deal wit' the situation as I played back the conversation in my mind.

"Why, Daddy, why?" Denie asked as she rocked in my mother's old chair.

The sad thing about it was, I'd hurt my baby girl so much, I didn't know where to begin. I didn't know how to give her answers.

"Huh?" was all that I could say.

"Why did you lie to me all these years about my mother?"

"Denie, I was tryin' to protect you. I'm not perfect. I've made plenty of mistakes in my life."

"That's an understatement."

"But to be honest, I'm not sure who your mother is. I mean I have an idea, but…"

"So you slept with that many women unprotected that you have no idea who my mother is?"

"Denie, when you were left at my door you were only a couple of weeks old. The doorbell rang and when Lisa went to answer it, there you were, with a note attached. Eventually, Lisa promised to forgive me for cheatin' and promised to raise you as her own. Deep down inside she was so mad at…"

"Fuck Lisa, and fuck you, too! That bitch always hated me. Look at what she did to me. I'm scarred for life because of her. But you know what, I should blame you for how fucked up she is. Is my birthday really November 29th? Do you even really know how old I am? My brother always warned me on how fucked up you were, but I never listened. No, my daddy could never do any wrong."

"Denie, what do you want from me? Baby, I'm sorry. You're all I lived for; you're the only thing that matters to me."

"Why, cuz you broke? Your money was all you cared about, and now that's damn near gone. Oh, so now that Lisa's deranged-ass is done with you, I'm a priority. That's bullshit!"

"Broke! Is that what you think? If I was broke there was no way I could've had a nursin' staff care for you around the clock. That was a $100,000 note right there. I'll show you broke!"

My daughter had hit a nerve and I was pissed. I remember runnin' down the stairs, and out the back door to the shed. After movin' several things around, I pulled out most of my stash. I never wanted my daughter to lose faith in me. Never would I be broke, I vowed to myself a long time ago. I raced back up the stairs wit' the gardenin' bag full of money and threw it across the bed.

"Broke is that bitch-ass nigga, Nelson, you love…not me."

The money obviously didn't faze her. "Now you wanna hate on the man that loved me, when you didn't!"

"You think he's so perfect. I watched that man fuck whores Denie. That's why I didn't want you to be wit' him. He lives the same life that I do. I always wanted you to have a better life. Am I wrong for wantin' better for my little girl? Damn, Denie!"

Not even wantin' a response and desperately needin' air, I left. Just like that. That's how I ended up spendin' the night wit' that trick, Shelly. As I got closer to home, I snapped out of my deep thoughts and questioned what I could say to Denie to repair what we had left. I wondered if I would've stayed and talked things out, maybe she would begin to forgive me, or even see where I was comin' from. Wit' my life in such turmoil, I needed my daughter now more than ever.

I pulled into the driveway, and got out my truck in slow motion. Practicin' what I was goin' to say, I finally got the courage to face my daughter. When I opened the door and the ADT alarm didn't go off, I got a little worried.

"Denie!" I called, but got no response.

Wit' all my family had experienced, I drew my .45 and slowly walked through my house to see what was up. After checkin' downstairs, I walked up the steps and checked every room, which were all clear. My heart dropped to my stomach right before I got to Denie's room. The last thing I wanted was her to be hurt…again. However, when I kicked the door open there was no one there. No Denie, no clothes, just a neatly made bed with a note.

Dear Daddy,

I need some time away from everything including you. Don't try and contact me I'll be okay. There are a lot of unanswered questions that no one can seem to help me with, so I'll just disappear. That way your big mistake (me) who ruined your marriage can vanish into thin air. Just act like I was never left on your door step. I don't have any identity here. I'll start a new life for myself, without you and anything associated with you. When you start feeling sorry for yourself and wondering what you're gonna do without your baby girl, remember... I'm no longer your baby girl. Go take care of your other daughter, you know the one you had with that whore Trixie. Maybe you can be a better father to her. I'm out! Wish me luck and thanks for the cash! That's the least you can do!

Denie (if that's even my birth name)

P.S. Oh, and tell your wife, Lisa that I'll never forget what she did to me. I owe her one because it's definitely not over.

What the fuck is goin' on, was all I could think to myself as I took a pillow from Denie's bed and threw it across the room. All that I had left, the only thing that mattered to me in this world was gone and there was nothin' I could do about it. I sat on the edge of the bed and held the letter as my eyes watered. I had to keep talkin' to myself. "Real men don't cry," I kept reiteratin'.

"Maybe I should've stayed and talked to her," I told myself as my phone started to ring. It was Juan.

"Yeah."

"I just called to tell you Ma had the baby."

"So. Why are you callin' me? Fuck Lisa and that bastard-ass baby. My daughter is gone thanks to that bitch. Fuck her!"

"What you mean Denie's gone?" Juan asked wit' concern.

"She left and obviously took my fuckin' stash wit' her!"

"Aight, well I just called to let you know wassup, but I guess you got your hands full, holla."

CLICK.

"Fuck!" I yelled before fallin' back onto the bed.

I was pissed. Denie had taken damn near all the money I had left and I didn't know what to do. I'd been chillin' from the streets lately wit' all the chaos goin' on wit' Uncle Renzo, so I needed every bit of cash I could get. Denie was my heart, but she'd crossed the line fuckin' wit my bread. She was definitely on my shit list!

Chapter Three
JUAN

Ever since I was sixteen years old, I longed for this moment of being my own man. Not having to ride on the coat tails of Rich. No more people saying, "*Oh, that's Rich's boy. He good peeps.*" No more of that shit. I hadn't heard that in months, which felt good. I had finally made a way for myself. Gaining respect on the streets on my own meant a lot to me, and there was nothing anyone was going to do to take that away. In jail, I'd met a lot of connects, but I just wasn't that trusting of people. So badly, I wanted to be done with dealing heroin since I witnessed firsthand what it had done to my mother. I had a plan. I was gonna make it outta this game untouched.

No matter what she'd done and who she'd become, I loved the woman who raised me; the woman that she was, before the drugs, before the rape, before Rich destroyed her innocence. I loved that woman, and I was determined to get her through these hard times. I was determined to get her back to the old Lisa. I loved my mother to death, but lately she had been getting on my nerves. She and her drama always put me behind schedule, so I texted my man to let him know I'd be about twenty minutes late. Ever since my little sister was born last week, my mother had been calling me every five minutes like I was her baby's father. Damn, didn't she know there was a reason why I didn't have any kids?

As I made my way down South Dakota Avenue, and

jumped onto Route 50, my phone rang. Looking at the caller ID, I had no idea who it was.

"Yeah, who's this?"

"Wassup my nigga, this Cornell. You trying to go to Lux tonight?"

"Damn, what you got another new number?" I asked.

"Yeah, man this chick I was hittin' from Detroit keep hackin' into my phone, even my damn Twitter account. Yo' she started trippin' when I told her I wasn't tryin' to put a ring on her finger. Man I'm tired of these bitches thinkin' they gonna get saved," Cornell replied.

"Is this the one you met when you played with the Pistons?"

"Yeah, she was cool at first, but when I got traded to the Wizards last season, I didn't talk to her as much and so we kinda fell off. Man, I'm just tryin' to play ball and make some money. All that other shit is irrelevant."

"I feel you man. I don't have as much paper as you, and these bitches even get on my nerves," I said with a huge grin. "Well, I gotta make a run. Lux sounds good. I'll meet you at the club about 12:30. I'll text Brittney and let her know we coming through so she can grab us a table."

"Bet."

Cornell Willis was my man. He played basketball for the Wizards and was probably one of the few dudes I hung out with who wasn't wrapped up in the street life. We met last year at a club's valet when we both pulled up at the same time with the same color SL. I had just gotten mine and couldn't wait to pull up in it and have the girls sweating my new ride. Wondering who the nigga was, we exchanged looks until we got to the front door of the club…both wanting tables, of course. When we were told there was only one left, I lost it on the promoters, who ended up giving me a couple of bottles of Ace of Spade if I was willing to share a table with the nigga. I was a little hesitant at first because I didn't usually fuck with corny-ass athletes, but he ended up being cool as shit.

It was history from there. He ended up giving me my money back for the table at the end of the night and even picked up the bill. I was never a nigga who accepted handouts from dudes, but since I gave him one of my girls for the night, he was appreciative. He was a real nigga, with swag, like me. We started hanging out from that day forward. In and out of town, we did it big. Finally, it felt good to have someone in my circle that wasn't a fucking leach. He had a legit bankroll; something I would get one day.

Breaking out of my deep thought, I concentrated back on the task at hand, and that was getting my paper straight in the DMV area before I took my venture to ATL. My man, Kwame that I were going to meet tonight since he'd been talking non-stop about some dude named Malik from Atlanta. He was supposed to be this paid nigga down there and by the way Kwame was sweating him, I couldn't wait to see what he was all about. With us expanding in DC by the day, adding down south to our roster, would be the come up I needed. Kwame needed me and my paper, in order to make this major deal happen. Originally, I was supposed to meet Malik at a strip club on New York Avenue, but with our Virginia partners needing to re-up, I didn't want to discuss business in front of him. That first date would just have to be on hold.

Fifteen minutes later, I pulled in the parking lot of a pool hall in Landover. One thing I hated about going there was the smoke. I hated cigarettes with a passion. As soon as I walked in, the smell of old tobacco instantly hit me in the face. Trying my best to ignore the stench, I walked past several flat screens with preseason basketball games on, and headed to the back. The one thing about the hall I did like was the fact that it wasn't a hot spot for a younger crowd, making it a real low key place to handle business. When I spotted my crew across the room, I made my way toward them, ready to handle my business.

"Look at Pretty Boy Rico Suave, always late. You gotta make a grand entrance huh?" Kwame joked.

They always teased me calling me a pretty boy, or some

type of Spanish joke. Not just because my father was half Columbian, but because of how I looked. Everyone always thought I was Dominican because of my hazelnut complexion and curly hair, but as soon as I opened my mouth to talk, they knew I was black. No accents here.

Looking around the table, my Virginia partners as well as the rest of my crew were already there. Instantly, I was pissed off because I noticed an unfamiliar face sitting beside Kwame. I figured it had to be Malik. It was clear that Kwame had disregarded my orders.

"Who's the new face at the table, Kwame?" I asked sarcastically.

"Oh, this my man from ATL, Malik. You know…the one I was telling you about."

"Wassup my man. Listen, can we talk to you once we conduct business with our partners here? Kwame can hit your phone to let you know when we're done," I stated.

"Oh alright that's cool," Malik replied with a smirk.

As soon as he walked away, I continued with our meeting never missing a beat. I could tell Kwame was mad as hell, but I didn't give a fuck. That's what he got for not listening.

"Wassup my niggas, y'all ready to make some more cash?" I inquired.

"Hell yeah," Kwame's twin brother, Kyle answered.

He was a rookie, but loyal, so he was a part of our team. Kwame had been locked up a couple of times when we were juveniles so their mom tried to shelter Kyle as much as possible. However, when he saw the money that was coming in, he was determined to get in on a piece of the action. My crew consisted of Kyle, Kwame, Man-Man, and Willie.

We vowed that we were married to the game and our motto was and always would be *money over bitches*. Growing up together, they all looked up to me, which was a gift and a curse sometimes since that caused a rift between me and Kwame. He hated me being the leader of the pack. I always had the baddest chicks, the hottest cars, freshest gear and no matter how much he tried to be in competition with me, he could never fuck with my swag. That was the one advantage of being Rich's son. The disadvantage…the fact that I now hated him for what my mother had become. But it was cool. What I had planned for Rich was surely going to be the ultimate pay back.

Kwame tried his best to act as if he was equal rank, but he knew that I fed him. It was because of me that his family ate. Our Virginia partners trusted our crew because of my name alone. The respect on the streets was because of me and I called the shots. I let him show his muscle a little bit, but then shut him down the moment a decision had to be made. For example, the dudes from VA were trying to get us to go in with them on a new venture they had taken on in North Carolina. However, I quickly turned them down. I appreciated them trying to look out, but it was best if we kept the same territories with them for a while. They still needed us to supply them so either way, I was getting paid.

Once the meeting was over, I let Kwame know Malik could come back over. With irritation, Kwame shook his head before walking over to his man, who sat at the bar with a beer. Within minutes, we were face to face.

"Malik, I apologize about what just happened, but I just don't like to mix different crews and make others feel uncomfortable," I said.

Malik gave me a pound. "It's all good. So, what's up? Is DC ready to merge with ATL and get paid?"

"Well, I'm always game to get more money. Kwame has been speakin' highly about you since y'all been hanging out. He told me you're doing major things down in Atlanta."

"He good people," Kwame butted in.

Malik nodded. "Yeah, I hear the same thing about you, Juan. Kwame told me you might wanna move down south soon, so he thought we all could put our paper together and make some major moves."

"Sounds good. Maybe me and Kwame could fly down and see what's good," I responded.

"Let me know when you trying to come down so we can meet up and talk business," Malik added.

After listening to Malik and Kwame tell us stories about all the fine bitches in Atlanta along with everything else except getting paid, I knew it was time for me to go. If Malik was the foot in the door I needed to make shit happen in ATL, then I would definitely use him. I had a drink with the crew, talked shit for a few more minutes then finally rolled out to go meet Cornell at the club.

● ● ● ● ● ● ● ● ● ● ● ● ● ●

It took me no time to get downtown. With money on my mind, it was time to celebrate what was soon to come. I was ready for a night full of hot chicks, good music, and popping bottles. It was time to spend some doe and fuck some hoes. New York Avenue was jammed pack. Some football players were hosting the party. The Redskins played the Cowboys and won so it was crazy tonight! After hitting a couple of back streets, I made it to the front of the club's valet. The Ethiopian valet dudes knew that I left hefty tips, so they rushed to park my car.

"Yadi, wassup my man. You gonna keep me out front right?" I questioned.

"Yeah, Juan I gotcha."

I made my way to the front right side where the private entrance for the VIP was. As usual, the regular line to get in was wrapped around the corner. For late October, it was kinda cold outside so it was crazy to see the half-dressed girls freezing their asses off. A couple of them that I slutted on some late nights from time to time, tried calling my name asking if I could get them in. That only meant they would be at my table sucking down my liquor all night. I wanted some new shit tonight so I acted as if I didn't hear them and kept walking. After giving a couple of pounds to the promoters and owners of the club, my waitress ushered me up to my table. I knew Cornell was already there since it was going on one o'clock. I couldn't help but smile as we made our way through all the groupie bitches who were trying to get through the ropes to get a quick come up for the night.

"Wassup my nigga!" Cornell yelled over Young Jeezy's song, *Lose My Mind*.

"Yo, who are these fine females you got with you tonight?" I asked, looking around at the fresh meat. Cornell always had bad bitches around him. That was the norm.

"You know how we do it! It ain't no fun if the homies can't have none!"

We both started laughing. It was on.

I likem' long hair, thick red-bone, open up her legs to filet mignon... Lil' Wayne blazed through the speakers. As I pumped my fist to the music, one of the girls came up on me and started dancing.

"That's how you like it. Long hair, thick red bone, huh? Well, baby this all me, no weave," she proudly stated.

She swung her long streaked blonde curly hair around and started grinding on me like she was determined to give me a shot of ass tonight. "My name is Cherry, and yes I'm real, real sweet," she whispered in my ear.

After she was done flirting, Cherry and her homegirl put on a performance, grinding and kissing all over each other. They were both fine as hell, so I knew it was going down at Four Seasons in Georgetown tonight. After giving Cherry enough conversation for me to get her and her girl to leave with me for the night, a familiar face caught my eye from across the room. It was my ex-girlfriend Ciara.

We'd broken up over a year ago and she was to blame for my distrust in women. After having a baby with another nigga, I never put my trust in another broad. She was with a couple of her girlfriends in general population. When she was with me she stayed in VIP, now I guess she had to party with the regulars. When we finally made eye contact, that was my cue to make her jealous.

I grabbed Cherry, then told her and her girl it was time to

bounce. After I hit Cornell off with some money, I let him know I would be at his game tomorrow, before me and the girls rolled out. As we made our way through the crowd, all of a sudden I felt a cold drink splash in my face. It burned the shit out of my eyes.

"Fuck you, Juan!" Ciara screamed.

Before I could even respond, security was carrying her ass out. I'd never been the type to hit women, but shit might've been different this time if I had the opportunity to get at her. I decided to let it go as me and my jump offs made our way to valet. My car was right out front, and since I was driving my two-seater SL, Cherry jumped in with me and her friend followed us to Georgetown. My cell phone rang as soon as I started the car. It was Ciara.

"What, bitch?"

"How can you do that in front of my friends? You know…"

"After what you just did…fuck you and your friends. Man, I'm busy. Lose my number!"

After I pulled off, Cherry gave me a puzzled expression. "Look, I'm a pretty girl. I don't fight over niggas, so if you got drama I can just…"

"Listen, that's my ex which means she don't have any type of say so in what I do. I'm trying to fuck you and yo' homegirl tonight. I'm not thinking about that bitch."

"That's all I needed to hear! Trust me, you're gonna love this good pussy." Cherry reached in her bag and pulled out a blue X pill. "This is all I need to fuck your brains out tonight."

Any girl I ever fucked while they were on Ecstasy always gave me a good night of pleasure, so my dick instantly got hard. Before we even made it off of New York Avenue, Cherry had already unzipped my jeans and pulled my dick out of my boxer shorts. As she massaged my tool, a smile suddenly appeared on her face.

"Damn Juan, you got a big dick! As pretty as you are, I would've never thought."

"I bet you can't fit it in your mouth," I bragged.

"Wanna bet. I'm the best fuck in DC. Watch my work."

At that moment, Cherry put all nine ½ inches of my dick in her mouth. She was definitely a pro, which made it easy for me to bust all in her mouth.

"Damn, girl!"

"Told you," she said as she swallowed all of my babies and licked her lips. The whore was definitely talented.

After we got the room, me and the girls went straight upstairs and had a night of fucking pleasure. When they started off eating each other, Cherry's instant aggressiveness turned me on.

"Lay back, bitch," she demanded to her friend as she lifted her dress and exposed her clean shaven pussy.

Cherry used her tongue piercing to make the girl squirm as she quickly flicked it across her clit. I loved to watch two bitches fuck. The shit was like a work of art. As my dick began to throb, Cherry made her friend cum until she cried. I'd experienced plenty of threesomes in my day, but had never seen a girl get turned out like that. After admiring Cherry's skills, it was my turn. Taking off my clothes, I quickly slid a condom over my dick before laying back on the bed. Getting either one of these sluts pregnant was definitely out of the question.

"Damn, are you really gonna make me suck your dick with a condom?" Cherry asked as she got on her knees.

"No disrespect, but I'm trying to stay clean. You got me once in the car, and I normally don't fuck around like that."

"Why? It's not like I got something. What the hell can I give you by sucking your dick?"

"Man, just give me some head and stop talking so much." I didn't give a shit if she got upset.

"Yes, sir," Cherry complied as she put my tool in her mouth.

While Cherry worked her magic, her friend came from underneath and started sucking my balls.

"Damn baby, what's your name?" I asked.

"Kita," the girl answered in between her wet slurps.

Like Cherry, she was also damn good at what she did. "I like your style," I said with a silly smirk.

After licking my balls, Kita was ready to return favors to Cherry. Positioning herself directly behind Cherry's ass, Kita began to spread her cheeks then moved directly toward her pussy. Listening to Cherry moan turned me on. Even Kita made me want to fuck her just from the way she had Cherry going. I eventually pulled away from Cherry once her concentration turned from me to Kita. As I went to put on another Magnum, I watched Cherry turn on her back so she could give Kita a better angle. Moments later, they both started pleasuring each other as if it was some type of competition of who could make who cum first. It was funny to see them both so competitive. I laughed to myself as I wondered who would have the best pussy sucking skills. As I stared at Kita's big round ass, I was determined to get inside of her.

As soon as I got the condom on, I went straight to Kita. She instantly let out a loud moan as I stroked in and out of her tight hole. I could tell Cherry was getting jealous because she immediately stopped focusing on Kita and put my balls in her mouth.

"Damn Juan, when are you gonna fuck me?" Cherry said in between licks.

Before I could answer, Kita started yelling so loud, I'm sure the people in the next room heard her. That's all it took before I took the condom off and came all on Kita's back. Even though I was out of it, Cherry was determined for me to fuck her. I never had an issue with getting my dick hard especially while looking at her extra large Double D's swinging in my face. Cherry got right back on my lap after I put another condom on and rode my dick like a cowboy from Texas. I had to admit, her pussy was the best I'd had in a long time. Not to mention, her head game was on point. I had fun with Kita, but Cherry was definitely the main course of the evening. After several rounds of sex and several nuts later, I passed out with thoughts of hitting them both off with a stack for their services.

However, Cherry was definitely gonna be on speed dial when I needed a convenient freak.

Chapter Four
LISA

"Come on Carlie…that's a good girl," I whispered to my baby girl as I nursed her.

It was a blessing that after all the trauma and emotional stress I'd gone through over the past couple of weeks, that I was still able to produce milk. I made a promise to God that I would stay clean if he saved my daughter. And I was determined to do just that. When she was born she only weighed three pounds, four ounces, and had only put on nine ounces in the past month. I continued to pump until I was able to nurse her, and today was special because it was the first day that she actually was able to latch on.

Looking at Carlie and her features made me think of Denie, especially with her deep dimples and light cinnamon complexion. Now, I knew my plan had to work to pass off Carlie as Rich's child because she really looked like him. Since Uncle Renzo had revealed Carlos and Rich were brothers, I see why my daughter favored them both. As I nursed my princess and enjoyed the moment of being a mother again, my cell phone began to vibrate in my purse. Knowing I couldn't answer since the private room I was in was so close to the NICU, I ignored the call until it continued to vibrate.

"Whoever this is, is ruining my moment," I said to myself as Carlie stopped sucking. Thinking she might be done, I put her over my shoulder then proceeded to softly pat her back until I heard a small burp. "Awww, that's a good girl," I said in my best baby voice. "That's mommy's girl."

When my phone started vibrating again, I sighed then placed Carlie back in my arms. Watching out for a nurse, I quickly grabbed my phone then placed it up to my ear. "Hello," I whispered.

"Bitch, what type of games are you playin'? My lawyer just called and told me that you're filin' for child support for that lil' crack baby you got over at the hospital!" Rich yelled.

NICU or not, there was no way I was gonna let him talk to me like that. "Rich, fuck you. She's not a crack baby. I don't smoke crack, asshole. If you don't want me to let Renzo know about what you did, it might be in your best interest to go along with the plan. Carlie is your daughter if anyone asks," I replied with a devious smirk.

"Fuck that! You're the reason why Denie disappeared and you want me to help you take care of a child that's not mine. You trippin'. You fucked my brother bitch, then got him killed. You fuckin' tramp!"

"Well, I raised your daughter that you had on me muthaucka! What's the difference?"

"The difference is you tryin' to fuck wit' my bread, and wit' all the cruddy shit you've done, you don't deserve a dime."

"With all the shit you put me through you owe me your life. Now, if you want to enjoy the few miserable years you have left on this earth, you'll play by my rules, or I'll see to it that Renzo puts you in the bottom of the Atlantic Ocean. Or would you rather be where Carlos is?"

I could tell that last comment stung because Rich was quiet for several seconds.

"Who the fuck do you think you are? That blow got your mind trippin' if you think I'm payin' you child support."

"Try me, Rich. I'm through with being your wife. I can't wait until I'm rid of your ass. See you in court, asshole."

"I don't want your washed up junkie-ass anyway, you

fuckin' whore!"

"Once my lawyer is done with you, Rich Sanchez you'll be my whore. We'll see who ends up on top in the end."

CLICK.

Carlie must've sensed I was upset because as soon as I hung up, she started to cry. The last thing I wanted was for her to be upset, so I rocked my baby to calm her down.

"It's okay, sweetie. Rich took your daddy away from us, but we'll get him back right through his pockets. No one will stop me from making sure you have the world. That's the only way your father would've wanted things to be for his princess."

Just when Carlie drifted off to sleep, there was a knock on the door.

"Yeah, come in," I said, thinking it was probably Nurse Brooks.

However, when Ms. Stupid Ass social worker walked in wanting to talk, I instantly regretted allowing her access. I'd been avoiding her for weeks because I didn't want anyone to try and take my daughter away from me. The promise I made to God still stood strong. I didn't want anything to do with heroin, and I meant every word. My daughter's life was almost sacrificed because of my negligence, and I was determined to live for Carlos through our daughter.

"Well hello, Mrs. Sanchez. I've been trying to get in touch with you for almost a month now. Did you get any of my messages?"

"No I didn't. Why are you here?" I asked with a serious attitude.

"It's protocol that we try and get you help to fight your addiction so that you're able to be 100% for your daughter. I just need to ask you a few questions to evaluate your situation."

"Addiction? The only thing I'm addicted to is shopping."

"Mrs. Sanchez, denial isn't going to help you. Trust me. I'm on your side, but I need to make sure that your daughter is not at risk."

"What do you mean my daughter is at risk?"

"Do you know how many times I've seen babies die from negligence?" the social worker questioned.

"Look, I'm not going to neglect my daughter. Here my daughter is fighting for her life and your unsympathetic-ass waltzed in here approaching me like I'm some kind of strung out crack head!"

"Calm down, Mrs. Sanchez."

"No, I'm not going to calm down. Maybe once you leave then I can."

"How long have you been using?" she asked with a straight face.

This bitch just will not leave, I thought. "Using? I don't have a habit. You're not gonna take my daughter away from me!"

At that moment, something snapped inside of me. I got up and ran in the bathroom with Carlie in my arms and locked the door. There was no way I was going to allow anyone to take all that I had left of Carlos away from me.

"Just leave me and my daughter alone!" I yelled.

"Mrs. Sanchez, please you can't avoid the situation. I'm here to help you, now open the door," the social worker pleaded.

"No!" As I shook uncontrollably, Carlie began to cry. "Leave us alone, you're upsetting my daughter."

"It's not sanitary for her to be in there Mrs. Sanchez. Her immune system can't fight off the bacteria!"

"Just leave us alone! You're not taking my baby. She's all I have left of him. She's all I have left!"

Tears streamed down my face as I held my daughter close to me. I quickly sat down on the floor with my back against the door. A few minutes later, I could hear the social worker talking and a familiar sounding voice talking.

"You need to talk to your friend. Can you let her know that I'm leaving, but I'll be back. My card is on the chair."

"Okay, I'll talk to her," the voice responded.

I could hear heels coming closer to the door and then there was a knock.

"Lisa, are you alright in there?"

"Go away!"

"Come on. I didn't fly all this way to get the cold shoulder."

When I finally opened the door, Marisol stood there with gift bags and a ton of, "It's a Girl" balloons. *What the fuck is this bitch doing here*, I thought.

Chapter Five
LISA

I was instantly appalled. Since Marisol was no longer my friend, I didn't give a fuck about her anymore. Now, I basically viewed her as just Carlos' wife…nothing more. *How dare this bitch come up in here uninvited*, I asked myself. *Prancing her ass in here with gifts for my baby like this is a shower.* Little did she know we had much more in common than she knew about. Little did she know that her kids had just inherited a baby sister. We both loved Carlos, but at least I was the last person he'd made love to before he passed away. He died in my arms and here she was, still in limbo wondering where he was.

I had to admit though, the bitch looked good in her Tom Ford sunglasses, fitted True Religion jumpsuit and knee high Chanel boots. She seemed to be back on her game even though I've could've sworn the last time we talked she told me that she'd lost twenty-five pounds. Looking down at my frumpy, Adidas track jacket and old Seven jeans, I was a tad bit jealous, especially since I still hadn't dropped the baby weight. I couldn't wait to get back to my old self again.

"Hey girl. Why are you giving these nurses a hard time? Let me see that baby girl," Marisol said with a huge grin.

As I walked out of the bathroom, I looked around the room to make sure the social worker wasn't trying to trick me.

'That bitch wasn't a nurse," I replied. Picking up the social worker's card, I ripped it up then threw the tiny pieces of paper in the air. "What do you want, Marisol?"

"Damn…it's like that. I came to see what made you have another baby by Rich's crazy-ass? Let me see my little cousin. Can I hold her?"

"Umm no, I need to put her to sleep. She's had a rough day. How did you know that I was here?" I asked sitting back down.

"Well, if it wasn't for your husband, I wouldn't have known anything since you don't return my calls anymore."

"Correction…ex- husband."

"What is going on with y'all? You both seem so bitter. I mean I've known you guys forever and I've never seen you both like this," Marisol said, sitting the gift and balloons on the table.

"What did he tell you?"

"He pretty much said that you had a baby and he wasn't sure if it was his, which I knew was a lie. You've never cheated on Rich in your life."

Don't be so sure about that, I thought as she continued to talk.

"He can kiss my ass with that dumb shit though because that little girl looks just like him. What's her name?"

"Carlie," I said with pride.

"Cute. Anyway, he went on to say how much he hated you and how you'd gotten wrapped up with some dude who had you addicted to blow," she carried on in a sarcastic tone.

"He said what? He's just looking for a way to weasel his way out of his responsibilities since I don't want his ass anymore. Fuck Rich!"

"Well, I'm not here to talk about him. I came to talk to you. You know I fuck with the powder from time to time, but damn Lisa. You can't let it consume you."

She'd definitely hit a nerve. "Look, don't come in here judging me, especially if you're listening to Rich's sorry-ass. Have I ever judged you? Did I ever come to you and say you need to stop getting high when you and Carlos would be fucked up and I would be watching your kids. I was always your friend. And while we're on that subject…how you treated me at my mother-in-law's funeral was unforgiveable."

"So, you're still mad at me about Rich fucking with my friend Jade?"

"Not mad, but disappointed. There's a difference!" I yelled. When Carlie started to stretch, I told myself to calm back down.

"Lisa really, are you serious? I told you I had nothing to do with that. They were sneaking behind me and Los' back. We had no clue for a while. They're both grown. They did this, not me and Los."

"I could never be mad at Carlos for your actions so stop saying *me and Lo*s," I imitated.

"Lisa, I love you. We go back too far for us not to be a part of each other's lives. I need your friendship as much as you need mine, so let's just start over and be there for each other." Marisol reached over and hugged me.

To get her to shut the fuck up and leave, I agreed to reconcile with her. After Marisol shed a few tears and I rolled my eyes in my head, she initiated another conversation that irritated my nerves even more than the first one.

"Lisa, I miss my husband so much. To go through my daughter fighting Leukemia without him was traumatic. My father-in-law is doing all he can to get to the bottom of Carlos' disappearance. I swear to you Lisa, when I find out who did this to me and my family I'm gonna make sure they die of a slow, miserable death. I'll make sure that their family suffers, too. They will feel the wrath of a fucking wife scorned."

The more Marisol talked, I felt like I wanted to throw up. It was only a matter of time before Uncle Renzo found out that Rich killed Carlos because of our affair. It played in my head over and over that Renzo was doing all he could to get to the bottom of this ordeal. The Columbians just weren't to be fucked with. I'd heard several stories from Rich about things that Uncle Renzo had done to people who crossed him. The one that stuck out in my mind the most was when Renzo abducted this guy who stole from him and mailed his fingers back to his wife before they killed him. As Marisol went on and on about how Renzo would kill whoever fucked with his family, I knew she meant it and I was scared shitless because I knew she meant every word. The last thing I needed right now was to be on his bad side.

As Marisol spoke, I envied her as I looked at her long blonde streaked hair. *What made Carlos love her so much*, I thought to myself? Grabbing my own chin length locks that had grown since the rape incident, I began to think. *Was it that she was Puerto Rican*? I mean she lived in his home, drove his cars, and here I was depending on my son to take care of me since my ex-husband wasn't giving me shit. Suddenly, when Marisol started giving Rich praise, that shit snapped me out of my deep thought.

"Girl, I don't know what I would've done without Rich's support throughout these months since Carlos has been gone."

"What?" I asked, annoyed as ever.

"Rich has been amazing. I mean…he hasn't had that much money, but he's given me whatever he could. More importantly, his gave me his shoulder to cry on. He's definitely been there for me. I mean the girls just love him."

"So, you mean to tell me, I've been depending on my son to help me make ends meet and this bastard has been playing house with you making sure y'all good. Are you serious?"

"Lisa, calm down. He hasn't given that much. Besides, my daughter is sick. She's on borrowed time," Marisol replied.

"So is my daughter! You know what, I need you to leave. Get out now!"

As much as I tried to hold back the tears, they still managed to make a grand appearance. My tears were mainly about missing Carlos though…not about Rich's no-good ass. Marisol tried to reach out and hold me, but I pushed her away. After telling her to get out several more times, she finally left. There was no way I could take being in her presence another moment.

As she walked out, Nurse Brooks walked in.

"Are you okay, Mrs. Sanchez?" she asked.

"Please call me Lisa."

"We heard you yelling."

"I'm sorry about that. I'm just stressed right now," I said, holding Carlie's hand.

"Well, Lisa, do you mind if I pray with you."

"No, not at all. I could use a good prayer."

Nurse Brooks was like a God sent angel. She must've known I was going through something. As she laid her hands on me, she gave me an instant reminder of my father. I missed him and really needed his presence right now, but my pride wouldn't allow me to call.

"Father God in the name of Jesus, we ask you to watch over this mother and her new bundle of joy. You know her trials and tribulations and I just come to You with this family and ask You to lay Your hands on them, Father. Give this mother the strength to overcome any harm that comes her way. We pray that this baby will get the energy to gain the weight that she needs and grow to be a healthy girl. We come to you Father because we know You heal and that's what we're asking you, God to heal us and to help us live in your light. We thank you God for your blessings, and Jesus name we pray, Amen."

I cried as Nurse Brooks held me as if I were her own child. It felt like I was at home with my dad. It was obvious that he'd never stop praying for me because it felt as if she'd been sent to watch over us.

"Do you feel better now?"

"Actually I do. Nurse Brooks, I just want you to know that I'm not an addict. I just made some bad choices from going through so much in my life. I vowed not to ever use again and I'm living for me and my daughter. She means the world to me."

"Ms. Lisa, I believe you. I'll talk to your social worker and let her know that you're capable of handling your baby."

"Really? Thank you so much." I stared at my beautiful

baby girl. "When do you think she'll be able to go home?"

"Well, you know it's all about weight gain now since she can finally breathe on her own. Did she nurse well?"

"Yes, she did pretty good for her first time."

"See, Carlie is a fighter. At the rate she's going, I'm sure it'll only be a couple of weeks before she's able to go home. Now, it's time for me to take her back. I hope you had a good visit."

"You made it that way. Thanks again."

Before Nurse Brooks took Carlie back, I gave her a kiss on her forehead and told her I loved her. All of a sudden, I felt a little better. As I walked down the hallway, I peered into the window of the NICU and watched as Nurse Brooks played with Carlie. She was my guardian angel that I needed in the storm I was going through. However, I knew it was only a matter of time before the light at the end of the tunnel would soon come. I would get my time to shine with Carlos looking down on me.

Chapter Six
RICH

This fuckin' day couldn't come fast enough. Today, I would finally be free of Lisa Renee Sanchez's deranged-ass. I knew I'd put her through years of hurt, but nothin' compared to her makin' me lose my daughter's trust and killin' my brother. Her ass was lucky to still be alive. There were many days I'd planned out her death in my head, but just couldn't make myself do it for some reason. As long as she stayed the fuck away from me…I guess I could deal wit' the fact that she was still breathin'. However, I still told myself the next time that bitch got out of pocket, her fuckin' luck was gonna run out.

It was hard gettin' out of bed, but there was no way I was gonna miss this important day. It's crazy how once upon a time I would've moved the earth for her ass. She was the center of my universe, but now I felt like she was just weight on my back. My hate had overpowered any love I ever had for her. She was tryin' to destroy my life and I was fed up wit' her bullshit.

Finally hittin' my alarm for the third time, I got out of bed, and headed to the bathroom for a hot shower. When times got tough I could always count on Denie or my mother to help pull me through. Now, I didn't have either of them. I'd contemplated sellin' my mother's house for quite some time and gettin' a condo downtown since it was just me. I didn't need all of the space and the memories of my mom made it even harder to live here. I began to think about what a strong woman my mother was and how she stayed with my father even after findin' out he'd cheated wit' my Aunt Celeste. I missed her desperately and still blamed myself for not bein' here when she died.

After gettin' in the shower, my mind drifted once again to my time wit' Marisol the night before. Wit' all that she'd gone through between her daughter Mia and Carlos' disappearance, my guilt slipped in and I decided to treat her to a nice, intimate dinner at Timothy Dean's restaurant in Baltimore. I thought back to when she first walked in. I could tell that she was definitely inchin' her way back to her old self. Her confidence screamed *I'm that bitch* when she arrived and I knew it was wrong, but that shit turned me on.

Lookin' sexy as hell wit' skin tight jeans, a cropped leather jacket and an embellished tank top, her appearance demanded attention. To top it off, she was blinged out in the wrist, hand and neck areas. Her diamonds would easily blind you, especially the canary diamond cross that dangled between her cleavage. However, the more I stared at the necklace, I quickly snapped back to reality when thoughts of Los entered my mind. I was wit' him when he bought it for her and could remember the proud look he had on his face like it was yesterday. Knowin' the dinner had a hidden agenda, I quickly got my mind right and told myself to stay on task. Little did Marisol know, she was going to be my shield from Uncle Renzo. He loved Marisol like a daughter and because of this, I needed her on my side...I needed her to trust me.

She always loved me from when we were young, and understood how we all had made mistakes. We understood each other, and accepted one another for who we were. Not to mention, we shared the common goal of bein' ruthless and from the streets. She had dudes afraid of her on both coasts, east and west, and her ride or die mentality was kind of sexy. She demanded respect and definitely got it. She wasn't weak like that bitch Lisa. She was a thoroughbred, and I liked that shit.

When Marisol eventually brought up Lisa's name durin'

dinner and told me about her concern, I wasn't the least bit interested. But I tried to play the part. I remember laughing when she said that Carlie looked exactly like me. She tried to lecture me on how I needed to be there for my daughter while she fought for her life. Marisol of course wasn't aware of all of the betrayal I'd experienced wit' Lisa, and how she was responsible for Carlos' death. I planned to keep it that way for a while. She didn't need to know the truth 'til the time was right.

After I dodged the Carlos and Lisa questions, she then began to ask about Denie. Wit' that bein' a sore subject for me, I instantly became distant. The more she pried, the more I blamed Denie leavin' on her teen rebellion and bein' mad at me about Nelson. Marisol's concern for Denie made me uncomfortable knowin' that I couldn't tell her what was goin' on. Denie and Marisol had always been close, so it was normal for her to show such deep concern. The more she got agitated about me bein' indirect and uncomfortable wit' her questions, I knew it was time to go. That was my clue to wrap dinner up and get back home.

Ending my trip down memory lane, I finally hopped out of the shower and grabbed my towel. Seconds later, I heard my phone's text message alert go off. It was Lisa.

I don't want any excuses today to get our divorce postponed any longer. Dress your best and say a prayer, because you're gonna need it.

"Bitch, kiss my ass," I said, wishing she could hear me.

Damn, I hated that bitch more and more by the second. She was crazy if she thought I was payin' for that fuckin' baby. Makin' my way back to the bathroom, I got my clippers out and started to trim my new beard. As I looked at myself in the mirror, I just didn't look like myself. My eyes were blood shot red and I was in desperate need of a haircut. Lately, I'd been keepin' it cut close, but once my thick curly hair grew out, I looked like one of those Al B. Sure type of niggas, and that's not how I rolled. I hadn't even hit the gym in months, so my once muscular build was also startin' to fade. Since I'd been fucked up about my bread, my appearance had definitely taken a backseat, but I vowed to get myself together soon.

The beard trim was all the groomin' I could do since time was tickin' away. I had to be out of the house in less than fifteen minutes to ensure a parkin' space in the garage and still be on time. Walkin' into my closet, I pulled out my Hugo Boss black suit and all of my Louis Vuitton accessories, from the cufflinks, to the belt then topped it off wit' wine colored loafers. My attire was on point, but my look just wasn't 100%. I could feel it. However, despite the way I looked, it was time for me to get this divorce shit over wit'.

After drinkin' a protein shake, I jumped in my Range Rover and headed downtown. There was still enough time to make it if there wasn't too much traffic. Drivin' down Michigan Avenue, I turned on the radio and landed on 93.9. Russ Parr and his crew were trippin' as usual and got a couple of laughs out of me. It was so much on my mind I definitely needed to laugh. Right when I was in a calm place, my phone rang and I answered it without even screenin' the call.

"Yeah, what's up?"

"Rich…it's your Uncle, long time no hear. Where the hell have you been?" he asked in his strong Columbian accent. My heart instantly sunk into my stomach.

"Wassup Unc'? I've had so much goin' on. Denie has disappeared and I have no idea where she is."

"Rich, your personal life is your business. My business with you is finding out who killed my son. You've been ducking my calls for months and Marisol tells me she just had dinner with you last night. I can't believe you still haven't found out anything yet. This is bullshit!"

"Unc', I've been bustin' my ass tryin' to get leads on what happened wit' Los and I haven't come up wit' anything."

"Well, I guess you're gonna need Marisol's help then. Since you can't seem to do a man's job, I'll have Marisol get to the bottom of things."

"Damn, Unc that was straight disrespectful. Can't you understand that I'm goin' through a lot right now? First, I find out that my cousin is really my brother thanks to secrets you and my mother kept. Then on top of that, somethin' happens to him, and I have no clue where to look or who to ask, and now I'm on my way to court to finalize my divorce from Lisa."

"Will you stop ramblin' on like a damn woman and just get shit done!"

Tryin' to hold my composure, all I could say was, "Alright."

"Speaking of Lisa…that's another thing. What's going on with her? Every time I've called her, she just breaks down crying and hangs up."

"The bitch is crazy. That's what's wrong. I'm done wit' her ass!"

"What could she have done to you that would top all the shit you've done? Shit, my wife had a baby with my brother and I still stayed with her and raised him as if he was my own. You young kids are always in a hurry to just give up. We went through so much more than you and still held it together."

"I'm just not down with secrets and shit!"

"I'm sure you've held things from Lisa and she doesn't know all you've done. Did you forget that girl found out you had a baby by her friend at your mother's funeral?"

"I don't give a fuck! Lisa ain't shit. Y'all think she's innocent, but that shit is a wrap wit' me and her."

"Like I told you before, she knows too much, Rich. You're making a big mistake. You're in too deep to let go of a woman scorned. She could ruin the business."

"She won't, I promise you that."

"Well, I just don't wanna have to put out an order to…you know."

I knew exactly what he was talkin' about. He didn't want to have to order me to kill the mother of my kids.

"She had a melt down when Marisol saw her at the hospital. She seems to be unraveling," Uncle Renzo continued.

"I got this handled."

"You betta, and more importantly, I want answers about my son no later than this Friday, or I'll have to go off of my own assumptions and I don't wanna do that."

"Alright, I gotta…"

Before I could finish my sentence, my uncle had hung up on me. I knew he had suspicions of me, but I had to take care of my Lisa drama and then I could take care of him and Marisol. I had a plan, and since Marisol was obviously reportin' back to him, I knew my plan would work.

Lookin' at the clock, it was ten minutes 'til ten and I was several minutes away from the court buildin'. I had to be in court at ten a.m., so I started to panic. I ended up forgettin' my last court date due to me dealin' wit' Denie's recovery, so there was no way I could be a no-show at this one. After that incident the judge told my lawyer if I missed another appearance, I wouldn't be happy. I didn't need Lisa to luck up on what little bread I had left that easy.

As I made my way up New York Avenue, I turned off to a side street to dodge the traffic and noticed a black Suburban turn right behind me. Usually I wouldn't trip, but the dark tint made me uncomfortable. Makin' a quick lane change, I instantly became concerned when the Suburban followed suit.

Who the hell is that, I thought as I pressed on the gas a little harder.

Quickly thinkin' back to me and Uncle Renzo's conversation, somethin' told me that it could've easily been some of his people. He could definitely work fast, and for all I knew the truck could've been followin' me since I left my house. At that point, I made another turn down P Street to see if they would follow, and just as I thought, they did. Now, I was ready for war. I went into my secret stash in my dash as I drove eighty miles per hour down a one way street. I didn't obey any traffic signals as I put my .45 caliber on my lap. If I had to blast a nigga in broad daylight, I would. It was either going to be him or me. And I didn't have any plans on checkin' out today.

Moments later, the SUV made an aggressive power move. The truck sped up, driving wildly and tried to get on the side of me, but I took a quick left down another street. I took the Range Rover to the limit, goin' through numerous puddles and potholes.

I tried my best to dodge them, but as soon as I thought I'd lost them, they pulled on the side of me at the light. As soon as I saw the dark tinted window roll down a little, I was just about to point my pistol, when suddenly they pulled off. All I could see was the top of someone's head, but it appeared to be a Spanish or white person which made my suspicions true. That was classic Uncle Renzo tryin' to see if I was paranoid. I was sure he suspected somethin', but just couldn't put his finger on it. If it came down to it and Uncle Renzo had his men followin' me, he would've been a couple of men short on his team. I was definitely ready to blast them niggas… family or not. Fuck it, Uncle Renzo could get it too if he was tryin' to play wit' my life.

Chapter Seven
LISA

The sight of that bastard Rich rushing through the door made my stomach turn. I couldn't believe his ass had the audacity to show up ten minutes late. I was praying he didn't show up at all in a way so that the case would work in my favor. Looking at the sweat pouring from his face, I began to shake my head wondering why he looked like he'd just ran a 10K marathon. No matter how many designer labels he had on, he looked as if he'd been hit by a tractor trailer. His clothes were wrinkled and he was in dire need of a haircut.

"I'm glad you could join us, Mr. Sanchez. Please come in and have a seat," Judge Deena Bower said in a sarcastic tone.

"Sorry, Your Honor. There was so much traffic and…" Rich tried to say.

"Save it, Mr. Sanchez," the judge replied. "I've heard every excuse in the book, and I'm not in the mood for lies this morning. Your tardiness is inexcusable. You need to be prompt in my courtroom. Do you understand?"

Rich shook his head. "Yes ma'am."

I hadn't heard that nigga be polite in years.

"Okay, let's proceed," the judge continued.

After I gave him a *fuck you* look, I was ready for war. "Let the games begin," I whispered to myself.

Rich's lawyer was just his type. He usually went for light

skinned girls, but she was a brown skinned honey, who looked like Kandi from the old group Xscape. Short hair, slim, but curvy with a big butt; I knew they'd fucked at some point in his life. I wasn't sure if she was a jump off from the past, or if she was one of his recent affairs, but I could tell by their body language that there was something going on. Rich was very charismatic as he explained to her why he was late and the way she looked at him, you could tell it was more to their relationship. I knew that man like the back of my hand.

"Your Honor, my client Lisa Sanchez has been married to Juan Sanchez Sr. for over twenty years. During this marriage they had three children; Juan who's twenty-three and currently lives with my client, Denie who's seventeen, and currently lives with Mr. Sanchez, and Carlie Sanchez who is a little over a month old and currently fighting for her life in Holy Cross Hospital," my lawyer stated.

"I'm sorry to hear that," Judge Bower interrupted.

"Thank you, Your Honor," I replied as my lawyer continued.

"Umm…Your Honor, I'm sorry Denie is eighteen. Her birthday is…today actually," my lawyer stated.

I could instantly tell from the look on Rich's face that he'd completely forgotten about Denie's birthday. He looked crushed. I on the other hand displayed an instant frown when I thought about what happened to me on this day last year. It was something that I desperately wanted to forget but couldn't.

"Mrs. Sanchez's life with her husband was a complete nightmare for her. She dealt with physical, emotional, and mental abuse. Mr. Sanchez's infidelity has caused my client to suffer from STD's as well as one of Mr. Sanchez's affairs resulting in a child with one of her close friends. Mrs. Sanchez is requesting the following from Mr. Sanchez due to her pain and suffering for over two decades. Spousal support due to the fact that Mr. Sanchez never allowed my client to work. He wanted her to stay home and be a homemaker and take care of the children."

"Objection, Your Honor, Mrs. Sanchez is still young. She's

in her late 30's and should have no problem with getting back into the work force," Rich's lawyer objected.

"With a brand new infant, raising kids since the age of sixteen, and never having a job? Yeah…I'm sure that'll be easy," my lawyer countered.

"Ms. Williams, please wait and hold your objections until after Mr. Leach completes the list of what his client is requesting," the judge announced. "Objection overruled."

I shot Rich a smirk and directed my attention back to my lawyer.

"We're also requesting for Mrs. Sanchez to keep the house that she currently resides in with their son Juan Sanchez Jr., at 17305…"

"Man, hell no, that's my mother's house!" Rich blurted out.

Never would I have imagined that Rich would play this dirty. He had the house put in his mother's name over a decade ago to keep the Feds off his back. Now, he wanted it back.

"Mr. Sanchez, have a seat and respect my courtroom!" Judge Bower ordered.

Rich apologized as my lawyer completed my list of demands. Rich was furious. Even though I knew his bar Bottom's Up and his strip club were cash cows, I knew they were cover ups for his illegal businesses and I needed him to have some type of income to pay me. With that in mind, I just asked for his t-shirt and corner stores in Southeast. I figured that they could be good income on a rainy day if he ever were to be sent off to jail.

The next thing I requested was to keep my X6 of course and all of my jewelry. My intentions and motives were to make sure I was never put in a bad position ever again like I did when Rich went to jail. I was thinking of things that could be sold if money was ever needed. The last request sent Rich over the edge; my request for child support. He squirmed in his seat and whispered to his lawyer.

He was trying hard to hold his composure as I continued to smile at him. He knew that smile meant play nice or else. My advantage over Rich was that my lawyer Mr. Leach knew so much about him since he represented Rich for years. This case was a walk in the park for him. He figured the child support would be where we would win big. With the cost of childcare expenses these days and Rich's reported income, I could be looking at a minimum of $1800.00 a month. That's the least he could do for taking Carlos away from my daughter, especially since he'd been helping Marisol.

It was now Rich's lawyers turn to let the judge know what Rich opposed and what he was willing to do.

"Your Honor, my client is very disappointed at his wife's accusations and would like to see what proof she has to prove the abuse she's suffered."

"Mr. Leach, does your client have any proof of abuse. If not, this could be all hear say," Judge Bower questioned.

"The children witnessed his abuse. I'm sure their son would have no problem with testifying on his mother's behalf," Mr. Leach replied.

"I'm sure he would, Your Honor, since their relationship is strained," his lawyer responded.

Just like I thought, he'd fucked her. She had way too much emotion in her response for it to just be a professional relationship.

"Mrs. Sanchez, if you don't have proof, maybe photos, a police report, a medical report of some sort, or more than one witness, then I'm going to have to disregard your claim of abuse," Judge Bower said with sympathy.

"No, I don't," I answered.

"Your Honor, as far as the businesses are concerned, my client is in the process of selling both of the establishments that Mrs. Sanchez is requesting. There are actually contracts on both properties," Rich's lawyer announced.

"Your Honor, if that's the case, my client is requesting 75% of the profit from the sales of both properties," Mr. Leach blurted out.

"I'll make a note of your request, Mr. Leach. Please continue Ms. Williams," Judge Bower replied.

"My client does not agree to Mrs. Sanchez's request to keep the home in NW Washington where she currently resides. This home belonged to his mother and since her passing, anything attached to her is sentimental to him so he'd like to keep this property. With that being said, Mr. Sanchez is willing to give Mrs. Sanchez $10,000 to assist with a down payment on a home of her own."

"Oh, hell no! That's my house, you're not gonna take my house from me, Rich!" I screamed.

"Mrs. Sanchez, take your seat now. You will respect my courtroom as well!" the judge yelled while banging the gavel.

"I'm sorry, Your Honor," I said, taking my seat.

"Your Honor, my client is willing to pay a lump sum of $25,000 in spousal support to assist with Mrs. Sanchez with getting her life together and making an investment for her future. However, my client is requesting a blood test for Carlie Sanchez, the youngest child. Therefore we do not agree to the request for child support."

"A blood test, Rich? You bastard! Is that how you wanna roll? You don't want to fuck with me Rich!" I yelled out again.

"Order! Have a seat Mrs. Sanchez. No more disrespect in my courtroom will be allowed. You've been warned," the judge demanded. "Counselors, you might want to advise your clients that the next outburst in my courtroom from either party will result in someone going to jail. I have no problem with holding either of you in contempt of court," Judge Bower said in a calm but stern tone.

Both lawyers agreed and Judge Bower then directed her questioning to Rich.

"Mr. Sanchez, is this some type of ploy to buy time or are you accusing Mrs. Sanchez of infidelity? My patience is wearing quite thin with you both."

"Your Honor, I have reason to believe Lisa was havin' an affair, because she told me she was seein' someone else. My wife and I weren't even intimate around the time she got pregnant, so that's why I question paternity," Rich replied in a bitch-like tone.

He smiled at me as if he had one up on me.

"What do you have to say about this, Mrs. Sanchez?" the judge asked.

"I can't believe him. All that he has put me through all these years. I just can't believe him. He knows he's the father," I responded, knowing that I was actually lying. I was almost at a loss for words.

"Alright, here's what I'm gonna do. There will be a two week continuance on the case until the paternity test results are back. Mr. Sanchez, if you are the father of this child, you will pay child support, so be prepared. Let me give you a date now." Judge Bower went back and forth with the lawyers until they landed on a date that we would be back in court December 6th at nine a.m.

My stomach instantly did somersaults. There was no way I was going to win anything now. I knew that Judge Bower would definitely look at me differently once those test results came back. Rich had just put a monkey wrench in my plans and I was going to make his ass pay. As mad as I was, I wish I could've knocked the smirk off of his face. My blood boiled.

As soon as I heard court was adjourned, I jumped out of my seat and strutted out of the courtroom. Mr. Leach, I was sure needed to talk to me, but I couldn't bear to be in that court room any longer. Passing through the hallway, there were so many baby mamas and baby daddies arguing over child support and anything else under the sun.

"Piss, piss, excuse me miss, can I talk to you for a minute," all kinds of obscenities were being yelled my way.

I just ignored them and kept it moving. I had no time for ignorant-ass niggas. I was ready to work on my Plan B to get Rich's money and pay him back for all the hurt he'd caused me.

As soon as I made it out of the court building, I bumped into that bitch Trixie who Rich cheated on me with. She even had her daughter with her. I was ready for her ass to jump out there and say something slick to me, and with the day I was having so far, she was liable to get her ass whooped in front of her daughter. I didn't care if she was Rich's child or not.

"Hello, Lisa."

That tramp had the audacity to try and speak to me, but I rolled my eyes and kept it moving.

"Wow Lisa, you still not speaking. Damn you still mad that I fucked your man," she added.

I stopped and turned around. "Bitch, fuck you!"

"You're not my type, and if I did fuck you, you would've been over Rich years ago," she shot back.

"If I did roll like that, I wouldn't fuck a whore like you. Oh, and by the way you're wearing that scar well!" I said sarcastically with a smile.

I needed to remind that bitch of the beating I'd put on her at her salon. That for sure hit a nerve because she started fussing and cursing like the hood rat she was. Just when I started to walk off again, Rich came out the court room.

Instantly, her daughter Juanita ran up to Rich. "Daddy, daddy!"

"Hey, baby girl," he said, picking her up and twirling her around. "Trixie, why do you have her down here?"

"Why? Are you concerned that I'm gonna take your ass to court?" she asked.

"I could care less if you did or not," Rich countered.

"Well, if you must know, a friend of mine goes to trial today, so I came down here to make sure he was good."

I already knew that was going to set Rich off.

"You triflin' bitch, you better get my daughter away from here."

"Triflin', are you serious? You just started being a father to your daughter in a matter of what…a week, and now you want to judge my parenting?" Trixie asked.

"Keep talking shit. You gonna get fucked up, Trixie!"

Damn I wish Judge Bower could come outside and watch this. Then she can see how much of a fucked up person Rich really is, I thought.

"Is that how you act in front of your three year old daughter? I don't know how you and Lisa get down in your household, and no matter how triflin' you might think I am, my daughter ain't use to this ignorant shit you trying to pull."

"Like I said, get my daughter from down here. She needs to be at home looking at cartoons or some shit, not at a courthouse with some dude you probably fucking," Rich replied.

"You better be lucky I ain't down here taking your ass to court! Come on Nita," Trixie said as she walked off switching from side to side. She probably thought Rich was looking at her ass, but he'd already walked off and wasn't paying her any attention.

Letting out a loud laugh, I walked off and made my way to the garage. As soon as I got to the parking attendant, I was furious because I'd given him an extra $20.00 to park my car on the main level so I didn't have to walk that far. Looking around, I knew he'd gotten over on me.

"Where's my shit?" I asked.

"On level three," he said, pointing up.

"You should give me my damn money back," I said, snatching my keys out of his hand. "Are you even allowed to work in this country?" I asked the Ethiopian attendant before storming off.

I didn't think my day could get any worse. Before I made it to the stairwell, I could hear Rich's voice yelling at the parking attendant as well. He'd obviously been bamboozled, too. Putting some pep in my step to avoid any contact with Rich, I could hear his footsteps getting closer. As my luck would have it, he ended up catching me as I hit the car alarm on Juan's new Benz. What was the likelihood of the dumb-ass attendant parking our cars side by side?

Out of all these damn parking spaces he couldn't have found a different one, I thought to myself. I knew the drama was on the way.

"How'd you like court, you coke sniffin', whore? Oh…wait you do heroin, right? You thought you was gonna get my bread without a fight. You got me fucked up!"

"Rich, fuck you! You're over there taking care of Marisol

and her kids, and now I see you even taking care of Trixie's so you're gonna take care of mine, one way or the other. Trust me."

"Marisol is a strong woman who handles her business and takes care of her kids. You on the other hand are always sittin' around waitin' for me to take care of your dumb-ass. Those days are over!" he yelled as he got in his truck and rolled his window down letting out a huge glob of spit that landed right on my arm. "And tell your son, he's never gonna learn. He's drawin' way too much heat wit' that hot-ass car. Look at those rims and shit!"

"You think you got one up over me! We'll see how big your balls are when I tell Uncle Renzo what you did!"

I was so pissed when he pulled off that I quickly took off one of my Louboutins and hurled it at his back window as hard as I could. Seconds later, his truck stopped. Rich jumped out and looked at his back window. There was a small crack right in the middle.

"Bitch, you cracked my fuckin' window, now I'ma crack your head open!"

Without a seconds notice, Rich lunged at me, catching me by my hair. I knew that someone might hear me, so instantly I screamed to the top of my lungs. The first smack to my face stung like hell. At that point, I knew I had an instant black eye when my nose hit the hood of Juan's car.

"Stop, Rich!"

"Hell no! You've dodged a couple of ass whoopins and a death sentence. For what you did to my daughter, I should've been killed your ass!" he yelled as he gave me another blow that knocked me this time to the ground.

My Gucci bag fell right along with me and all my belongings, including my cell phone to the ground. I had a choice to cover my face or fight back and run the risk of him doing more damage. Balling up in a fetal position, I took my beating like a man as he kicked me in my ribs.

I screamed again, but the last blow knocked all of the wind out of me. Moments later, I could hear a group of people coming down the stairwell and that's what saved me. Rich caught wind that someone was coming and jumped in his truck.

"This shit ain't over!" he said, pulling off unnoticed.

Chapter Eight
JUAN

There was always some shit when it came to my mother. With the constant drama between her and my father, or her drug habits, all of her issues were wearing me thin. She asked me the night before to go to divorce court with her, but I knew how she rolled. I would've definitely been up on the stand testifying and I didn't have the time or energy for all that shit. My plans when she came home, were to show her all the Ralph Lauren and Juicy Couture clothes that I'd bought my baby sister from the mall. I thought that would make up for me not being there for her at court. However, all that family shit went out the window when she called and told me to come get her from some parking garage near the court building. Her voice was very faint and she sounded as if she'd been crying, so I knew it had to be serious.

Luckily, I was on my way from Pentagon City, so I was able to make it downtown in no time. She told me she was on the P3 level which was at the top of the garage, so I parked my truck on the street and walked so I could drive my Benz back to the house.

When I got to my mother, I couldn't believe the state she was in. There were a couple of young dudes who'd stayed with her until I got there, so I gave them a few dollars for looking out and not calling the police. Her face was bruised, nose a little swollen, and her eye had a mark under it. I knew we had to hurry and get home to start working on her eye before it got any worse. By her just giving birth over a month ago, her body was still fragile. I knew the pain that she described wasn't her just being dramatic.

"Let me take a wild guess on who did this. Rich, right?" I asked.

She slowly nodded her head. "Yes."

"Why did you let him do this to you? What happened?" I yelled.

"He's crazy. He beat me because I threw my shoe at his truck," she said, holding her side.

"Why did you throw the shoe? Why didn't you just leave him alone?" It sounded like I was the parent.

"Can we please just go?" she begged as I helped her in the passenger seat.

Pulling out of the garage, I was in a rage. I couldn't even think straight as I envisioned Rich pounding on her. The days of him putting his hands on my mother were going to come to an end. Rich needed to know that I was a grown-ass man, not a little boy anymore so if he wanted to beat on somebody, he should come my way.

Looking over at my mother laying back in the seat, her bruises gave me flashbacks of the days when I was a child and couldn't help her. The more I thought about all she had to put up with, the more pissed off I became. Picking up my I-Phone, I called that nigga Rich; ready for war. As soon as he answered the phone, there was no hello, he instantly started talking shit.

"If you callin' my phone about that bitch, Lisa, I don't wanna hear that shit."

"Look I'ma say this for the last time. The next time you feel the urge to put your fucking hands on my mother, come fuck with me. Go beat up them other bitches in the street you deal with."

"Juan, you can jump yo' self out there if you want to, cuz you can get it, too. That bitch ain't gonna send me death threats talkin' about she's gonna tell Unc wassup, then crack my windshield and think it's all good. Wife or not. She lucky she still breathin'."

"Man, I said what I had to say."

CLICK.

I hung up on his ass. Never was I the type of dude who argued. My maturity level was too much for that type of shit. I wasn't the one for drama. I left that gay shit for the ladies and bitch ass niggas. It was just a matter of time before I put Rich in jail where he belonged. I knew how to get to him and he would soon pay for hurting my mother.

My mother of course had left out some major details of what sparked the fight between them as usual. She didn't tell me that she'd threatened to tell my Uncle Renzo about Rich's involvement in Carlos' death. That was a major no, no and I'd told her on many occasions that she needed to chill with that whole situation. At some point, she had to listen. If not, someone was bound to get hurt.

When we pulled up to the house, I helped her inside, then up to her room. I thought I would give her some time to get herself together before we had the Uncle Renzo lecture. While she rested, I went downstairs to the movie room to watch some of the highlights of the Lakers game since I didn't get a chance to watch it. Kobe ended up giving the people forty-five points allowing the Lakers to win, which meant my man Cornell owed me $500 from our bet. I thought I'd call him to give him a hard time.

"Wassup my nigga, you got my dinero?"

"Man, go ahead with that, we ain't shake on that bet."

"Don't start that shit. You seen my man Kobe kill them folks last night," I replied.

"I got you man. You know we play New York tomorrow. We going out after the game too, you rollin'?"

"You know what man, I got a better idea. Hook me up with some courtside tickets for me and my mother. Instead of hitting a club, maybe we can go out to the W rooftop downtown for drinks afterwards. She's going through some shit and I think she might need to get out."

"Isn't that cute, the mama's boy takin' his mother out for

drinks." Cornell let out a huge laugh. "Man, I got both of y'all. You bringin' anybody else, don't you got a sister? What's up with her, how old is she?"

"Cornell, stop playing man. My sister is actually taken, plus she's eighteen which means she's too young for you."

"Alright man, I'll see you tomorrow. Since you ain't trying to hook me up, I guess I'll go let off some steam in the gym."

"Shut up man!" I laughed before getting off the phone.

When I heard dishes rattling in the kitchen, I knew my mother was up. No matter how much she probably wasn't in the mood for a lecture, it was important for me to let her know she was playing with fire when she threatened to tell Uncle Renzo about Carlos. I placed the T.V. on mute.

"Hey Ma, can you bring me a Red Bull in here?"

"Yeah, I'm fixing me a bowl of fruit salad, you want some?"

"Yeah, thanks."

Up until this day, my mother had never failed me. She always took care of me, and that's why no matter what, I would always be by her side. Moments later, she walked in the movie room with a colorful bowl filled with all of my favorite fruit.

"Thanks."

"Anything for my baby boy."

"Man, I ain't no baby, I'ma grown man."

"Well, you'll always be my baby no matter how old you are."

"Look, Ma, it's some things I want to talk to you about."

"Shoot, what's up?"

"Wait…how are you feeling? You didn't lay down long."

She sighed. "I'll live. I took some pain medicine, which helped a little bit. As long as my ribs aren't broke, I'm fine," she replied before placing a pineapple in her mouth. "What do you wanna talk about?"

"Well, the first thing I've wanted to ask you for a while is; what made you lie for Rich and raise Denie as your own?"

She sighed again. "I didn't do it for Rich. I did it for Denie.

When I first laid eyes on Denie, I instantly fell in love with her. It wasn't about Rich cheating, he always did. It was about me having the daughter that I always wanted. Back then, before all of the buildup of hurt and pain, I had more of an innocence about me. I cared, I had a heart. I couldn't believe someone would leave a newborn baby on a doorstep. I decided to keep the secret and take care of her. Not for Rich, but for Denie."

"So, what happened to you, Ma? Why did you torture Denie the way you did?"

"Juan, I knew this question was coming. Since the warehouse incident, I've been trying to put my breakdown in the back of my mind. I'm a strong believer that your experience makes you into the person you are. Come on Juan, along with all the verbal, mental, and physical abuse, I'd been raped and abducted because of your father's mistakes. I was tired. I really do feel bad for what I did to Denie and I want to reach out to her and apologize one day. I still love her. It wasn't me. Sometimes I don't know who I am."

She started to break down and cry. I hated to see my mother upset.

"Okay, Ma, no more questions. Let's make this a good night. I have a great evening planned for you tomorrow. After I handle my business during the day and you visit with Carlie, we're going to the Wizards game. Courtside seats, baby!"

"Really?" she said all spoiled. "As long as I can put on enough make-up to cover these bruises then I'll go."

"You'll be fine."

Then I remembered I hadn't given her the gifts I bought Carlie, so I went to go get them. She instantly lit up.

"Oh my goodness. Juan, that was so sweet of you. To finally have a daughter of my own, and for you to accept her even with how she got here, means a lot to me. I know you don't approve of the relationship I shared with Carlos, but I loved him. He was there for me when I was low, and Carlie gives me that piece of Carlos that I need to move on, and get my life back on track."

Once she said that, I remembered that the purpose of me wanting to talk to her was to address the Uncle Renzo topic. Even though it might've set her off again, I had to address this issue with her no matter what.

"Speaking of you and Carlos, Ma, Rich told me that you threatened to tell Uncle Renzo about what happened. Do you realize that if Renzo knew that, he would not only kill Rich, it would put me and your life at risk? Uncle Renzo would kill all of us without a blink of an eye."

"I just want Rich out of my life!"

"Uncle Renzo is not the way. Do you trust me?"

"Of course I trust you."

"Well, if you never listened to me before, know that I have a plan for Rich that we both will benefit from. Just trust me. When you go back to court and you don't get your child support, or if the judge says we have to move out of this house, don't put up a fight. Know that I got your back and the plan I have for Rich, he ain't gonna be ready for. Ma, just be easy. Trust your son, I got this."

●●●●●●●●●●●●●●●

The next morning I got up and went to several important meetings in order to make sure my plan for Rich was going in the right direction. My day was long but productive and I got a lot accomplished. When I made it back home, it was six o' clock and I couldn't believe my mother was ready to go. She looked like she was really trying to make a statement. She had on some tight Seven jeans with a long Alice & Olivia silk shirt. When I looked down at her feet, I had to object.

"Ma, who wears four inch heels to a basketball game?"

"Well, I'm single now and you never know who I might meet," she said sarcastically to get under my skin.

"Whatever, let's go."

We made it downtown in forty-five minutes due to all the traffic on 16th street. Once we finally arrived, we got our tickets from the will-call box and made it to our seats right before the game started. My mother was so excited which made me happy to see her in such great spirits. When Cornell was introduced in the starting five, I let my mother know that's who my friend was.

"Damn, he's fine. How old is he?" she asked, placing her new bob-styled hair behind her ear.

"Too young for you," I answered in an annoyed tone.

Cornell got his man and led the team in scoring with thirty-two points. Basket after basket my mother cheered for him as if she was his mother. She was so into the game that it was actually funny. You would've never guessed her life was in such disarray the way she carried on. However, despite his efforts the Wizards fell short of two points and lost. After the game, Cornell left us two family passes so we could wait for him. When he finally came out, my mother tried to play it cool, but I could tell she was a little star struck.

"What's up my man, I thought you weren't bringin' your sister?" Cornell whispered as he gave me dap.

"Cornell, this is my mother, Ms. Lisa. Ma, this is my man, Cornell."

"Hi Cornell, you can call me Lisa, and thanks for inviting us. I had a great time."

"Thanks, Lisa. You're welcome to be my guest anytime." I could tell that he was definitely checking her out. I couldn't blame him though. Even though she's picked up some pounds, my mother still had the body of a twenty-five year old.

"So, what's up, you ready to roll? You bring some chicks for us to hang out with?" I said to throw a wedge between whatever chemistry that was starting to build up between the two of them.

"Naw, man. It's just us three at the W tonight for a few drinks. I gotta leave early in the mornin'. We play Houston tomorrow. I'm really not tryin' to hang out late."

"Alright, meet me at the 6th St. Garage entrance so we can ride over together," I suggested.

"Alright, cool."

When we got in the car, I gave my mother the no dating my friends speech, but of course she didn't act like she was phased by anything I was saying to her. When we got to the W, it was crazy. Once the valet attendant took our cars, we made our way to the front of the line. Groupies were on the prowl in full effect. Every other chick sung, "Hey Cornell, Hey Juan."

You could tell my mother wasn't use to this, but she played it cool. When we got off the elevator and made it upstairs, my mother was in her comfort zone. She wasn't expecting such elegance with all the trashy chicks that were fighting to get in. As soon as we made our way to the table, I spotted Cherry at the bar.

"Not speaking tonight, Juan?" she aked.

"What's up, babe?"

I gave her a hug and a small squeeze on the ass. She was looking damn good and her sweet perfume instantly made me think of how she made me feel the last time we were together. We made arrangements for the night, but the only problem was she wasn't driving and I didn't know how I was going to allow her and my mother to be in the same vehicle together. I had to have her tonight and was determined to make a way.

Once I caught back up with my mother and Cornell they seemed to be hitting it off quite well. You would've thought they'd known each other for years. I was instantly irritated. Cornell was a good dude, but I knew how he rolled. He was just like me and I just didn't want my mother to have anymore drama in her life. When I sat down, they were laughing and carrying on like two best friends.

"What's so funny?" I asked.

"Cornell is a trip. I was telling him that we were watching Madea movies last night and he was over here reciting lines. He does a good imitation of Madea's brother, Joe."

I wasn't enthused. "Oh, really."

My mother looked at me strangely. "Yeah. What's wrong with you?"

"Nothing. Look Ma, I'm ready to go. I gotta take you home because I got something to do tonight."

"Damn Juan, we've only been here for twenty minutes. I'll just catch a cab, go on. I'm not ready to go. I'll be alright."

"I'm not leaving you here," I replied like I was the parent.

"Why not? I'm not a child. Besides, there's a taxi stand right outside the hotel," my mother informed.

"Juan, it's all good. I'll drop her off on my way home. I can just go I-495 home, it's cool."

"Alright Cornell, but take care of my mother the way you would want me to take care of yours," I said, with a wink as he gave me a pound.

"Of course," he replied.

Something was telling me that leaving my mom with him was a bad idea, but I had to fuck Cherry tonight so I took that chance.

Chapter Nine
LISA

Finally, I could say I had a great night. Cornell was such a nice guy and I really enjoyed his company…so much that he invited me to go to his game in Philly the following week. We even exchanged numbers, but I didn't want Juan to know just yet. I knew I had to prove to him that I was going to be a responsible mother again, so it was way too soon to brag to him about another man. Trying to be strong, I went upstairs to my room and made sure I didn't call Cornell to come back and quench my thirst for affection. Since I knew Juan wasn't coming home, and I was feeling horny from all the drinks, I would've loved to fuck him. He was 6'7 with skin the color of Jack Daniels whiskey and a smile that made me weak at the knees. To top it off, he had a charming smile and a body full of tattoos; just like Carlos. He was beyond sexy and I guess the urge for me wanting to fuck him was probably because I was so damn lonely. Not to mention, with the exception of my ten inch vibrator, I hadn't had sex in months.

Taking off my clothes, I got into bed and started to please myself. As I rubbed my breast, I closed my eyes and thought of Carlos. I played with my nipples while I held the vibrator between my thighs and pressed it tight against my pussy. Feeling the vibrator up against my clit had me in a trance. Changing the speed from slow to fast, I moved my battery operated friend into a circular motion until my clit started to throb. Suddenly, I felt my insides cringe and a powerful release of fluid running down my thighs. The more I thought about Carlos, the harder I came.

"Oh, shit," I said as my body shook uncontrollably. It felt good to be having a much needed orgasm.

As I continued to lay there, a noise coming from down-stairs, instantly had me paranoid. With my past experience, I knew not to ignore it. Grabbing my gun from under the bed, I slowly walked down the steps and before I could make it to the foyer I heard heavy footsteps walking in my direction. With my heart rate beating out of control, I was scared and wondered if it was the al-cohol that had me tripping.

"Juan, is that you!" I yelled out. Feeling on the wall for the light switch as soon as I found it, the intruder appeared right be-fore my eyes in my foyer.

"Oh my God!" I yelled as I fell to the floor.

"Hey Lisa, surprised huh? I hope I didn't scare you," Car-los said in a soft tone.

"I thought you were dead. I've been lost without you," I said as I stood up and walked closer to him. I had to touch him to see if he was real.

"It's really me Lisa."

"I'm sorry Carlos for what Rich did to you. I'm so sorry. He said he would kill me if I told anyone." I started crying and ran to him as he held me. It was really him. The love of my life was alive. "How did you get out of the car? How did you sur-vive?"

"Before I tell you anything, no one can know that I'm not dead. When is Juan coming home?"

"He won't be home until tomorrow. I promise I won't tell anyone. I missed you Carlos. Where have you been all this time? Why did you stay away from me so long?"

"Let's go upstairs and talk," he suggested.

As we walked up the stairs I could tell he wanted to touch my naked body, but he also seemed a little jumpy and paranoid. In-stead of coming on to me, he sat on the edge of the bed and con-tinued his story.

"All I remember is waking up to this guy and his wife. The guy saw the car being dumped in the water. He actually worked security overnight at the docks and saw everything. He was able to use his tow truck to get the car out of the water and found me in the trunk. His wife is a retired surgeon and nursed me to health."

"My prayers were answered. I prayed for you to come back to me. Why didn't the couple go to the police?"

"Well, they feared for their lives. They felt it was up to me to go to the police if I chose."

"I mean, how? I just don't…"

"I can't stay long, no more questions. I just wanted to see what's been going on with you. I see you gotta a new boyfriend. Look like he got some doe."

I instantly shook my head. "No. He's not my boyfriend. That was one of Juan's friends just giving me a ride home."

"So, you let Juan's friends give you a kiss on the cheek?"

My eyes widened. He obviously had seen everything. "He was just being nice. How long have you been following me?"

"Oh, I've been watching everyone from a distance for the past couple of weeks. What's been keeping you at the hospital?"

"Carlos, you're not going to believe me, but we have a daughter named Carlie. I named her after both of us."

"What, we have a child?"

"Yes, she's the reason why I've been at the hospital so much. I had her early, but she's getting better. Let me get my phone so I can show you a picture." Quickly, I dumped my bag on the floor to get my phone and showed Carlos the pictures of our beautiful little girl.

"She's really mine," he said, as sadness came over him. I knew he was thinking about his other daughters. I wondered if I should tell him about Mia's Leukemia, but quickly dismissed it. I thought it was best that I kept our moment about us.

"Yes baby, she's ours."

The more I stared at Carlos, the more I couldn't help myself. I had to have him. Straddling behind him I wrapped my hands around his buffed body and started to give him a massage as I kissed him on his neck and whispered a gazillion I love you's in his ear. My pussy was so wet I just needed to feel his sexy lips sucking all of my juices. Of course Carlos couldn't resist me any longer and threw me back on the bed.

"You want me to suck this pussy, Lisa?"

"Yes, baby, suck this pussy."

At that moment, Carlos flicked his tongue across my clit and started to go to work. Damn I missed him so much that I couldn't help but cry tears of happiness. "Carlos, I'm about to cum baby, I'm about to cum!"

He hummed on my pussy and let me cum all over his face. As I came, he lifted my ass and started to stick his tongue in and out like a snake. I needed to taste him so I made my way around and put his stiff hard dick in my mouth as he started to eat my pussy again. Sucking on the head of his dick and playing with his balls, he moaned. I didn't even get five strokes in before he busted all over my face. I missed everything about him even the scent of his semen. This man was my heart, and I loved every part of him. I was ready for my man to have me any way he wanted to.

Getting on top, I put his dick back inside of me and rode him like my life depended on it. He felt good as he pulled and sucked on my nipples. When he put his hands around my body and placed his finger inside my ass, that nasty shit made me go absolutely insane. I didn't know which way I wanted to cum first.

Calling out his name, I stopped because I wasn't ready to have another orgasm yet. I wanted to have Carlos all night. Getting up, I positioned myself on my knees. It was his choice which hole he wanted to enter. He chose my ass, and I was okay with it. Anything Carlos wanted from me, he got. This was something that I only had done once before against my will, but for Carlos, I would do anything. I clinched the sheets and took it like a soldier. It hurt a little at first, but I quickly got the hang of it and started fucking him back. After many different creative positions we made passionate love all night long. It was the best night of my life.

Carlos made me promise that I would never tell anyone he was alive. He agreed he would spend the night with me and made me feel loved as he held me until we fell off to sleep. His arms felt secure…safe.

The next morning I woke up naked, hot, and wet. When I turned over to grab for Carlos, he was gone and I was devastated. As I got out of bed, my phone rang. Thinking it might've been him, I grabbed it hoping his voice would be on the other end.

"Hello," I answered in an anxious tone.

"Ma, Marisol just called me and said she was on her way back in town,"Juan said.

I was beyond disappointed. "So, what, I don't give a fuck about Marisol. Why are you calling to tell me that?"

"Ma, be quiet and listen, Carlos' body was found. She's coming to identify it."

"What are you talking about *his body*?" *I just saw him last night*, I thought.

"His body, Ma. They found his car in the Chesapeake Bay."

I placed my hand over my mouth. "Oh, my God!"

"Yeah. She's been trying to call Rich too, but can't get a hold of him," Juan informed. "Look, remember what we talked about with Uncle Renzo. I'm not sure if he knows yet, but you have to be easy or you know the consequences."

"It can't be him. It can't be Carlos. I gotta go!"

I was confused and completely delusional. The amazing night that I'd just shared with Carlos had obviously been nothing but a fucking dream.

Chapter Ten
RICH

Gettin' out of bed this mornin' was hard because my head was so heavy wit' all the shit goin' on. This past week had been absolutely crazy for me, especially runnin' into Trixie and my daughter. Even though I'd recently been tryin' to have a relationship wit' my four-year old daughter, I still got so mad at myself for fuckin a bitch like Trixie raw. It was never my plan to have a child wit' her. I guess this was one time my cheatin' had caught up wit' me. I knew it hurt Lisa to see Juanita run up and call me daddy, but I couldn't change the affair. We would soon be divorced so it really wasn't her problem anymore anyway.

The more I thought about our altercation two days ago, the more I realized that it was a bad idea that I let Lisa get to me. She could use me beatin' her ass against me in court and could really fuck my money up. Hopefully she was so fucked up in the head that she didn't think to take pictures of her face. I know that Juan wouldn't testify. My son might've been upset wit' me, but he knew the code of the streets. I didn't raise a snitch. There was no way he would be turnin' on me in a courtroom. Just when I thought to call him to make sure my assumptions were correct, my phone rang. It was Marisol.

"Rich, Rich oh my God!" she cried.

"Marisol calm down, why are you up so early? Isn't it six a.m. in Cali, what's wrong?"

"I tried to call you all day yesterday. I got an anonymous call from some woman saying that Carlos' body was dumped in Baltimore off this pier in…"

"Wait…hold up. Who told you that?"

"I don't know."

"What do you mean, you don't know. Did the voice at least sound familiar?"

"No, I don't know who it was. Anyway, I called the private investigator and they looked into it and Rich they found him!"

"How do you know it's him?"

"It was his car, Rich! They found it in the Chesapeake Bay. They want me to come and identify his body. Rich I can't do this alone."

I was speechless for a moment. "What do you need me to do, I got you."

"Well, I'm about to hop on the first flight out there. I'll be in D.C. by 3 o'clock your time. Can you pick me up from National airport?"

"Of course I can. Did you tell Unc' yet?"

"No, I don't want to upset him for no reason. I want to be sure it's him."

"I think that's best. Just take it easy, don't tell anybody what's up 'til we know for sure."

"Okay. Rich I don't want it to be him. I mean, I know he's been missing for a while, but I just kept telling myself that he was gonna come back. What am I going to tell my girls?" Marisol sobbed.

"Let's just hope for the best. Try to keep it together at least 'til you get here."

She let out a slight sigh. "Okay, I'll try."

As soon as I hung up wit' Marisol, the first person I called was Juan. Even though he already knew what was goin' on, I let him know that he had to talk to Lisa to make sure she knew the importance of holdin' herself together. She could definitely blow this thing up and we could all be dead. I made sure I stressed the word *all*, so he knew that his life could be at risk as well. He understood and said he would try and talk to her again. My conversation wit' Juan made me feel that I could trust him and my court case was solid.

As my mind began to race, and all I could think about was who the hell could've tipped Marisol off to where Los' body was. I started to get even more paranoid. Shit, I didn't even know that Marisol hired a private investigator. The more I thought of it, the more I wondered if he was the person followin' me that day. No matter what, I couldn't be connected to my brother's death and I wanted to make sure that Lisa didn't fuck it up for us all. *How did my life turn upside down like this in a matter of months*, I wondered to myself. There was someone followin' me, Uncle Renzo was indirectly sendin' me death notes, my daughter hated my guts, my bread was gettin' lower and lower by the day, and now they'd found Carlos' body. Life was fucked up for me.

Wit' my head poundin', I took a couple of Advils, and laid back down to try and get rid of the overwhelmin' amount of stress. I propped my head up wit' a couple of pillows before gettin' lost under my down comforter. Driftin' off to sleep, I dreamt of the good memories Carlos and I once shared. Damn, if only I'd known he was my brother things could've been different. I missed him so much. Wakin' up in a cold sweat a few minutes later, it finally hit me, I was a murderer. I was the one who pulled the trigger and took away my brother's life. Even though my brother betrayed me and had an affair wit' my wife, he didn't deserve to die. If I would've found out under different circumstances, I wouldn't have killed him. Our motto was always money over bitches, and I had to go and fuck that up. None of that hurt as much 'til now.

After sittin' in bed and thinkin' for what seemed like hours, it was time for me to go get Marisol. Despite the outcome, I had to be strong for her. I owed her that much. Gettin' in the shower and puttin' on my clothes was the easy part. Drivin' to the airport, pickin' up Marisol and listenin' to her cry wasn't as bad as I thought either. However, once we pulled up to the Coroner's office on Preston Street was when it felt like my Nike boots were filled wit' cement. The sad thing was Marisol and I had different emotions. She had hopes that Carlos might still be alive and that the body found wasn't his. Me on the other hand...I knew it was him and the guilt was eatin' at me by the minute.

After goin' through all of the processes it was time to see Carlos' remains. Surprisingly, they allowed both of us to view him, after Marisol went off on one of the medical examiners. It was so cold in the room where his body was kept that we both began to shake before they even lifted the white sheet.

"Now, I have to warn you that the body is badly decomposed due to it being under the water for so long. It probably isn't even gonna be recognizable, but because bodies decompose faster in the air and underground surprisingly there was a small amount of tissue remains that has some markings on it. We believe it may be a birthmark or tattoo that you might be able to recognize. If not, then we'll have to count on dental records," the assistant medical examiner stated. "Are you ready?"

Marisol shook her head. "Yes."

My eyes immediately filled wit' tears, and the guilt set in even further when the examiner finally lifted the sheet. As much as I'd prepped myself, I was still shocked at what I saw. There was no hair, no recognizable body parts, just bits and pieces of gray colored tissue that smelled like rottin' fish. Luckily, I caught Marisol before she fell to the floor.

"Ma'am, are you okay?" the examiner asked.

"Yes, I'm sure she'll be fine. This is just too much. Can we hurry up and get this over wit'?" I said, holdin' onto Marisol's arm.

"Sure. As you can see in this area of tissue, there's a marking that appears to be tattoo or something," the examiner pointed out.

Tryin' to get a closer look, I stared in the area that he was referrin' to and could easily make out part of the tattoo that used to be on Los' arm; a tattoo that had the initials M.O.B. which stood for Money Over Bitches. When I looked at Marisol, it was if she knew.

"It's him! That's my husband," she said, then cried quietly.

"Can you give us some time alone, sir?"

"Of course," the medical examiner answered as he placed the sheet back over Carlos' remains.

"Oh my God, Rich it's him."

I shook my head. "I know."

"I want you to stay with me please," she cried.

"I wouldn't dare leave you." I stepped behind Marisol and put my arms around her as she stared down at the sheet.

"First, Mia is diagnosed with Leukemia, and now it's confirmed that my husband is gone. What am I gonna do without him Rich? Carlos was my everything!"

"I'm gonna be here for you through it all. Anything you need from me, I owe it to you."

"We need to be there for each other."

I instantly noticed the slip up. However, Marisol was so distraught that she didn't even realize that I said I owed her.

"Whoever did this to my husband is gonna get an old fashion, slow, Columbian death. Rich, I've killed before over money and loyalty, but this shit is on another level. They will pay," Marisol stated.

"Umm, excuse me. I'm sorry to interrupt you guys, but we're not allowed to have you in here alone for an extensive amount of time. So if you…"

"No, please don't make me leave my husband. Please don't!" Marisol screamed 'til we finally carried her out.

Once they sat us in another room, we were told that although they believed Carlos died from drownin' because his remains were found in the trunk in the car, the state still demanded that they perform an autopsy. Hearin' that, I wasn't sure how I felt. I was positive that once they studied his bones, they were sure to find evidence of the gun shot wounds. From there it would probably be a homicide investigation, which really would cause some drama. The last thing I needed was the cops sneakin' around my crib and askin' me questions.

On the way back to my house, Marisol's eyes were blood shot red from cryin' and probably lack of sleep. I let her know that she didn't have to go to her house in Potomac and be there alone, so she agreed stayin' at my house would be best. Once we finally made it back from Baltimore, I helped Marisol out of the car and into the house. She was out of it, but was coherent enough to ask for some water to take a couple of Excedrin PM's. Before she passed out, she let me know that it was okay for me to call Uncle Renzo. She obviously wasn't in the mood to talk to him, and little did she know, I wasn't either.

After Marisol fell asleep, I gave Juan a call and updated him on what was goin' on. He knew that it would only be a matter of time before Uncle Renzo would be in town on our heels; ready to blame whomever he could for Carlos' death. Juan assured me that his conversation wit' Lisa went well and that I had nothin' to worry about. Apparently, she was on board and knew that any slip up would put all of our lives at risk. After hangin' up wit' Juan, I built up the courage to call my Uncle. The phone only rang once before he answered.

"Yes, Rich, what is it?"

"Hey Unc' umm, I don't know how to say this but umm…"

"Spit it out Rich, what are you trying to tell me, time is money."

"Well, umm.."

"Land the plane Rich, I'm handlin' business. Don't fuck with my money. Is it my son? Is that what it is?"

"Yes. Today me and Marisol went to Baltimore to view a body and it was Los'."

"What the fuck do you mean?"

"Well, she got an anonymous call from a woman sayin' that Los' body was dumped in Baltimore."

"What!"

"She called her PI and asked him to look into it. He called…"

"So, the cock sucker that I'm paying looked into this without contacting me. He'll be dead by the morning. This is unacceptable. Why didn't Marisol call me, where is she?"

"She's upstairs sleep. She's really out of it. This is hard for us all. Marisol's intentions were to find out if the tip was real or was some bullshit before she called to let you know anything. That's why I'm callin' now."

"Oh my God! You better find out who's responsible for this, Rich. His blood is on your hands. What kind of shit did you get Carlos wrapped up in?"

"Nothin'! You're the one who kept a secret and didn't tell us we were brothers, and now you're pointin' blame at everyone but yourself!"

"Don't you dare talk to me with disrespect!"

"We're all mournin', Unc'. We're all hurtin'!"

Before I could go any further, the phone went dead. Now, I was convinced that I was on borrowed time and I knew that I would have to act fast in order to survive.

Chapter Eleven
LISA

Over the past three nights, I'd been dreaming about Carlos nonstop. Dreams of us raising a family together and moving away to some low key spot in Europe. It felt so good that sometimes I wanted to stay asleep especially during our passionate lovemaking sessions. Even when I wasn't asleep I constantly thought about the times we shared together and what could've been if he wasn't ripped away from me. Something told me that despite his marriage to Marisol eventually he would've left her for me. His body language often told me that he wanted me to be his girl, and I knew if he'd gotten the chance to see Carlie...that would've been the icing on the cake.

I constantly flooded my mind with good thoughts of him. Not the fact that someone had contacted Marisol about the location of his body. Not only did I block out what his remains must've looked like, but I didn't even want to think about what Uncle Renzo had planned to do now that Carlos' death was finally confirmed. My main focus was to somehow keep my name out of anything relating to his murder and to protect my beautiful baby girl. If Uncle Renzo ever got suspicious, Rich was gonna have to deal with that shit on his own. He was gonna be the one to go down...not me.

In a rush to see Carlie, I quickly got dressed, throwing on a fitted turtleneck and a pair of jeans, with my black fur vest and matching boots. Even though I shouldn't have been concerned about appearances, I tried to be on point when I visited Carlie to erase the perception the hospital staff had of me. Especially that nosey-ass social worker who'd already labeled me an unfit mother. I hated that bitch, and needed her off my case.

Thirty minutes later, I pulled into a parking space and power walked up the sidewalk, slushing my feet through the water from all rain we'd been getting. As I made my way into the hospital and up to the NICU, I spotted Nurse Brooks. With an outdated Northface jacket on, it looked as if she was getting ready to start her shift.

"Well, hello Lisa. How are you feeling this cold winter morning?"

"I'm okay, any updates on my baby girl?"

"She's definitely progressing and has been able to do a better job at mastering her feedings. We're just hoping within the next couple of weeks her lungs will develop even more so she can be ready to come home with mama."

"Yeah, I would like that a lot."

"I'll keep praying for you and that beautiful daughter of yours."

"Thanks I'm going to need it."

"You'll be fine. Now, let's go and get you all ready so you can nurse that baby girl and think about her coming home to you. That's all that matters right about now."

"You're right. Thanks for being so caring," I said, as we both got on the elevator.

Within a few minutes, Nurse Brooks got me set up in my private nursing room with Carlie, who was fast asleep. As I held her, I admired the way she was fighting for her life and yet still managed to look so peaceful. It was as if she didn't have a care in the world. It made me think about how I let the small things in life bother me so easily. At that moment, I decided to whisper a sweet poem to her that my father used to say to me when I was little.

My sweet precious baby girl, do you know that you're my

world.

 Laying there without a care at peace, rest my child enjoy your sleep.

 Before I could continue, the sound of my voice must've awakened her because her eyes slowly began to open.

 "Hey, sweetie. You ready to eat for mommy."

 I pulled out my right breast, lowered my bra then placed my nipple by her mouth, but she wouldn't latch on so. "Come on Carlie. You need mommy's milk."

 After trying this for at least five minutes, I decided to give up. The last thing I wanted was for her to be hungry so I called Nurse Brooks in to give me a bottle full of the breast milk I'd already pumped. Happy that the hospital was able to store my nutrients, I couldn't help but smile when Carlie took the bottle like a pro.

 "That's it. Eat up so you can get big. Mommy needs you to come home," I said, playing with her soft jet black hair.

 After only drinking one ounce, I stared down at her as she peered up at me. Even though it was a priceless bonding moment, I started to feel sad when thoughts of my daughter growing up without a father entered my mind. I really hoped that I could give her a life of happiness and raise her differently then I'd raised Juan and Denie. A world without drugs and violence. In the Sanchez family, that appeared to be a perfect world, but I was determined to become a better mother. I was gonna do things right this time.

 All of my thoughts were suddenly interrupted when my phone rang. It was Cornell. He'd been calling me for days, but with all that was going on, I hadn't accepted any of the calls. Realizing that he was very persistent, I finally decided to answer.

 "Hello."

 "Wassup stranger?"

 "Why did you say that?"

 "Well, I haven't talked to you since we met so that qualifies you as a stranger. What's been up? You alright? You sound like you just lost your best friend."

"I sorta did? You know we had a death in our family, so I was dealing with that. Plus,
I've been busy visiting my daughter in the hospital. It's just been very stressful."

"Oh, I'm sorry to hear about your loss. Should I call back at a better time?"

"No, it's fine."

"So, how old is your daughter?"

At that moment, I'd totally forgot that Cornell and I had yet to discuss Carlie. I knew that what I was about to say could possibly scare him off, but if he wanted to fuck with me he had to accept her, too. "She's a newborn. She'll be six weeks tomorrow, actually." Silence immediately fell over the phone. "Hello."

"Umm...yeah I'm here. I didn't know that you'd just had a baby," Cornell replied in a disappointed tone.

"You didn't ask," I said with a smile. I hoped sarcasm would lighten the mood. "Is that a problem?"

"No, not at all. As long as you ain't with her father we should be straight."

Please, if her father was still here we wouldn't even be talking right now, I thought. "No, he passed away."

"Damn, everybody in your circle is fallin' off," Cornell said with a slight chuckle."

"Very funny. You better be glad I have a sense of humor."

"So, how's the baby? Why is she in the hospital?"

"She was born a bit early," I replied. There was no way in hell I was gonna tell him about the drugs, so I hoped he didn't ask. "She's building up her strength and getting healthier every day. I just got finished feeding her actually."

"Don't you sound like the sweet mama?"

"I'm just enjoying the only peace I have in my life right now and just trying to concentrate on my future with her."

"Well, am I goin' to be a part of that? That future thing sounds good to me."

His comment made me blush like a high school crush. "If you act right. You know how you athletes are."

"Man, I'm tired of hearin' that. One thing I can promise you, when I have a woman that I'm in love with, I treat her as if she's the only lady on this earth."

"Blah, blah, blah. Haven't I heard this all before?"

"Alright Miss Lady, you either gonna let me take you out and give me a chance, or I'ma let you think what you want about me and wonder later about what could've been."

"Wow, did I hit a nerve, sir?"

"No, I just don't want to go back and forth about what I can do to change your life and what you're used to. It's too early in the morning for that."

"Well, what are you doing up anyway? Where are you?"

"The early bird catches the worm," he said, letting out a slight laugh. "Naw, for real I'm about to hit the gym for a few hours. So, is it a date or what?"

"It's a date. Come pick me up around six."

"Bet."

"And Cornell, don't tell Juan."

"I won't. Kiss the baby for me," he added before hanging up.

Shocking myself, I couldn't believe I'd decided to go on a date with him. For some reason he put me in a better mood and at that point, I started to think that maybe he was what both Carlie and I needed. I knew once Juan found out he would be furious, but I didn't care. Cornell was a millionaire and if I played my cards right, he could potentially be my future for me and Carlie. Since Cornell didn't have any kids and didn't appear to have a girlfriend, I was sure that I could make my way into his life. No baby mama drama was a plus and I knew that with him only being twenty-eight years old, I could work my mojo.

After my visit with Carlie, I ran a few errands and by the time I made it home, I only had an hour left before Cornell arrived. Although I could've used a power nap so I could be well rested, I quickly hopped in the shower and lathered up in my favorite vanilla bath gel. Even when I got out, I kept the vanilla scent going with the lotion, and body spray. I knew that he would go crazy from the aphrodisiac scent.

Going in my closet, I placed the tip of my index finger in my mouth trying to decide what to wear. It had been years since I'd gone on a date, so I had to impress. *I can't even call me and Carlos' rendezvous real dates*, I thought then stopped at my shoe section.

Since he was 6' 7' I was sure that my five inch Gucci platform boots would put me only a foot away from his gorgeous lips, so I decided to grab them. Making my way to my lingerie drawer, I put on a sexy black Badgely Mischka thong set. I had no intentions on letting Cornell see it tonight, it was just that I needed to feel sexy in order to open up and show him the real Lisa. Since I'd been nursing Carlie, my breasts were looking quite yummy and I knew that it was important to wear something sexy enough to tease him. At that moment, I thought it was a good idea to put on my black fitted Cavalli dress that tastefully hugged my curves.

Once I got dressed, I sat at my vanity and started on my hair and make-up. Searching through my numerous eye palettes, I decided on three warm colors so I could create a great smokey eye. Looking in the mirror, I admired my new look. Thinking back, I couldn't believe that I'd let my hairstylist Jermaine, give me a choppy bob. With the exception of when those bastards cut off my ponytail, my hair hadn't been this short since the tenth grade, but I liked it. It gave me more character and pizzazz.

After I completed my look, something suddenly came over me. I was convinced that I needed to go on the internet to see what the media had to say about my date before he arrived. As I opened my laptop, I wondered if it was a good idea, but the nosey side me made me proceed. Once my laptop was loaded, I went to my Google search engine and typed in Cornell Willis' girlfriend. I knew that if he'd ever taken a picture of him and some woman, it would be posted on at least one gossip blog.

There was nothing under images, but there was a link to

some pro athlete girlfriend website. As soon as I began to read the posts, it was unbelievable how all types of jump offs went on the site and posted their sexual experiences with different athletes. Surprisingly, there weren't too many things on Cornell. One girl just said he was an asshole and extremely cheap. I figured she must've been an *after the club chick* he'd hit and rolled out.

When I couldn't find anything else on Cornell, I started to explore other players and couldn't believe what these girls were saying. Most of them were married, which led me to believe that their wives couldn't possibly know about the website. This was one of the main reasons why I didn't want to date an athlete. Then I thought about it. I was married to a drug dealer for almost two decades and he cheated the whole time. At least these guys had guaranteed money and a real job. The more I thought about it, the more enticed I was to give Cornell a chance. Grabbing my phone out of my purse, I texted Cornell to see how far away he was. I wanted to get out of the house before Juan got home. As soon as he texted back to say he was less than ten minutes away, I heard Juan punching in the ADT code to enter the house. *Shit, just my luck.*

"Ma, where you at?" Juan yelled out.

"I'm upstairs in my room." I could hear him running up the stairs as his diamond chains clinked together. "Well, don't you look like a rapper?" I teased.

"And don't you look like you got a hot date. What's all this about?"

"Nunya."

"Yeah, that's how you going on me? We keep secrets now?"

I sucked my teeth. "Okay Juan, but you have to promise not to get upset."

"Spill it."

"I'm going on a date with Cornell."

"What? Man, didn't I ask you not to talk to him? That's my man, and he is only twenty-eight. With everything that's going on, you're going on a date with him?"

"Yes, I am. Besides, he'll be twenty-nine in January. So technically I'm only 9 ½ years older than him, and he seems like a really nice guy. Don't try and make me feel bad for going out, Juan. You were the main one wanting me to get past the Carlos situation. I need a moment and something to get my mind off of things."

"Ma, I understand that you're trying to get your mind off some things. You're stressed and I understand why, but he's my boy. We hang out together. We mess with chicks together. It's just not gonna work and I don't want anything coming in between our friendship."

"Juan, we're both grown. Damn, you act like I'm trying to marry him tomorrow. It's just a date."

"Man, wait 'til I talk to that nigga. He didn't tell me he was taking you out."

"That's because I asked him not to."

He shook his head. "Well, don't come crying to me if he hurts you. Remember y'all grown." Leaving out of the room, Juan went back downstairs before I could respond.

My son had never seen me with anyone besides Rich and was obviously having a hard time dealing with it. I was trying really hard to get over Carlos and I knew Cornell would be a good person for the job. Moments later, the front door slammed. I knew Juan was upset, but I had to do this, just to see if this was what I needed.

Just as I started to re-apply my lip gloss, my phone rang.

"Hey, I'm outside," Cornell said. "I think I just saw Juan peelin' off down the street."

"Yeah, I'm sure that was him. Let me grab my coat. I'll be out in a minute."

As I walked downstairs, butterflies filled my stomach. A part of me was excited while another part was nervous. Turning on the alarm and locking the door, I made my way down the driveway to his black on black Bentley coupe. With my nerves all over the place, I prayed that I didn't slip and fall. Embarrassment wasn't an option right now.

Unexpectedly, Cornell got out of the car and helped me down the rest of the driveway. He looked great with his black leather jacket, Gucci skull cap and black Gucci boots. As he opened his car door for me, all I could think to myself was, *if Rich could see me now he would die.* Once Cornell got in the car, he grabbed my hand and kissed it.

"Hey beautiful, you look damn good."

"Well, aren't you the charmer, thanks. Do you always open the door for your women, or just on the first date?"

He smiled. "I don't have women. I have friends I'm cool with. And I do give respect to women. I have a mother and a sister that I want to be respected, so I make sure I treat women as I would want the women in my life to be treated. Anyway, your aura demands respect."

"Oh really. Why do you say that?" I questioned as I thought about how I'd never been respected by a man.

"Well, you just seem like the type of woman who demands respect from a man. It's how you carry yourself."

"You're still not answering my question."

"I mean, it's hard to explain, but you make me want to treat you right. How is that for an answer?"

"It's good as long as you mean what you're saying and be a man of your word. I don't have time for games right now."

"I will. I'ma make you love me, watch."

"Whatever!" I said as we both laughed.

He had game, but I was determined I wasn't going to be played with by another man. As Juan crossed my mind, I wondered if he was just being overprotective or if he was genuinely concerned because Cornell wasn't good for me. I liked Cornell so far, but I just had to make sure I held my head and stayed in control.

We drove for fifteen minutes making small talk and listening to Trey Songz. When we finally made our way into downtown Silver Spring and pulled up in front of Chipotle, my mouth dropped. I thought to myself, *is this nigga serious.* I was dressed for a romantic evening, not for an after school snack. All I could think was *how the fuck is this nigga gonna say he's taking me out to make me feel better and now we're at a fucking Mexican fast food restaurant*. I hoped liked hell he was testing me.

"So, Miss Lady, do you like Chipotle?"

"Actually, I love it," I replied with a huge smile. "Their salads are the best."

"Are you alright if we have dinner here?"

I had to play it off. "Of course, but are they open?" I asked, looking through the window. "I don't see anyone else in there. Plus it looks a little dark."

"Yeah, they are open."

When Cornell parked, we walked hand in hand to the front door. All I could think of was the girl on the blog saying how cheap he was. *Maybe her ass was telling the truth*, I thought as Cornell opened the door.

"Hello, Mr. Willis, we were expecting you. Is this your lovely date?" a short white man with a burrito t-shirt asked.

"Yes, this is Lisa."

"Hi, Ms. Lisa, welcome to Chipotle."

"Thank you," I replied with a confused expression.

"Follow me," the man stated.

Once we made it further inside, there was a candle lit table for two. There were no other customers, just two Chipotle employees and us. At that point, I was so impressed with Cornell's efforts, it didn't matter where we were eating. All that mattered to me was the fact that I felt special again; a feeling that I hadn't experienced in a long time. The date had just started and I didn't want it to end.

After we ordered our food, I listened to him talk about his family. He told me that his mom was a single mother and raised him and his sister on her own. His father had left to go to the store to get milk when he was only six months old and never returned. Neither him or his sister who was two years old at the time had memories of him. He'd just recently met his father three years ago, but didn't trust him since he felt he was back in his life due to his status. The more Cornell spoke about his absent father, the more he became upset, so he decided to shift the conversation and inquire about my upbringing. I was usually a private person, but being married to Rich you got used to dodging questions when people tried to pry. After Cornell poured his heart out to me, there was no way I could be secretive about my family with him.

"I can't believe I let you in like that on the first date," Cornell said, as he held my hand. It appeared as if he was starting to trust me already.

"Well, I'm sure we'll be sharing many stories in the future," I replied with a slight grin.

"I have a better idea. Share with me right now. Were you raised in a two parent home?"

"Actually, I was. I'm a preacher's daughter."

"Oh yeah, you know what they say about those sweet preacher's daughters," he joked.

"Whatever, Cornell. Anyway, I had my son when I was young and my parents forbid me to see Rich, Juan's father. I was young and was determined to keep my baby and be with the one I loved. Rich was my life and you see I chose my son, so my father threw me out of his house. I had to depend on Rich to take care of me and my son. Skip to a few years later, Rich started to change, which I saw but was in denial like most women. He started spending more and more time with other women, his uncle, cousin…well brother, but that's another story in itself."

"What was the crime in that?"

"Because he got caught up in the streets. He almost died in a car accident and severely injured his knee which threw away all of our dreams of him one day being in the league. All of his scholarships and dreams went out of the window and that's when our lives changed."

"Damn. So, how did it change?"

"He got knee deep in the game and the rest is history. I really didn't have a relationship with my dad after that, and my mother and I never got along, so Rich was all I had."

I noticed I was starting to talk too much. The number one way to turn a man off. But I felt so at ease talking to him that everything just started to roll off of my tongue. He made me feel like I could trust him for some reason.

"So, I guess I'll call you Ginger, huh. Like in the movie *Casino*."

"You're not funny. That life is all behind me now." As soon as I started to spill again my phone rang. It was Juan. I didn't want to argue with him so I sent him to voicemail three times.

"I see you a busy lady, somebody lookin' for you. Am I holdin' you from your man?"

"That's Juan…smart-ass. I don't feel like hearing his mouth. You know he has a problem with me seeing you."

"He'll be alright. I'll take good care of his mother," Cornell replied.

Before I could reply, Juan sent me a text. You need to get home now! Rich is tripping about Uncle Renzo.

My nerves all of a sudden went crazy. I didn't know what to do, so I panicked. All I could think about was, *maybe Uncle Renzo found out what happened.*

"Oh my gosh. Cornell you have to take me home. I have a family emergency!" I yelled abruptly.

"Is Juan alright?"

"Yeah, we just need to go."

"Okay, no problem."

I texted Juan back to let him know that I was on my way home. Even though we never got a chance to eat, Cornell took care of the waiter and we headed back to my house. It was a very quiet but fast drive back. I didn't know what to expect at home and I guess Cornell got the picture because the questions instantly stopped. Once we pulled up in the driveway, Cornell parked and hopped out to open my door. When he proceeded to walk toward the house with me, I stopped him.

"No, I'll be okay. You don't have to walk me inside. Thanks for a great evening."

"You're welcome and I am walking you inside. That's what gentleman do," Cornell insisted.

Not wanting to debate, I allowed him to follow me. As soon as I opened the door, I dropped my purse in the foyer and ran straight to the living room. "What's up, Juan? What happened?" I asked.

"Man, you alright? You had your mom worried," Cornell added.

"What the fuck is this about? Y'all a couple now? You come in here all concerned like y'all have known each other for years. This is a family matter and…"

Cornell must not have closed the door all the way, because before Juan could finish, Rich came in like a mad man.

"Who's hot-ass Bentley is in my driveway and why the fuck y'all got the door opened like that?" Rich yelled as he walked through the door.

Obviously Juan and Rich were both in a rage, and I didn't know how to get Cornell out of the line of fire.

"Man, like I was saying, you need to roll out," Juan said as he gave Cornell a stern look.

"Cool," Cornell said then turned to me.

"I'll call you later," I said to assure him that I had his back. Moments later, he gave me a kiss on the cheek and left.

Rich was pissed off and in shock. I knew that I'd hit a nerve. When he walked toward me, Juan quickly blocked his path.

"Don't even think about putting your hands on my mother."

"You goldiggin'-ass whore! Damn, you fuckin' your son's friends now? You that desperate for a come up, bitch?"

"Why? Are you mad because he got more money than your broke-ass!" I shot back. I was tired of Rich and didn't care anymore.

"Both of y'all stop! Can we discuss the reason why we're here," Juan spat.

"Juan, if you asked me to come home from my date to lecture me again about how I need to act if Uncle Renzo or Marisol asks me something then…"

"Ma, I don't give a fuck about your date. We need to discuss the importance of when we go to the funeral, memorial or whatever Marisol is planning that we're all on the same page. That's the reason I called you to come home," Juan replied.

"Oh my God, Juan do you think they know? I don't want to be wrapped up in this shit!" I yelled in a hysterical rage. I ran to the couch, sat down then buried my face in my hands.

"I should've killed this dumb bitch on BW Parkway," Rich said, annoyed with my reaction.

"Rich, we have to act like a family now. I'm not trying to die because of y'all fuck ups. Ma, be easy. Uncle Renzo is probably gonna try to break you, but you gotta be strong if you want to see another day."

I was quiet for a few seconds. "Okay. I'll be strong."

As soon as Juan got up to go to the bathroom, Rich came over to me and slapped me so hard I saw stars.

"Bitch, this is all your fuckin' fault," he said as he left out the door.

Chapter Twelve
JUAN

As Cornell called my phone for the third time in less than an hour, I hit the ignore button once again. I just wasn't in the mood to talk. I'd been avoiding him since he'd taken my mother out two days ago, so hopefully at some point he would get the message. I just wasn't ready to deal with that shit especially since I was trying to be there for my mother. Even though she wouldn't tell me, I knew something had happened between her and Rich that night.

When I walked back into the living room, she seemed to be in a daze. Not to mention, the red mark on her face showed signs of an assault. No matter how many times I begged her to tell me, she just kept giving me some dumb-ass excuse about the red mark only being makeup. I knew she was covering for that nigga, and wished I could've caught his ass in the act. Already dealing with the Carlos situation, it was important to me that I got my mother through this hard time. More importantly, I just didn't want her to slip back into a place where she would turn to drugs to cope.

As I got dressed for Carlos' memorial service, I was beyond ready for all of this shit to be over with. Looking through my closet, I decided on my Rock and Republic Jeans with my D&G striped sweater. Since the service was at their house, I didn't really feel like dressing up. My Prada loafers and fur bomber would be as dressy as I got.

Sitting on the edge of my bed as I put my last shoe on, I thought about how I could make my way into Uncle Renzo's organization without Rich. I wanted to keep my plans for Rich separate so it wouldn't interfere with me getting money. If everything worked out, I had plans to leave town and start over in Atlanta. I knew that Uncle Renzo was a hard one to convince, but I had a plan to make him trust me. With him and Rich at odds, and Carlos gone, I knew that I could stick it to Rich if I got Uncle Renzo to allow me to take over Carlos' part of the business. This would definitely put me in position to get some real money and leave this game all together, so both of my sisters and my mother would be in a better place.

I thought about Denie a lot and always hoped that she was doing okay. For the past couple of weeks I tried calling her, but she hadn't answered any of my calls. Hoping she would eventually come around, I figured I'd give her the space she needed. I commended her for leaving and taking that nigga Rich's money. He deserved everything that he had coming to him.

My Rick Ross CD was on blast as I got ready. Checking myself out in the mirror, I picked a small piece of lint off my sweater right before my mother stormed through the door.

"Why the hell do you have that music turned up so loud?" she asked.

"Damn, what's up with you? Coming in here with all that attitude," I said, turning the music down.

"I'm sorry. I had a rough morning trying to feed Carlie at the hospital. I had a moment thinking about Carlos and how I'm gonna have to raise her alone. I know Rich isn't gonna stand up, especially with that stunt he pulled in court demanding a paternity test."

She sat next to me on the edge of my bed and looked down. It always hurt me to see my mother in pain. Since I was a teenager, I protected her and did what I could not to make her feel alone. It really upset me when whatever I tried to do to make her happy wasn't enough.

"Ma, I asked you this before but maybe I need to ask again.

Do you trust me?"

"Of course, Juan."

"Well, why is it that no matter what risks I take and what I do to make you happy is never enough?"

She looked up. "No, I appreciate you so much. I'm sorry that I make you feel like that. I love you more than anything in this world."

"Then just trust me that Rich won't be an issue for long. It's just a matter of time and we will be free of his bullshit."

"Why do you keep saying that? He's like some type of fucking villain in a scary movie. He just never goes away. Just when you think he's gone on with his life, he finds a way to come back and make my life hell."

"Well, know that I'm doing all I can to make that nightmare go away and give you happiness."

"He doesn't even want me to have this house. What will I do for money? After a while I know this will all go away and I won't have anything. I've never had a real job, no skills. I just don't know what to do. Rich was all I've known, all my life, and just when I began falling for Carlos, Rich ruined everything."

"Ma, we have less than an hour before the service so let's continue this conversation in the car. Besides, I have some questions I need answers to."

She looked at me with a funny expression before agreeing. Moments later, we made our way to my car. As soon as we pulled out of the driveway, I decided to go in and start my questioning.

"So Ma, whatever I ask, please be honest."

"What is it, son?"

"Why did you go out with Cornell? Was it for the money?"

She gave me the look of death. "Are you serious?"

"Yes, I'm serious. Why Cornell, why my friend?"

"Juan honestly, at first, I did look at him as a come up. I looked at him as an opportunity to get ahead in life legally. But after spending time with him I got to know another side of him. He let me know the guy off the court. He wasn't the superstar player, *Mr. Three* everyone else sees. He was just Cornell. With all of the fancy restaurants I've been to in my life, my date with him had to be one of the best."

"Where did y'all go?"

"We went to Chipotle in downtown Silver Spring," she said with this huge smile.

I was confused. "What? That nigga is a fool. The chicks always said he was cheap. How can he spend thousands in the club popping bottles of champagne, but can't even take my mother to a nice restaurant?"

"No Juan, you've got it all wrong. He had the place cleared out. It was just the two of us in the restaurant sitting at a table by candlelight. Now, don't get me wrong, when we pulled up at first I was like *what the fuck*, but after showing me all that, I knew then that my night would be full of bliss."

She seemed happy. I knew that I was trying to protect her, but maybe I needed to stop being so hard on the both of them. Maybe Cornell was what she needed to stay off of drugs and keep her life on track. Even better, maybe this would help her get past both Carlos and Rich.

When we arrived at Carlos and Marisol's house in Potomac, MD it was just as I remembered. I hadn't been there since I was younger, but the house was still off the chain. After having to be buzzed into the gate, the long brick driveway led us to the house. With at least seven bedrooms, the house on Newbridge Drive was huge. Looking at the 9,000 square foot home, Carlos was definitely getting paper, even more so than Rich thanks to Uncle Renzo. And I was willing to do whatever it took to be living like that, too. I wanted Uncle Renzo to take me under his wing and teach me everything I didn't know. I could be the protégé that he needed me to be.

There were a few cars parked in the circular driveway, but I didn't see Rich's car yet. Once we parked and went inside we were greeted by Marisol. My mother and Marisol didn't say two words to each other. Instead, they just looked each other up and down. The funny thing about them both was, they were both wearing the same pair of boots which I thought was hilarious. Women were so petty at times. This wasn't the time or place for my mother to be acting annoyed with Marisol so I thought I'd remind her to be easy so we didn't run into any issues.

I grabbed her arm. "Ma, please no drama today. Marisol is mourning her husband, so you need to respect that. We don't need no shit."

She looked at me like I'd just called her a bitch. "Juan, don't forget who the mother is. I'm fine. I know what I have to do."

At that moment, her attention quickly drifted from what we were talking about as she caught a glimpse of Carlos' name with angel wings tattooed across the top of Marisol's back. Her dress was open in the back, which I thought looked quite sexy, but of course my mother was instantly pissed.

"No, that bitch don't have a big ass tattoo of Carlos' name on her back," she said, rolling her eyes. "That shit looks terrible."

"Ssshh," I replied as we took our seats in the theater room.

They had completely transformed the room for the service and it looked great. There was an urn with a huge photo beside it of Carlos, Marisol, and their two daughters along with a slide show of Carlos' pictures throughout his life. There were a lot of photos of Rich and Carlos during holiday celebrations or while they were all on vacation. Every time a picture appeared with Marisol in it, my mother frowned then sucked her teeth.

"Why do we have to keep seeing her? She's not the one dead, Carlos is."

Her comments were irritating the shit out of me. Suddenly, our attention was drawn to the back of the room when we heard Marisol get excited when Rich came in. Both my mother and I looked at each other with weird expressions.

"What the hell was that all about?" my mother asked.

As I was about to answer, I noticed Uncle Renzo walk into the room. Since I knew him and Rich had some tension between them, I thought what better time to go and talk to him.

"I'll be back, Ma," I said getting up. I made a b-line straight to the most important person in the house. "What's up,

Unc'? How are you holding up?"

"Well, under the circumstances, I'm trying my best to mourn my son's death and handle it the best way possible."

"I can understand that. I'm really sorry."

"Well, whoever is responsible for this will definitely be sorry. I'm going to send a clear message to everyone that I have a million dollars for whoever can give me information, and I mean concrete information on who did this to my boy. Somebody will talk, I'm sure."

"I guess that's the way to do it. What's the old saying, money talks and bullshit walks?"

He nodded his head full of silver hair. "Yup."

"Unc, I know this might not be the best time to talk about this but…"

"Where's your mother?" he asked, totally ignoring me as if he knew what I was about to ask.

I pointed. "She's sitting down in the front."

"Let me go say hi to her."

As he walked off, I felt as though my dreams had walked off right along with him. Like a lost puppy, I followed behind him determined to finish my conversation once he greeted my mother.

"Hi Lisa sweetheart, how's everything? Don't you look lovely?" Uncle Renzo stated.

"Hey Renzo, I'm so sorry about Carlos," she said as she turned to him. She seemed startled like she'd seen a ghost.

"When are you going to come out and visit your uncle?"

"Umm, well you know Rich and I are going through a divorce right now, and it is getting very…"

"I didn't ask about Rich, I asked about you. Oh my goodness, before I forget, congratulations on the baby girl. Marisol told me she's adorable."

"Oh, thanks."

"Maybe I can come by the hospital before I leave town to visit."

"I would like that," my mother replied. As she started to get emotional, she got up to go to the bathroom.

"Don't worry Unc', she'll be alright. She's just going through a rough time right now, but I try to help her get through everything," I said.

"You've always been good to your mother. I told your father that Lisa is a good woman and he should've stuck it out."

"Well, he's not a good husband and she deserves better, so she'll be okay without him."

"Maybe, but he lost a good one. Juan, when you get a good one, hold on to her. A good woman is hard to find these days."

"I agree. But Uncle Renzo, can you hear me out for a minute? I want your advice on something." I thought that I needed to change my approach to make him look at me as a protégé as well as an opportunity to get more money.

"What's that son?"

"Well, I was looking into trying to break away from Rich completely and eventually joining your team. Our relationship has always been broken and the only reason I deal with him is on business, that's it."

He paused for what seemed like forever. "Juan, I don't know about that. I really don't want to be responsible for something happening to you in this business. You're a good boy. Look at what happened to Carlos. I introduced him to this life, him and your father. It shouldn't go beyond their generation. You need to make something out of your life boy. You're still young. Get out while you can. You already dodged jail once, with one hell of a rabbit's foot."

Damn, I hope he don't go into how I got out, I thought. "It's too late. I'm already in too deep. This is all I know, Unc. I promise you I'll be loyal to you, even if it takes me helping you and Marisol get to the bottom of Carlos' death."

I was desperate. I needed him to know that he could trust me. After a little more convincing I was finally able to break through to him. It seemed like he was willing to give me a chance. With Carlos gone, he said he needed me, and asked how I felt about working with Marisol. I agreed and let him know it wouldn't be an issue. Never before had I worked with a woman, but

Marisol was different. Despite how pretty she was, her ass was ruthless, and like one of the boys. I knew my mother wouldn't be happy about it, but I had to do what I had to do. When it was time for the memorial service to begin, I saw Rich shoot me a puzzled look wondering about my intense conversation with Uncle Renzo. Little did he know, I was ready for the big league and I couldn't wait to shut him down.

Chapter Thirteen
RICH

What the hell could Juan and Uncle Renzo be talking about, was all I could think of as the memorial service started. Most of the time Juan was so busy tryin' to fuck women, he didn't have time for long conversations with anybody. My mind wondered in so many different places as I thought back to the day that I killed my only brother. His last words, *I love you Rich,* played in my head as I stared at one of his pictures. Him havin' love for me was never a doubt in my mind. He'd obviously just gotten caught up. I told myself over and over, if I'd known he was fuckin' Lisa before catchin' them in the motel room, things probably would be different.

That bitch Lisa would be the one in pain right now. I would've put Marisol on her so fast she wouldn't even have known what hit her. That bitch was responsible for all the trouble in my life and as long as she lived on this earth, I would see to it that she had a life of misery. Especially since she'd made me lose the two most important people to me. As soon as that blood test came back and the judge could see how much of a whore she was, then everything wit' the divorce would work in my favor. That bitch was gonna pay. I cut her a dirty look as she sat there lookin' miserable and cryin' as if Carlos was her damn man.

Marisol was in so much pain. Even though Uncle Renzo and I barely said two words to each other, she sat between us as we both took turns comfortin' her. After the priest spoke and prayed over Carlos' ashes, there was a soloist who sung and then it was time for family and friends to speak about their memories. Many I hadn't seen in years. When I saw Carmen, Los' six year old daughter get up and speak, I tried my best to hold back my tears.

"I remember when my daddy used to take me to the zoo. It was fun. My daddy used to always take me to get ice cream. I miss my daddy and I hope my granddaddy gets the bad man that killed him."

Loud cries came from different parts of the room, but Marisol was the loudest of them all. She stood and held Carmen as they both sobbed uncontrollably. Knowin' it was my fault, knowin' I'd filled the room wit' so much pain and knowin' there was nothin' I could do about it made me feel like shit. For once in my life, money couldn't fix my problems.

Following Carmen, Uncle Renzo got up to speak. He looked like he was agin' so much. Never before in my life did I wish the old man would just croak, but I needed the added stress of him comin' after me out of my life.

"I have many memories of my boy, but the one I would like to share with you today is one that will hopefully make you realize how much he meant to me and how much his caring, self-less personality had an effect on everyone in this room. It hurts me to tell you all this, but there are very few of you who know this story. When Carlos was born, my late wife Celeste and I, we both knew that he was a special child. The only problem was I was sterile and there was one of two things, either Carlos was a miracle or my wife had conceived with someone else. The fact that I was sterile was something that I hadn't shared with my wife, so I went on praying that my son was a blessing."

I couldn't believe Uncle Renzo was about to tell that story in front of everyone. Now wasn't the time. I looked at Juan as he put his head down. I couldn't help but wonder why. Uncle Renzo got a little choked up, but held it together and continued.

"One night when Carlos wasn't even a year old I got a

phone call from my sister in law saying she had something that she wanted to tell me, but would like to keep it amongst us. That was the night I learned that my Celeste had an affair with my brother while I was in jail. That explained a lot. I held this in all of these years and still raised my nephew as my son. He meant the world to me and I knew that I had to put my pride aside and raise him as my own. I know that many of you are in shock wondering why I chose to speak of this now, but we are among friends and family and that's why I chose to have this ceremony in an intimate setting. I wanted to let all of you know in front of my Carlos, that no matter what, he will always be my son and I loved him. We had great memories and as I deprived my brother of raising his son as some of you might think, the only way I could deal with the betrayal, was to be a man and be his father. I knew he was the only child I would ever have and the only regret I have is keeping this from you Rich. I'm sorry and I'm sorry to you, to Marisol, my daughter. Now, I feel my heart is no longer heavy with keeping the truth from you all."

Marisol was in complete shock and gasps shot through the room. I thought it was my duty to get up and save the service. I thought maybe I could win back my Uncle Renzo's trust if he felt like I had his back. When I got up to speak I caught eye contact wit' a familiar face that I didn't want to see, not now. If she got up to speak, she would ruin everything. It was Jade. She sat alone in the back tryin' to be unnoticed. I was speechless. She made me feel like she had my life in her hands. She held all the cards since she knew what I'd done. And since Uncle Renzo was in a confessin' mood, I prayed that he didn't rub off on Jade.

For a while, I stood there and nothin' would come out of my mouth. My thoughts were no longer on Carlos, they were on how I could kill Jade. After standing there, finally Marisol snapped me out of it.

"Rich, are you okay?" Marisol whispered.

Respondin' wit' just a nod, I snapped out of my daze and started to speak. "I'm sorry. Umm, this is really hard for me. So, now I guess you all know that Carlos was actually my brother. But

I want to let you know Uncle Renzo, that we loved each other like brothers without even knowin'. We were always brothers. We were never cousins. I loved him wit' all I had. Man, you talkin' about a good dude. He was all that and then some. He would give you the shirt off his back and I'm sure everyone sittin' here knows that. We definitely had our moments, but when I needed Carlos, he was always there. When I was away, he helped my family as much as he could and I'll always be grateful for that. The bond we had was somethin' that not even death could take from us."

Before I broke down, I managed to hold it together so I didn't look guilty. Marisol then got up and spoke, while I prayed that Jade was gone by now. The entire time I spoke, she shook her head like I was a hypocrite feedin' my audience lies.

"First, I would like to thank everyone for coming to share in the homegoing for my husband. Memories of such a humble loyal man, I don't know where to begin. Even though we all know that God doesn't make mistakes, I'm gonna be selfish and say, my husband didn't deserve this. We still had more memories to create, more years to share as husband and wife. Now, my girls have to grow up without their dad and that's what hurts the most. After months of telling my girls that their dad was coming home soon, it's hurts to know that he'll never walk back through the door. When my daughter was diagnosed with Leukemia and I had to hold her and tell her everything was going to be okay, even though I had no idea where Carlos was, it hurt like hell. I just don't know what to say to you right now about good memories because I'm hurting right now. I want to take somebody out. I want whoever that did this to me and my family. I want them to hurt like I do. I want to destroy them, I want…"

Before Marisol could go any further I pulled her away from the podium then helped her back to her seat. She cried like a baby in my arms. Soon, the kids gathered around cryin', too. It was such an emotional moment. Seconds later, I finally stood up and thanked everyone for comin' before lettin' them know where they could go get food and refreshments. Before I was done, Marisol stood back up and interrupted me.

"I'm sorry everyone, I just want to be alone. Can you all please just go?"

"Gladly," Lisa responded as she stood up and rolled her eyes.

All of a sudden, someone started clappin' like they were at an awards show.

"Rich, you're so damn good."

Everyone instantly turned in Jade's direction.

"I can't believe you can just stand there as if you really care when this is all your fault!" Jade blurted out.

Everyone's eyes bulged, especially Uncle Renzo's and Lisa's as Jade made a swift exit. If I thought I could've gotten away wit' it, I would've pulled out the gun that was tucked in my waist and took Jade's ass out right there. I could feel my temples thumpin' on the side of my head along wit' my heart that started to beat out of control.

"I have no idea what she's talkin' about," I said addressin' the small crowd. "Bitter bitch. I don't have time for this shit today," I said under my breath before lookin' at Marisol. I hoped she wasn't buyin' what Jade was sellin'.

Knowin' I had to act fast, I gave Juan a look which he knew exactly what it meant, and jumped out his seat. Jade had to go.

Chapter Fourteen
RICH

An hour after Jade's crazy eruption, Marisol went to her room once her cousin volunteered to take the girls for some ice cream and take Lisa home. Before Uncle Renzo left, he let me know he would be in touch wit' me before he went back to the West Coast. I didn't know how to take it, but I knew it couldn't be good. Wit' me owin' him money and Jade's outburst, it was clear I was on borrowed time. Textin' Juan every ten minutes, I wanted to make sure he was on her heels. It was important that he knew exactly where she was stayin'. I had to make sure that bitch didn't make it back to New York alive.

When I went up to Marisol's room to check on her before I left, she was a mess. "Hey, I was just comin' to see if you need anything before I roll out."

"Rich, do you have to go?"

"Why? Do you want me to stay?"

"Yeah. I just don't want to be alone."

I knew that I had to get at Jade and even though Juan was on top of it, his weak-ass probably had every intention of pullin' out at any moment. I needed to leave, but couldn't help but wonder if I stayed would Marisol be more likely to trust me. Or if I left would she know what I was up to? My mind raced wit' thought after thought. I had to make a choice.

Makin' my decision, I gave Marisol a kiss on her forehead

and let her know that I would be back to check on her by the end of the day. Gettin' rid of that trouble causin' bitch was way more important than consolin' a friend right now. As soon as I walked out of the house, Juan's name popped up on my phone.

"Tell me you got good news," I said, jumpin' into my truck.

"Man, I'm still following this bitch. We're on the BW Parkway. Damn near in Baltimore."

If Juan knew I put his mother out on that same highway, I'm sure he wouldn't be helpin' me right now, I thought. "She's reckless man, you can't lose her. Just continue to follow her for me, please Juan," I begged. "I'm just leavin' Marisol's, but it's not gonna take long for me to jump on 495. I'm gonna try and catch up wit' y'all as soon as possible."

"Wait…we're getting off on the Arundel Mills exit," Juan informed.

"Alright, don't lose her, I'm right behind you."

My son had definitely come through for me this time. I knew that he wasn't my biggest fan, but I'm sure he was aware that if we didn't work together on this, it could cost us all big time. It was a matter of life and death not only for me, but my entire family. Wit' my .45 on my lap, I raced down 495 and made it onto the BW Parkway in no time. I called Juan back just to see where they were a few minutes later.

"Where are you now?"

"She stopped to get gas right off the exit. Then she got some food at the Chick Fila drive thru. Now, I'm sitting in the parking lot of that hotel called Springhill Suites. It's right across the street from the mall."

"Oh yeah, I know which one you talkin' about. I'm like ten minutes away. If she pulls out again, call me back. If not, I'll see you soon."

"Aight."

When I made it to the Arundel Mills exit, I felt as if all of my issues about anyone findin' out that I'd killed Los would soon be over. I always had a gut feelin' that Jade was the one who'd tipped Marisol off about Los' body anyway, so I was more than ready to end her life. My adrenaline raced as I pulled into the parkin' lot and parked next to Juan. I quickly got out of my truck, and got in the car wit' him. I was surprised to see that he had on a Nationals baseball hat pulled down over his eyes.

"What's up man? She still in there?"

"Yeah. Her room is 524."

I was surprised. "Damn, I didn't think you were gonna be able to figure that out. I thought I would have to do her ass in the parkin' lot."

"Well, the dumb bitch was so busy on the phone she did-n't even realize that I'd followed her into the hotel. As she was checking in, I sat at the computer in the business center like I had some shit to do. My goal was to at least find out what floor she was on, but the rooky nigga at the front desk actually told her the room number right before giving her the key. It was like this shit was meant to be."

"Damn, I guess it was. I appreciate you man. Soon all this shit will be over wit'. Was she by herself? Did she have more than one cup wit' her food?"

"She by herself, and she only had one cup."

"Cool, so I guess we can sit here for a couple of minutes and check out the area before we move in and…"

"Oh, hell no!" Juan interrupted. "I'm done. I did my part. Shit, I ain't no killer."

"Man, I need you here wit' me. I can't pull this off by my-self. At least be the lookout nigga."

"No. Like I just said, I did my part. All the other shit you planning is gonna have to be done on your own because I'm not killing nobody! I'm out. Now, get the fuck out my car, Rich!"

Just when I thought things were headed in the right direc-tion wit' us, he always found a way to fuck it up. "Man, Juan fuck you! Punk-ass!" I yelled then got out and slammed his car door as hard as I could. It was times like these when I missed Carlos. He was always down for whatever and never bitched up.

I was pissed. Juan obviously didn't realize the benefit for all of us if Jade was gone. I watched him pull off irritated. Little did his bitch-ass know he was an accessory regardless if I did the deed or not.

I laid low in my car and waited for about thirty minutes which was as long as I could wait. Gettin' out of my car, I put my gloves on then put my gun in my waist wit' the silencer already attached. Makin' sure there was no one around, I crept to the front of the hotel, then waited for the clerk to go in the back before I walked inside and made a mad dash to the elevator. Hopin' no one saw me, I mentally prepared myself for what I was about to do as the elevator stopped on the fifth floor.

Once I made my way to the door, I listened first to see if I could hear her talkin' to someone. Since the only thing I could hear was the TV, I knocked on the door. I knew if I tried to cover the peep hole, Jade probably wouldn't answer, so I decided to duck down so she couldn't see me. It wasn't the best plan, but it was my only one.

"Who is it?" she said in a soft tone.

"Room Service," I replied, disguisin' my voice.

"Room Service, I didn't order anything."

"Well, I have an order for some chocolate covered strawberries. I'll just leave them here at your door. Please sign the bill and put it back on the tray when you're done," I said, still in disguise. My voice was about to crack.

"But I didn't order anything," Jade said again. I wanted her to think I'd left, so I was quiet as I listened to her talkin' to herself. "I didn't order any damn strawberries. Hello?"

I hoped like hell Jade's curiosity would get the best of her and she would eventually open the door. After waitin' for what seemed like forever, and as luck would have it, she finally removed the lock and opened the door. I felt like a kid at Christmas as I pushed the rest of the door open wit' my gun drawn. Tryin' to catch her before she screamed, I quickly covered her mouth then shut the door before pushin' her up against the wall.

My eyes were immediately drawn to the small .22 sittin' on the nightstand as if she knew she might be in danger. My mind began to wonder where she could've gotten the gun from as I pressed my gloved hand further against her face.

We stared at each other for a few minutes before I finally spoke up. "I just have one question. Why the fuck did you call Marisol and tell her where Carlos' body was?" When I removed my hand, Jade looked at me like she was afraid to speak at first.

"What the hell are you talking about? I didn't call Marisol and tell her anything. I gave you my word."

"Yeah right, bitch! You gave me your word, but you just tried to get me caught up at the memorial service today. Get on the bed!" I yanked her arm then made sure I grabbed her gun and put it inside my coat pocket just in case she felt brave.

"What are you waiting for? Go ahead and get it over with!" she yelled.

Jade was a soldier and rarely showed fear of anything. Both she and Marisol were a lot alike in that way, but today was a lot different than how she'd been in the past, she knew what I had come to do.

"Shut the fuck up!"

Jade had obviously just gotten out of the shower and looked sexy as hell in her white robe. Wit' it slightly open, her perky breasts were exposed.

"So, you got some new piercings, huh?" I said, commentin' on her nipples.

"Yeah you bastard, and I got my pussy pierced, too," she said exposin' her cleanly shaven nest. There was a piercin' right at the top of her lips. I knew I had a job to do, but my manhood got the best of me. I had to have her one more time before I killed her. When I flashed back to how good and wet the sex was, my dick slowly started to rise. *Damn, we could've been good together*, I thought.

"Is this what you want, Rich? Do you miss this?" Jade asked. She placed her hands inside of her pussy and started fingerin' herself. She then laid back and started pleasurin' herself as if she was havin' a party that I wasn't invited to.

"Come on Rich, you scared, come over here and fuck me."

"Turn on your stomach," I demanded as I pulled my pants

down and plunged deep inside her wetness.

She felt so good that I immediately lost focus and took my coat off, but still kept my gun in one hand just in case. Jade moaned as if she'd missed fuckin' me as much as I missed fuckin' her.

"I miss this good shit, Jade. Damn, why did you leave me?"

"Shut up, Rich. Stop being sentimental and fuck me," she demanded before throwin' her ass back on me.

She played wit' her clit and moaned then flipped around and laid on her back. She put her hands behind her waist to lift herself off the bed a little and started fuckin' me even harder. I had one hand on her waist while pointin' the gun directly at her head wit' the other.

She continued to fuck me before slowly grabbin' the gun and placin' the silencer in her mouth. I knew this bitch was a beast when she started suckin' the barrel like a professional porn star, which completely turned me on. She then started playin' wit' my balls and as soon as I started to cum the gun went off.

I stopped movin' instantly. "Oh shit," I said lookin' down at her lifeless body.

Even though I'd pulled the trigger by accident, I succeeded wit' my plans. I hated to kill a bitch wit' such good pussy, but she had to go.

Chapter Fifteen
JUAN

When I woke up this morning I saw that I had several missed calls from Rich and Uncle Renzo. I'd gone to bed early the night before after I listened to my mother complain about Rich and feel sorry for herself once again about Carlos. It seemed as though anytime Carlos' name came up her whole world came to an end. The damsel in distress move was getting old and definitely wearing thin on my nerves. Sometimes I wished that I didn't always have to worry about her, especially since I needed to focus on my life for a change. It was time for me to start concentrating on me.

It's crazy how when you get older, the roles of parent and child eventually reverse. I'd gone from needing my mother and Rich to them needing me. I didn't mind helping out Rich every now and then, but the stunt he'd pulled the day before pissed me off. I knew that I had to follow Jade because I couldn't risk her exposing my mother, but I didn't sign up for being a fucking accessory to murder. Shit, I wasn't a killer. All I wanted to do was make money, hit a couple of chicks, and pop bottles from time to time. Street life is all I'd ever known, but I'd been lucky enough to make it without having to really prove my street cred. Carlos and Rich had paved the way for me in that sense. Selling drugs was a far stretch from killing muthafuckas and I needed it to stay that way.

As soon as I was about to get out of bed, my phone rang. I

sighed when I looked at the caller ID.

"What's up, Rich?" I answered in a dry tone.

"Man, you duckin' my calls now. I been callin' your ass all night."

"What do you want? I ain't got time to argue with you right now."

"Look, I'm still your father. I'm not one of your little bitches, so be careful when you're talkin' to me."

"Well, stop actin' like one."

"Muthafucka, I needed you last night and you wouldn't answer the phone, but as usual I handled everythin'. There's no need for you to try to duck me! I took care of everythin' without you, slim."

"Look, I'm a grown-ass man. There's no need for me to try and duck your fucking calls. If I don't want to talk to you then I'll say just that. If I don't answer then that means I'm busy."

"Busy doin' what? Fuckin' some broad. That shit could've waited," Rich shot back.

"No, I was busy comforting your wife all night. It seems that's been my job for as long as I can remember. Some shit you should be doing!"

"Juan, you know what…"

The phone went dead because I hung up on his selfish-ass. Little did that nigga know, he wouldn't have to take care of everything if it wasn't for me. I could've easily reminded him of that shit, since he'd had a memory loss, but just wasn't in the mood to deal with it.

After I hung up, I gave Uncle Renzo a call to see what was up. He let me know that he was going to come see me in less than an hour to continue our conversation from the day before. Quickly agreeing to his visit, I didn't want to pass up my opportunity to get him to trust me. My goal was to not only get Rich off the streets, but get what I needed to go legit and turn my money legal. I wasn't quite sure what I wanted to do yet, but I was going to figure it out along the way.

• • • • • • • • • • • • • •

Uncle Renzo arrived forty-minutes later, ready to discuss business. I was so happy my mother was at the hospital with Carlie because I didn't wanna have to play interference the entire time he was at the house. In her reckless state of mind, she was bound to say something stupid that would make him suspicious, and I didn't need that stress right now.

When I opened the door, Uncle Renzo wasn't alone. He was with his right hand man, Armondo, who looked like he was straight from the Italian mob. Because they were so opposite, I never understood how they ever became business partners. Everything about Armondo reminded me of Al Pacino. From the way he talked to how full his hair was on top. He had a strong Spanish accent and the two of them together would intimidate the baddest of all gangsters.

"What's up, Unc'? Hey Armondo, come on in."

We made our way through the foyer before taking a seat in the living room. No one ever went into our living room, but I wanted to have a more serious tone for the meeting.

"So, how are you son?" Uncle Renzo asked. From the dark circles under his eyes, it seemed like he hadn't slept in days.

"I'm cool. I'm glad that y'all were able to come see me before you left town."

"Well Juan, I like your style and I think that you'll be a great asset to the business, however there are a couple of things that concern me about you," Uncle Renzo stated.

"Really? Like what?" I inquired with a worried expression.

"I think that my first concern is that you're Rich's son. I'm not sure that your loyalty would be with me or with him. He just didn't handle things the way I would've liked him to when Carlos went missing, so I basically cut him off from the business. If you end up working for me, Rich can't be informed of anything we do. He's probably bitter, so I don't trust him now."

"That's understandable," I replied.

"Plus, there are too many questions and I need them answered before I can completely take on trusting you. Now, I'm not sure if those answers are going to come from you or from Rich, but I need to get to the bottom of who did this to my son." Uncle Renzo cracked his knuckles and gave me a stern look.

I shook my head. "So, what is it that you need from me? I need to prove to you that I can be trusted."

"I need to know where your loyalty lies. I mean to be honest, it should be with Rich. He gave you life."

"Fuck, Rich. He gave me life, but he never taught me how to live it. I've watched him beat and disrespect my mother for years. He's out for self and I just…"

Uncle Renzo cut me off. "Okay, that's enough. Now, my next issue is, you're too emotional. It's obvious that you were raised by Lisa."

"Damn, so what are you saying? I act like a woman?" I asked with a frown.

"No, I'm saying you wear your emotions on your sleeve. You have to learn the poker face. Before we can do business together, the flashiness, spending money in the club and driving all these expensive cars, is not gonna work. That shit is too hot. That draws the Feds and that's attention I don't need."

"Alright, I can dig that."

Armondo finally spoke up. "Okay here's my question. What happened with your jail situation? How did you beat those charges untouched?"

Instantly, a lump formed in my throat. He'd completely caught me off guard and I didn't know how to respond. Luckily, my mother came in the door a few seconds later yelling my name and asking me to come and help her with the bags.

"Umm, excuse me fellas," I said, getting up. I walked into the kitchen wiping the beads of sweat that had popped up on my forehead.

"Here," my mother said, handing me two grocery bags.

"Uncle Renzo and Armondo are here Ma, so don't ruin

anything," I whispered as she rolled her eyes and went into the living room where they were. As I put the milk in the refrigerator, I continued to glance back into the living room.

"Well, hello, you special gentlemen. You know I don't normally allow anyone to sit in my living room," she joked. They all laughed as both men gave her a hug.

"So, how's that baby of yours?" Uncle Renzo questioned.

"She's doing okay. She weighs a little over four pounds now, but we have to wait for her lungs to fully develop and gain more weight before she can come home."

Uncle Renzo sat back down. "So, is Rich being supportive of his new daughter, and speaking of daughters, how is Denie? We missed her at the memorial yesterday?"

"Well Renzo, Carlie is *my* daughter. As for Denie, she moved with Rich months ago and I haven't heard from her."

"Really? Now isn't that something. I know that Rich never got it right with Juan, but he has a weakness for girls. To not be there for Carlie concerns me a great deal. What's going on with him? Do you think it's about Carlos?" Uncle Renzo stared at her with great concern.

At that moment, I decided to interrupt them because I could definitely see my mother getting emotional. "You know how Rich is. Lately he's just been on edge and mad at the world. He's always been selfish, only caring about himself. This isn't anything new for us Unc. This has been the life we've always known since I can remember."

Taking a look at my mother, her eyes were watery and she was about to tear up. It scared me that she could put us all at risk.

"Lisa, why don't we go and get some lunch before I head out of town?" Uncle Renzo suggested. From that question, I knew he was suspicious.

"Umm, well…"

"Ma, why don't you go on upstairs and get some rest. You've had a rough morning," I quickly intervened.

"Yeah, that's a good idea," my mother replied then looked back at the two men. "I'm sorry you guys. Renzo, maybe we can do lunch another time."

"Okay Lisa, take care of yourself," he replied. We all watched her go upstairs before Uncle Renzo continued. "Juan, we need to head out. We have some business to take care of before we leave, but I'll be in touch. My only project for you right now is to help me find Carlos' killer. Once you've accomplished that, then I can trust you and we can move on to making you real dollars."

"I hear you loud and clear, a hundred percent."

As I walked them out, I noticed my mother at the top of the stairs.

"By Renzo, I'm sorry about Carlos," she said with a tissue in her hand.

"Lisa, it was nice seeing you. Call me anytime," Uncle Renzo responded.

"See y'all later," I replied before closing the door. When I looked up at my mother, I was ready to go off on her. What was the point of Rich killing Jade if my mother was going to be the one to let the cat out of the fucking bag?

"Ma, have you lost your mind? All I've asked you to do was be easy and keep it together. Anytime someone mentions Carlos' name, you fall apart. I'm tired of it!"

"Juan, you will never understand my guilt for why Carlos isn't here anymore. I know Rich killed him, but it's my fault he's dead. I was persistent that night. Carlos told me he had business to take care of, but I just had to see him. I should've waited to see him the next day. That's what he wanted."

"Ma, he's dead. Get over it. You can't keep blaming yourself. You didn't pull the trigger. Move on with your life. This shit is getting on my fucking nerves!"

The angrier I got, the more I raised my voice at my mother letting her know how disappointed I was. Suddenly, I was interrupted by the call I'd been waiting on since yesterday. It was the Feds. My mind began to wonder. Had they been tailing me when I followed Jade that day? Did they know she was dead? My mind raced as the phone rang for the third time. I knew I had to answer.

"Hello, this is Juan."

"Hey Juan, this is Agent Patterson, how are you?"

"I'm good."

"Well, I'm calling because we need to have a status meeting. Can you meet with us around three p.m. today?"

I was hesitant for a second. "Yeah."

"I'll text you the location around two. Does that work?"

"Yes, that's fine."

As soon as I hung up, the doorbell rang. Who the fuck can that be, I thought to myself as I walked toward the door. "Who is it?"

"It's your Uncle."

My eyes became two sizes bigger and my heart rate increased as I slowly opened the door. I was puzzled why Uncle Renzo was back.

"I forgot my cell phone in the living room," he stated.

"Oh, okay I'll grab it for you," I said, nervous as hell. I wondered how long he was at the door and how much of my conversation he heard with my mother. "Here you go, Unc." I handed him the phone. I tried my best not to let him see how edgy I was.

"Thanks, Juan. We'll be in touch."

"No problem. Have a safe flight back home."

When he finally left, my stomach couldn't stop doing flips. The Feds stressing me because I wasn't giving them evidence against Rich fast enough was only the start of my problems. Now, I wondered if they knew about Jade. I risked being in deeper trouble with them if they were following me or Rich. I had no idea what the meeting was about, and hoped like hell it wasn't more bad news.

At that moment, I started to ask myself if it was worth being in business with Uncle Renzo, especially with the fact that I knew what happened to Carlos. All this shit was starting to drive me crazy. I picked up my keys off the table in the foyer and told my mother I had to go. I needed some air.

• • • • • • • • • • • • •

While I drove to meet up with Agent Patterson, my anxiety started to kick into overdrive. The more I thought about meeting those pigs, the more my mind wanted to be done with this situation. All these years I'd been able to get through different types of situations in the streets, but now that I'd officially become a snitch, my choice of being in the game was obviously a bad idea. When the Feds came to me and offered me a deal when I got locked up, my first reaction was for them to get the fuck away from me with that hot shit. I'd never been a snitch and was raised with the motto *snitches got stitches.* My get out of jail free card for me to become an informant and take Rich down was absolutely ludicrous.

However, the more my mother slipped away and needed me to be there for her, the more I knew I had to do what I had to do. When I think back on it, my break down was when I found out she had started using drugs. On top of that blow, my lawyer let me know that I was facing five to twenty years. It really killed me that I went against everything I believed in to be turned out by the Feds, but my mother needed me. I wasn't about to leave her and let Rich be on top. It was time for his ass to go down.

As I pulled up and paid for parking, I couldn't believe those bastards wanted to meet them at the National Zoo. It was cold as hell outside. Who the hell went to the zoo in the winter? But I guess that was the idea of it. I'd even made sure I drove my low key Nissan Maxima to the meeting. Once I saw Agent Patterson walking toward my car, butterflies instantly filled my stomach. He was a middle aged white man, probably in his late forties with freckles spread across his nose. Usually he was dressed in a suit and a trench coat, but today he was in sweats with a Patagonia ski coat. I unlocked the door and he got in. Maybe that's how they dressed for snitch meetings.

"Well hello, Mr. Sanchez. How are you feeling today?"

This muthafucka acting like I'm on a job interview or something, I thought. "I'm good, what's up?"

"Well, this investigation isn't going as fast as we intended and my superiors feel that you're dragging your feet with getting information on your father. You remember our agreement, right?"

"Yeah, but I can't give you information that I don't have," I shot back.

"We need to gather some evidence or you're gonna have to wear a wire."

I looked at his ass like he was on crack. "Man, I told y'all before that I wasn't wearing no fucking wire. That was part of the deal as well, am I correct?"

"Now Juan, don't get snippy with me buddy. We need to close this case before the end of the year. And if not, then, well there will be consequences. Now, I have a couple of questions for you. Have you seen Rich involved in any transactions since we last met?"

"To be honest, Rich is broke and hasn't really been doing much lately. I think he lost his connect or something, and to sum it all up, he's been quite distant."

"Has he been to Baltimore lately?"

My heart sunk in my stomach. Did they know about Jade?

"Juan, has your father been to Baltimore?" the agent repeated.

"Umm, not that I know of. Look, Agent Patterson, I'll do my best at trying to get Rich to give me something within the next two weeks."

"You better. We're counting on you. If you want to be on the streets, then you need to get us Rich. Are we clear?"

I nodded and he smiled as he got out of the car without a care in the world for my feelings. He didn't care that he was asking me to hand my father over to them like he was some random nigga in the street. After all that shit, I needed a drink. And fast.

Chapter Sixteen
LISA

I walked into the courtroom two minutes before ten. Surprisingly, Rich and his lawyer were already there. He smiled like he had one up on me, which made me hate his ass even more. I tried to take my mind off of the inevitable, but within minutes I knew I would be humiliated when the test results were announced. Why Rich would expose my affair after all that I'd been through with him? He was lucky that I wanted to protect my son, because if not I would've exposed his worthless-ass to Renzo a long time ago.

Trying again to maintain my composure, I sat beside my lawyer as I prepared for one of the most embarrassing moments of my life. With my emerald green Diane Von Furstenberg silk blouse and BCBG pencil skirt, I even tried to dress as tasteful as possible so that the judge wouldn't think I was some type of slut or hoochie. At least when I was exposed, my appearance would be as professional as possible.

Five minutes later, the judge walked in the courtroom with a manila envelope in hand. *Shit, that's probably the test results*, I thought to myself.

"All rise," the bailiff announced just before the judge took her seat.

"Mr. and Mrs. Sanchez, I have made my decision on your divorce and I would just like to say that I'm very disappointed at the time that was wasted."

Glancing over at Rich, I was about to throw my pen at him from the way he taunted me. His ass was having a field day smiling and nudging his lawyer as this was all a joke. The judge was also annoyed with Rich's immaturity and started directing her attention to his behavior.

"Mr. Sanchez, I don't know why you think the welfare of this child is a joke. Is it something that you find funny?"

"Not at all, Your Honor. Not at all," Rich responded.

"You know what, I'm not gonna waist any more time on this. Before I go any further, counselors, do either of you have any more you want to add before I rule and reveal the DNA results of Carlie Sanchez?"

"No, Your Honor," they both said as she pulled the results out of the envelope.

"The DNA test results that I have before me states that Juan Michael Sanchez Sr. is the father of Carlie Gabrielle Sanchez with a paternity match of 99.5%."

The entire courtroom was filled with silence before Rich yelled out. "How the fuck is that possible? That baby can't be mine. Lisa was cheatin'! She cheated wit' my own damn brother!" He stood up like we were on the Maury Povich show. "There's gotta be a mistake!"

"Oh my goodness, he can't be my baby's father," I whispered in a state of shock.

"Order! Order! Mr. Sanchez, you have worked my last nerve and if you even think that you're going to disrespect my courtroom again then you're sadly mistaken. One more outburst and you're going to find yourself in lock up. I don't have a problem with holding you in contempt. Have I made myself clear?" the judge asked.

Rich nodded his head. "Yes, Your Honor."

"Mr. Sanchez, I'm ordering you to pay Mrs. Sanchez $1,400 a month in child support and $1,000 in spousal support. You will also be responsible for any medical care that the child is receiving now and in the future."

I was still in a state of shock and stared into space as the judge continued.

"Now, as far as assets go, Mrs. Sanchez you will remain at your current residence. I'm granting you sole ownership over that home. You will be responsible for all financial obligations. As far as the businesses are concerned, I'm granting all retail businesses to Mrs. Sanchez. Mr. Sanchez, since you have contracts on both establishments, and since you thought it was smart to try and close before I ruled, the funds from those sales will go directly to Mrs. Sanchez as well. I'll allow you to remain owner of your bar, Bottoms Up." The judge went on and on, but I couldn't seem to get pass her first announcement.

"Your Honor, may I say somethin'?" Rich asked.

"What do you have to say Mr. Sanchez, because I'm so tired of your shananigans?"

"Since I just learned that Carlie is my daughter, is it possible for you to discuss custody. Lisa has a drug problem and I don't want my child growin' up in that environment."

I looked at him like he was the devil. "What? You will never get custody of my fucking daughter!" I yelled.

The judge banged her gavel twice. "Mr. Sanchez, you've waisted enough of the court's time and money. You didn't even want anything to do with this child at first and now you want custody. Save the games for the playground. What I will do is honor you visitation. You're able to visit the baby while she's in the hospital, but only under supervision of hospital staff or Mrs. Sanchez. Once she's home, you can have visitation on weekends for the first three months. After that we can review granting joint custody as long as there's no sign of abuse or neglect. Do you have any objections, Mrs. Sanchez? Mrs. Sanchez."

"Yes, I do. I don't ever want him to see my baby," I quickly answered.

"Well, I'm afraid it's his baby too, Mrs. Sanchez so it's no way of getting around that. I'm sure you all will be able to work something out," the judge said. "Your divorce is final. Court is adjourned."

I was in complete shock when I heard her bang the gavel again.

"Oh my goodness, Lisa aren't you happy?" my lawyer asked happily, ready to celebrate. "The divorce is finally over. All the nonsense is over."

"No it's not, it just begun," I said as I walked out of the courtroom in a hurry.

"Bitch, I'ma get my daughter from your coke head ass! You think you gonna leave me with nothing and it's gonna be all good!" Rich blurted out.

Not giving a damn about anything he had to say, I made my way out of the courtroom. It was a must that I got out of there before I threw up. I felt faint…nauseous and needed some air. *What do I do now,* I thought to myself. I couldn't believe Carlie wasn't Carlos' daughter. As thoughts of how this could've happened, suddenly it hit me. The day Rich came into the house and raped me had to be the day I'd conceived. I couldn't believe it. Tears began to well up in my eyes as I stormed out of the court building.

When I finally made it to my car, I quickly got in and peeled out of the parking garage. I had no idea where I was going, and didn't care as long as it was far away from downtown D.C. Times like this I needed a friend; someone to talk to; someone who was willing to listen to my problems. As bad as I wanted to call Cornell, I quickly decided against it. It was too soon for me to bring any drama into the equation, so I decided to call my hair stylist Jermaine. He always had a way of cheering me up. Even though he didn't know all I was going through, at least he always found a way to make me laugh somehow. Just as I picked up the phone to call him, I had an incoming call. It was Juan.

"Hello."

"Rich just called me. Is what he said the truth?"

I let out a huge sigh. "I guess. That's what the results said."

"Well, now maybe you can put this whole Carlos thing

behind you. Carlie was what made it hard for you, Ma. Now, maybe you can let all that go."

"Juan, I gotta go." I wasn't in the mood for another one of his Carlos lecturing sessions.

"Hold up. Where are you?"

"I'm driving. You don't understand, Juan. I gotta go."

"Ma, maybe this is a good thing. You know how I feel about Rich, but now with Carlie not being Carlos' baby, it's less of a chance that Uncle Renzo will find out about your affair with him. We're closer to being in the clear with his death."

"Juan, I don't give a fuck about none of that shit right now, okay? All that was peaceful in my life has just been turned upside down and you think that I'm worried about Renzo. Fuck him!" I yelled as I hung up. I didn't know how I felt about it all. All the feelings I had were all a lie.

My emotions were a mess and I felt numb. Minutes later, I pulled up around 4th Street and as soon as I turned around, my supplier Black Moe walked up. By the look in my eyes he knew what I came for. I needed to slip away from my problems.

"What's up pretty lady? I ain't seen you in a while. Where you been?"

"Around."

He smiled. "You need something?"

"Yeah, I'm going through some things," I said, wiping my runny nose with my left hand.

After we did business, I pulled into a nearby parking lot and got straight to it. Pulling out my compact mirror along with the rest of my tools from my handbag, I took a line and instantly felt like I was on cloud nine. By the time I did the second line, all my problems had seemed to disappear. Laying back on the seat, I closed my eyes as the drugs took effect. At that moment, I could care less who Carlie's father was. All I wanted was another hit.

● ● ● ● ● ● ● ● ● ● ● ● ● ● ●

An hour later, I drove around until I found myself at Holy Cross Hospital. The more I thought back to Carlie's birth, the more I thought about how much she really did look like Rich. *Had I been in denial this whole time*, I asked myself? As I got out of the car and made my way inside the hospital, I kept shaking my head over and over. Even though I was still a bit high, I had to see my daughter. I had to look at her to confirm that she really was Rich's daughter.

"Fuck that DNA shit," I said, just before peering at Carlie through the NICU glass.

"Hi, Mrs. Sanchez," one of the younger nurses greeted me.

"It's Ms. Sanchez," I corrected her.

"Oh, I'm sorry. I can get you set up for your visit in your private room, Nurse Brooks is off today. My name is Tanya and I'm one of the NICU nurses on duty. Nurse Brooks told me that if you came by today to take great care of you."

"Thanks. I'm sorry if I was rude to you, I've just had a rough morning, that's all."

"No worries. Now you're here and whatever was so awful this morning couldn't possibly be more precious than that gift you have right here."

I just nodded and smiled as she went to get Carlie and set me up to nurse. The more my mind wondered, the more I couldn't believe the test results. I couldn't believe God was punishing me this way. I just knew he'd blessed me with a piece of Carlos to help me get through his death, but apparently that wasn't the case. As thoughts continued to swarm around in my head, Tanya placed Carlie in my arms. I just stared at her.

"Okay, I'll give you some privacy. Buzz if you need me," she said then walked off.

"How didn't I notice the exact resemblance you shared with Rich, Carlie? I should've known it. Look at your eyes. They're light brown just like his," I said to her as I continued to stare.

There was a blank emptiness inside my heart. I felt as if it had been ripped out of my chest and stomped on. I didn't know how to feel anymore. As my mind raced, I felt confused and alone.

Either it was time to nurse Carlie, or she felt my vibe because she started to cry. With my addiction being the cause of Carlie fighting for her life, I knew that me doing a line not even two hours ago was a bad idea, but I had to play it calm to make sure no one found out. Before someone got suspicious, I placed my nipple in her mouth and she finally latched on.

As I fed her, I thought about court. Even though the judge had awarded me pretty much all of Rich's assets, I was still down. Now I had money and really didn't need Juan or anyone else to take care of me, but here I was stuck with a sickly newborn baby by a man that I hated. Not paying any attention, I was interrupted by Tanya who quickly walked over to me like something was wrong.

"Ms. Sanchez, your nipple is covering her nose, the baby's choking."

My eyes widened as I pulled my breast out. "Oh my goodness Tanya, I didn't even realize it. Thank you so much." What scared me was the fact that I'd faked my reaction. *Did I try to suffocate Carlie on purpose,* I thought.

"You have to be careful, if her breathing tube comes completely out of her nose. She could lose oxygen, and that definitely could be fatal."

"Yes, I understand. Thanks again."

"No problem, she seems fine. The reason I came back was to let you know that you both have visitors."

I had no idea who that could be. Thinking it might be Juan and one of his random chicks, I nodded my head. "Okay, you can let them in."

However, as soon as the door opened, I noticed it was the last two people on earth that I wanted to see. Rich and Marisol.

"What the fuck are y'all doing here?" I asked.

Rich knew just how to push my buttons. Marisol's presence irritated me as she waltzed her ass in the room all dolled up like she was on her way to some type of major event.

"Bitch, don't start wit' me. You heard the judge. I came to see my daughter," Rich said.

"Oh, so now you care that quickly? You just called my daughter all types of crack babies and wished her the worst. Now you wanna run up here and act like you some type of caring father. And you got the nerve to bring her in here? Both of y'all get the fuck out!"

"Lisa, what's your deal? I don't know who you've become. I'm here for support and here you are coming at me as if I've done something to you. I lost my husband and you haven't even been there for me. But I call myself being the bigger person coming to see you and the baby for moral support," Marisol replied with much attitude.

"Marisol, you're not the only one who lost Carlos, we all did. Stop playing the victim," I shot back.

"Rich, I'm about to leave before I fuck her up. It's but so much I'm going to take," Marisol said with an evil scowl.

"Marisol, you know she's a little fucked up in the head. Now you see what I've been tellin' you all this time. Now you see what type of bitch you've been defendin' all these years," Rich told her before he looked back at me. "Let me hold my daughter." He walked toward me, but I quickly threw up my hand.

"Get the fuck back. I asked both of you to leave. Should I call security?"

"Is everything okay in here, Ms. Sanchez? There can't be any loud talking or noise in the hospital, let alone in the NICU. If you all don't keep your voices down, I'm gonna have to ask you all to leave," Tanya said in a very stern tone.

I patted Carlie's back. "I asked them to leave, but they won't go."

"Well, if you need me to call security I can but…" Tanya tried to say.

"Hold on, Miss. What are the rights here for fathers?

That's my daughter and I have a court order that states I'm able to visit my daughter. She cannot make me leave," Rich interrupted.

Tanya cleared her throat. "Listen, I don't want to be involved in your family issues. All I ask is that you respect the rest of the parents and their children, that's all."

"Okay, we will," Rich said as Tanya left.

At that moment, Carlie starting crying. "See, you made her upset," I said, patting her back even more.

"Rich, let's just go. You both have been through a lot today. Maybe it was too soon for you to come," Marisol suggested.

"Yeah, listen to your girl," I added.

"Alright, let's roll." Rich turned to me. "Bitch, I'm gonna get my daughter away from your ass one way or the other. You won't ever raise this one," he said as him and Marisol left.

I was so upset, but just kept rocking to calm Carlie down. I didn't understand how Rich could parade Marisol in here as if he wasn't the reason why she was mourning right now. He had some nerve. *Fuck them both,* I thought as my rocking increased. They had me so irritated at that point and ready to go. After buzzing the nurse so she could take Carlie back to the NICU, I was ready to leave. Usually, I felt bad when I had to leave my daughter, but this time was different. She was no longer my love child that I'd conceived with Carlos. She was a reminder of the night Rich made me relive being taken advantage of. She was a reminder of all the things that were wrong in my life starting with Rich. I needed to figure out my emotions. I needed a way out.

Chapter Seventeen
RICH

That bitch Lisa had to go. She'd already been awarded most of my shit in court, and now that slut was tryin' to keep me away from my daughter. Even though I was still in shock from when the judge announced Carlie was mine, there was no way I was gonna let that coke sniffin' bitch raise her. Lisa had beaten me at my own game. When I thought I was exposin' that cheatin' whore, it all backfired in my face. Now, I had to find a way to get my life back…startin' wit' Carlie. I just needed to prove that she was a coke head, which wasn't going to be hard. Hopefully after that, the judge would reverse the order.

I knew I should've killed Lisa's ass when we were in the warehouse, I thought. Never again would I spare another bitch's life based on sexual emotions or love. I banged my fist on the steerin' wheel as thoughts of Lisa and my money situation continued to dance around in my head. Now that my money had dried up so fast, I needed a quick come up. Especially since Uncle Renzo hadn't been fuckin' wit' me. The fact that he was gonna rely on Marisol to feed these streets instead of me, really had me fucked up. I really needed to make a way to come out on top and get my bread back.

Marisol and I rode in silence for about fifteen minutes when suddenly I felt her hand on mine.

"Rich, everything is gonna work it's self out," she assured.

"Man that sounds good, but Lisa knows that I have a problem wit' anybody who fucks wit' my money or my kids. She already messed me up wit' Denie." I knew I'd fucked up when that slipped out, because Marisol loved Denie as if she was her own. I knew she would want to know why I'd made that comment.

"So Rich, what really happened between you, Lisa, and Denie? Why do I feel like it's more to the story than you're leading me to believe? You just said she fucked you up with Denie. What do you mean by that?"

I sighed. "She always used to talk bad about me in front of my daughter and now Denie thinks that I'm a fucked up person."

"Where the hell is Denie?"

There was a deep concern in her eyes like she wanted answers. Marisol wasn't the kind of woman that you could tell anything to, so I knew I wasn't gonna be able to just blow her off. She was a boss bitch that went hard and demanded respect. Not to mention, she really loved Denie and genuinely always cared about her.

When we pulled up to my house, I looked over at Marisol who had her arms folded like a five year old child that wanted to stay up late on a school night.

"Look Marisol, Denie is just being a rebellious teenager. She's mad that I don't approve of her boyfriend. So she left to be wit' him."

"So, you just let her leave…just like that."

I shook my head. "Not exactly. One day I came home and she was gone."

Marisol stared at me for a few seconds. "Why the hell are you acting so calm? I mean, aren't you worried about her?"

"Of course I am. I just don't wanna push her away even further, so I thought I would give her time to cool down."

"Cool down? About what?"

I shook my head again. "Look, it's a long story."

"What was wrong with her boyfriend? Why didn't you approve of him?"

"He used to work for me and I didn't know they were messin' around. I've seen him do a lot of shit and I just didn't want that for Denie's life."

Marisol finally lightened up a little bit. "I can understand that, but what I don't understand is how Lisa fits into all that. I mean Lisa talking shit about you in front of Denie has always been the norm, so what did she do? Rich, I can tell you're hiding something from me and I wanna know what it is!"

Marisol was hip and it was hard tryin' to fool her. I really needed to change the subject fast.

"Come on Marisol, just let it go. I'm not in the mood to discuss Denie. Today has been hell. How about we just go in the house, I need a drink."

"Yeah, you're right. How about you get some rest and I fix you dinner? We can chill over some champagne like old times. Well, I guess minus Lisa and Carlos."

"Man, see that's why I love you. That sounds like a plan. I need a nap, and I haven't had a home cooked meal in a long time. What would I do without you?"

"Who knows what we would do without each other. This year has been crazy for both of us, but we need to help each other."

All I could think about was, *you're gonna help me, but you just don't know it yet*. She was my ticket to gettin' back on top and I had the plan that would have her beggin' me to be her partner.

When we walked in the house, it was cold as hell. I turned on the heat and then started the fireplace in the livin' room just in case Marisol wanted to chill in there. Makin' my way up stairs, I was ready to hop in the shower and get some much needed rest. As I got undressed my knee began to bother me. Ever since the car accident back in the day, I dealt wit' on-goin' pain, but since I had gotten shot, it was even worse. I decided that it was best that I chilled in the hot tub.

After fillin' up the tub and turnin' on the jets, I got in and immediately laid my head back. A minute hadn't even gone by before I started thinkin' about different ways to get my money right. My plan was to get Marisol to supply me and let me run my old territories again without lettin' Uncle Renzo know. I had a goal to gain Marisol's trust so we could eventually become partners. Then I could get her out of the picture all together and take over.

A smile crept over my face as I thought about bein' the top dog without anybody in my way. *Hell maybe she can help me get rid of Uncle Renzo first*, I thought. I knew that wit' him being around, there was no way I was gonna succeed wit' my plan. It was best that I take everybody out one by one.

After sittin' in the tub for almost an hour, I got out and put on a t-shirt and some Polo pajama pants when suddenly the smoke detector went off.

"Oh shit!" I yelled before runnin' downstairs to see what was goin' on.

When I ran into the kitchen, Marisol was fannin' a broom back and forth in front of the detector 'til finally it stopped.

"What the hell is goin' on?" I asked.

"Nothing I can't handle. It just got a little smoky."

"Well, I know you've said before that you can burn, but damn did you mean the house?" I laughed.

"Shut up. I thought you were taking a nap anyway. I'm not done yet."

"I was about to take one right before you decided to burn the house down."

"Whatever, Rich! I bet you're still gonna eat. Besides, my crab cakes are the bomb. I bet none of your bitches can touch me in the kitchen, and you know I'm hip to a couple of them…Lisa included."

"Lisa can cook," I said, defendin' her without even realizin'.

"That's not what Carlos said. He said her food was just okay. Taste this macaroni and cheese."

That shit pissed me off to hear Los and Lisa's name in the same sentence. When Marisol fed me a fork full of cheesy macaroni and cheese, I had to admit it was actually good. I was surprised.

"Not bad Miss Marisol, not bad at all. I'm impressed."

"Told you!" she said overly excited.

Marisol was a kid at heart under all that toughness, and that's what Carlos loved about her. She could be tough when he needed her to handle business in the streets, but could also be silly at times. He was really lucky to have her and always felt that they were perfect together. However, the whole time I envied what they had, he was fuckin' my wife behind my back.

Makin' my way back in the livin' room, I decided to lay on the floor in front of the fireplace and pop a bottle of Ace. A glass of champagne I was sure would ease my nerves and help get my mind right. In order for the night to go as I planned, I poured Marisol a glass of champagne and dropped a Roofie in her glass. She was a lush when it came to champagne, so I knew my plan would work.

"Ooh, I heard a bottle pop," Marisol said, comin' in the room wit' my plate.

Baked crab cakes, mac and cheese, greens, and cornbread. Either I was very hungry or the shit looked as if my man G. Garvin cooked it himself.

"Damn Marisol, I didn't know you could lay it down in the kitchen like this."

"I try, I try," she said wit' a smile.

As Marisol handed me the plate, I gave her the glass of champagne, makin' sure she had the right glass.

"Don't drink too much. You know how you can't hold your liquor."

Marisol sucked her teeth. "Please. I'm a heavy weight mister."

"Yeah right."

"I am." She gulped down her first glass as if she had something to prove.

Four glasses later, Marisol was beyond tipsy and laid on the floor tryin' to act as if she had it all together. But the more she talked, the more her words slurred. I knew it was only a matter of time before she would be all over me…beggin' for the dick.

"You're twisted already off of four glasses," I teased as she got up to take our plates into the kitchen.

"No I'm not. I'm good," she said stumblin'.

"No, you're not. Sit down. I'll get these," I replied before takin' the plates out of her hand.

Lookin' around the messy kitchen that Marisol had left behind, I placed the plates in the dishwasher, then wiped the counter and stove before realizin' it was completely silent in the livin' room. I thought Marisol had passed out 'til I suddenly heard my old-school slow jam CD playin'.

Yeah, this shit is workin' out exactly as planned, I thought to myself. I was ready to cash in, and loved the thought of Carlos' spirit watchin' me as I planned to fuck his wife. *Pay back is a bitch nigga.*

Dryin' my hands, I came back to the livin' room to find Marisol dressed in nothin' but a hot pink, lace thong set. Her breasts were at least a 36D. And even though I was an ass man, I couldn't help but stare at her. Her body was gorgeous.

"Marisol, what are you doin'?" I asked, tryin' to play it off.

"Don't act like you don't want this. I see your man poking out of your pajama pants."

Lookin' down, I saw that my dick was completely at attention. But after starin' at her body that looked like it belonged to a twenty-year old, I couldn't help it. By the time *Adore* by Prince came on, that was all she needed. Marisol started to do a striptease as she made her way down to the floor and landed in a split. As she moved her body back and forth like a snake, her long, cinnamon colored hair swayed from left to right.

As my dick began to throb, I could no longer contain myself. Walkin' over to her, I quickly pushed Marisol onto her back. Her thong had bows on each side that I decided to untie. But before I could finish the other side, she forcefully sat up and decided to pull my pants down so I could fuck her in her mouth.

"Come on Rich, I want you to cum for me. I want to drink your babies," she said, pullin' out my dick.

It didn't take long before she placed my tool in her warm mouth then started to move her head back and forth. I could tell she was a pro by the way she worked her tongue. Not to mention, she didn't let her teeth scrape up against my dick.

"Aahh shit, that's right. Suck that dick," I said.

"You like it baby. You like this deep throat," Marisol moaned in between slurps.

I was just about to answer when I suddenly pulled out.

"What are you doing?" she asked.

"I don't want you to regret this tomorrow. Do you really want this or is it just the drinks?" My plan was to play it off as if this was all a mistake.

"Does it fucking matter? You got a wet pussy sitting right here and you're questioning if you want to be inside of it. I need to be fucked Rich and I need it now! You gonna make me go get my gun and make you fuck me."

The sad thing about it was, I knew she was dead serious.

"Come on, Rich. Trust me, I fuck better than all those other bitches."

The more she talked shit, the more she made me want her. At that moment, I snatched her panties off, bent her ass over and went straight in her pussy from the back. She was right. Her pussy was the best that I ever had. Not only was it dripping wet, but she knew how to grip my dick just right.

"Rich, do you love this pussy?"

"Yes, baby. This pussy is good as shit."

"Well, fuck it like it's the best. Fuck me harder!"

Givin' her what she wanted, I pulled my dick out and put it right in her ass.

"Is this what you wanted? Huh?"

"Unhuh! Give me that big dick. I can take whatever you

giving. Fuck me Rich."

Marisol was obviously experienced in the anal department and showed it as she opened her ass so I could get it a little deeper. Her ass was so tight, a few seconds later I couldn't help but cum. As soon as I started to nut, Marisol turned around and sucked all of my juices, swallowin' every last drop. I thought Trixie was nasty, but Marisol had her beat. She continued to suck my dick 'til she got me back hard and jumped on top of me, ridin' my shit like I was a horse. We fucked all the way upstairs until she came and we ended up fallin' asleep in my bed.

Damn, I vowed to never fuck Marisol again from the mistake we made back in the day, but a nigga had to do what a nigga had to do.

Chapter Eighteen
JUAN

Sometimes I wondered, 'what the hell I'd gotten myself into', fucking with these Feds. The fear that I might have to give all this up one day if I was ever exposed as an informant, constantly fucked with my mind. Not to mention, if they know I was still hustling even though I was supposed to be clean, I'm sure they would send my ass straight back to jail. Hell, maybe they knew. Maybe they wanted Rich more than me. I knew that I was being greedy, but as long as I could get away with making money while I worked with them muthafuckas then that's the chance I was willing to take. I wasn't trying to go back to jail, but once this is all over, I needed to make sure that me and my mother had money to survive.

My main focus at this point was to stack as much paper as possible so that I could get things set up down south. My connect in Atlanta seemed to be quite solid. If only I could get Uncle Renzo to trust me, and give me even more territory, then I would have a quick way of getting paid even faster. At this point, stacking paper was my motivation so that when all this shit with Rich was over with, I could move and still be living life to the fullest. The more I pondered on what I could do to gain my uncle's trust, all of a sudden an idea smacked me in the face like a ton of bricks. I decided to give him a call instantly.

"Hello."

"Hey, Uncle Renzo, it's me Juan."

"How's it going, Juan? I hope you're calling because you have something for me."

"Actually, I do. I feel bad because I feel like I'm actually about to betray my father, but I feel there's something you should know. But only if we could keep this conversation in confidence."

"Of course Juan, what is it?"

"Well, I think you should know that about this time last year, my mother was abducted, raped, and held for ransom due to my father fucking this girl named Trixie. When he went to go get my mother from some abandoned warehouse, he was shot and the guys got away with a huge sum of money."

"I can't believe nobody told me this," Renzo interrupted.

"I know. I guess it was hard for them to talk about it. My mother took it bad. Anyway, my father and Carlos ended up finding out who was responsible and you know...got a little retaliation. His name was Mike."

"So, what does this have to do with Carlos' death?"

"Well, word on the street is that somebody from Mike's family killed Carlos. I don't think they wanted him to be found because they wouldn't win with a war, but that's all I could figure out from the streets."

"Really. Where are these guys from?"

"They're from Southeast, but that's all that I know."

"That's enough for now. Son, you did good, better than your father. I'll make sure he doesn't know what you've told me. I'm a man of my word and I'll make sure that you're rewarded for the information."

"No problem Unc'. I just want to help. Carlos was a good man."

"I'll be in touch."

After hanging up, it felt good to know that I'd gotten a few steps further for Uncle Renzo to trust me. I also knew that I was taking a huge gamble. It was my ass if Uncle Renzo knew that I lied about Carlos' killer, but it would at least give me time to work my way up in the organization and protect me and my mother from becoming a target. I knew once I had him completely on my side, I would be making the money I needed to stack up so I could eventually move.

Walking around my house, I pulled out my Louie duffle bag and threw in two outfits along with some underwear and toiletries for my quick trip to ATL. I was on my way to meet up with Malik, my newfound heroin connect and southern business partner. Me, Malik and Kwame had been talking about this deal for the past few days, so now it was time to make shit happen.

Before I left my house, I made sure I had all my money in hundred dollar bills so it made it easier to travel on the plane. I bought a couple of maternity Velcro belts that I could use to secure the money against my body so it wouldn't be detected. The last thing I needed was to be questioned by those fake-ass airport authorities, so I had to make sure everything was right. Besides, it wasn't everyday that someone flew on a plane with fifty thousand dollars. Fifty g's is what I had to have up front until I moved some product.

●●●●●●●●●●●●●●

Three hours later, I walked through Atlanta's Hartsfield Airport with a huge smile on my face. Not only had a weight been lifted off my shoulders since I was able to make it through security without a problem, but I was overly excited to be in the ATL; a place where I wanted to relocate and start all over. Not to mention, the fact that Atlanta had a hundred women to one man had me even more hyped. Even though I'd told myself this was going to be a short trip, if things popped off with a female, I didn't mind staying an extra day or two. My mind was busy with thoughts as I went to get my rental car, and drove off to the W hotel in Buckhead.

After I checked into my room and made my way up to my corner suite on the top floor, I thought to myself, *was this a good idea*? For a while I contemplated doing business with someone outside my circle, but since Kwame had vouched for Malik, I decided to go along with the deal. Kwame was supposed to fly down with me, but since something came up at the last minute I had to come by myself, which had me a little noid. I always knew Kwame was jealous of me, but when it came down to business, he was supposed to pull his weight.

His ass is gonna be the first one to try and cash in, I thought as I sat down on the bed. Just as I got pissed off, my phone rang. It was Kwame.

"Yeah, what's up you fake-ass nigga?" I said with a mild irritation in my voice.

"Man, cut that bitch shit out. Malik got you. I talked to him earlier and he told me y'all are gonna party tonight."

"Look, I'm just here to get my shit, politic a little and roll out."

"Nigga shut up. You know how weak you are for a phat ass. I heard y'all goin' to Magic City and Body Tap tonight. You know how they do in the "A". You're really gonna be ready to move down there once you experience the tittie bars. No bullshit, DC strippers ain't got nothin' on ATL."

"Damn, you ain't gonna represent your own hood. We got the best looking girls hands down. Fuck who got the hottest strippers, you can fly in to look at some ass, I'd rather have the hottest bitches around me 24/7. If I'm at the mall, grocery store, or in the club, DC ladies got it going on. You sweating these bitches down here like you from here or something."

"Stop bein' so damn sensitive. I'm just sayin' the ATL strippers are the shit. That's all facts."

"Anyway, what's up? I see you left me down here by myself. Malik seems cool, and I know you and Kyle vouched for him, but you know I don't trust no out of town niggas like that."

"Man, I keep tellin' you that Malik is straight. Plus, I told you that I had to handle some shit here and I didn't know it was gonna take that long. Just enjoy yourself. I'll be with you on the next trip, that's a bet. You my man."

"Yeah, okay. I'll holla at you later then. I'm about to lay down for a couple of hours before I have to meet up with him."

"Cool."

After hanging up, the conversation was confirmation for me that this was a bad idea. I'd been feeling uneasy about this trip when Kwame cancelled, but even more after talking to him. He always wanted me to help him get money, but never wanted to do what it took to keep the shit pumping. I couldn't wait to the day to get out the game. Despite who you thought *had your back*, deep down nobody could really be trusted.

My mind was heavy as I laid across the bed and fell asleep. Surprisingly, I dreamt of my ex-girlfriend Ciara for some reason. I hadn't spoken to her since the night I met Cherry and had no idea why she was on my mind all of a sudden. The crazy thing was, in the dream she'd just told me that she was pregnant with my child and that the baby was a boy. What took the dream to the next level was how excited I was when she told me. I started doing all types of crazy-ass flips and everything. When my phone rung and woke me up, I couldn't help but think to myself if the dream was some type of subliminal message. Was something trying to tell me that I needed to settle down?

"Yeah," I answered.

"What's up, Juan? It's Malik. You ready to have a little fun tonight."

"What time is it?"

"It's eight-thirty. I was gonna come scoop you around ten."

"That works. I'm gonna hop in the shower and get ready."

"Cool."

I was hungry as shit so the first thing I did was order room service. Hot wings and a Caesar salad would be enough to coat my stomach as I scanned over the menu. After getting off the phone, I quickly took off my clothes and jumped in the shower. The warm water hitting my body felt good and was much needed since I seemed so tense. Minutes later, I got out, wrapped my towel around my waist and laid out what I was gonna wear. Since it wasn't as cold as it was in DC, I was able to wear my black Burberry sweatshirt, dark blue True Religion jeans and my Gucci sneakers. I didn't want to look like I tried too hard, but at the same time I wanted to look like money so I finished the outfit off with my iced out Breitling watch and pave' platinum cross necklace.

When my phone rung exactly an hour and a half later, it was Malik letting me know he was waiting downstairs in a black Range Rover Sport. After grabbing five g's from the safe in the room, I made my way to the elevator. One of the disadvantages of being on the top floor was the elevator stopped a million times before I finally made it to the bottom. When the doors finally opened, I was in complete shock. The lobby looked like a club scene more so than a five star hotel. It was full of hot chicks with short ass dresses and platform pumps.

"Shit, I could've just chilled here," I said to myself as I continued to look around. I definitely didn't know that the hotel was a party spot.

When I made my way to the front entrance, Malik rolled his window down to let me know it was him due to the dark tint. Malik's truck reeked of weed as I jumped in the passenger seat and gave him a quick pound. Luckily, I'd sprayed my Creed cologne so I didn't smell like that shit when I got to the club. Malik had just finished rolling up a blunt when he introduced me to his man, Clint who was in the back seat. He was dark skinned with a bald head, and looked a lot like Wee-Bay from the Wire. He nodded his head, but that was about it. I guess the nigga was just as uneasy as I was.

"Wassup, my nigga! You ready to see some ass and make some cash," Malik said trying to divert my attention off of Clint's rudeness.

"I'm down. What's the plan?"

"You know we don't sleep much down here. We get our party on 'til five or six in the morning and then it's Waffle House time," Malik replied.

"So, when do y'all make time to get some ass? After the club?" I asked.

Malik smiled. "What real man is gonna pass up some ass? We definitely make time for that. We got you. We're gonna show you how we really do it tonight. Why do you think everybody moves to ATL? They get hooked. Trust me, your ass is not gonna want to go back home."

"Well, I'm ready!" I needed a quick vacation, and to get paid in the process was a slam dunk."

Our first stop was Body Tap. Surprisingly, there weren't many people there, so we rolled out and made our way to Magic City. When we pulled up the parking lot a few minutes later, it was packed. The parking attendants were turning around cars left and right. In DC if you were getting money, there was no question that you were respected on the club scene, so this was a test for Malik's street cred. When I saw the valet turn Malik's car around, I was immediately blown. I definitely didn't roll like that. I wasn't about to walk a couple of blocks or waste time looking for a parking space, so I quickly intervened.

"My man, what do you need to park our car?" I asked the attendant.

"We're completely full, please move your car," he responded then pointed in the opposite direction.

I took some money out my pocket. "Man look, take this three hundred dollars and park the car." When I handed the valet guy the doe, I didn't waste time getting out the car. "Come on. What y'all niggas waiting for?" I asked Malik and Clint.

When Malik looked at me like I was crazy, I knew at that point there was no way his ass was a boss. Where I'm from, money talks and bullshit walks, so that three hundred dollars wasn't shit. *Kwame set me up with the wrong ATL nigga*, I thought. It was time I showed him how real DC niggas get down.

When we walked up to the club, Malik knew the security dude so we were able to walk straight inside. I guess he was trying to redeem himself, but I still wasn't impressed. It was going to be a long night before his ass proved to me that he was a don.

A couple of people greeted Malik and some of the dancers gave him hugs as we walked toward our table. We hadn't even sat down before we started ordering bottles of Ciroc, Remy, and Moet Rose. Looking around the famous club, I was instantly in observation mode. I could tell there were all types of dudes that had status. From actors and rappers, to street dudes, you name it, people were out and obviously this was the place to be tonight.

It was funny how the guys battled each other making it rain to show everyone that they had money. It was like they were in competition with each other. One thing I had to agree with, the strippers were definitely better than ours. Phat asses and big tits filled every inch of the club, but there was one in particular who caught my eye. She had a caramel complexion with long hair down to her waist. Her eyes were naturally hazel and she had ass for days.

She sat on the side and waited for her turn on stage. Finally, when it was her time, I was curious to see what she was gonna do. I took a couple of shots to the head and got comfortable. At that point, Malik tried to hand me a blunt, but I passed. I let him know the drinking was my thing. I never was the one to fuck with weed, and wasn't gonna start now. Drawing my attention back to the stage, I was ready to see this fine ass chick do her thing as the DJ made his announcement.

"Coming to the stage we have an out of towner, but no stranger to Magic City. Straight from H-town, let's give it up for Miss Chasity."

The song, *Give Me That Becky* by Plies blasted through the speakers as she climbed her way up the pole, spun around and landed in a split. Her tricks and dance moves had the entire crowd going wild. Dudes were throwing money at her left and right. Finally, after I watched her for several minutes, I started feeling my drinks and found myself at the stage throwing her paper myself. I wanted to get her attention, which eventually worked because she popped her booty so hard at me I thought she was gonna throw her back out. While the other guys were making it rain, she was worth the Tsunami that I had going on. I had given her at least eight hundred dollars and in that case, she was fucking tonight for sure. She was so hard to resist that a couple of the other dancers decided to freak her out on stage. It was one hell of a show. I needed another drink, so I decided to walk back to my table.

"Man, what's up with that chick? I'm trying to hit her tonight," I said to Malik over the music.

"Who, Chasity? She cool, but she's definitely gonna charge you. She don't come here all the time but she cool wit' a lot of dudes. She come in town, make her money, then bounce to the next city."

"I need you to hook that up," I responded excitedly.

"So, I guess you ain't going to Club Dreamz tonight, huh?" Malik questioned.

"Man, I'll hit that joint next time." I said after I popped another bottle of Moet. I was definitely ready to go in on Miss Chasity. Just when I was on the last bit of my bottle, she made her way to our table.

"I'm Chasity, and you are?" she asked in a soft southern accent.

"Juan."

"Well, Juan where you from, because your accent don't sound like you from down here?"

"I'm from DC."

"Oh yeah, I know a couple of dudes from up there that live in Houston now. Thanks for supporting me."

"It's all good, I just like what I see, that's all."

She reached over and whispered in my ear. "Well, if you like what you see, I'm sure we can get out of here. I can show you much more. Especially if you're willing to give up some green for some cream."

I couldn't help but smile. "Miss Lady you ain't said nothing but a word. You driving?"

"Yeah, I got a rental. I'ma get dressed and then we can

bounce. Just give me about thirty minutes."

"Cool.

As she walked away, I grabbed her ass, causing her to look back and smile. I was more like Rich than I could admit.

"So, I guess you good for the night, huh?" Malik asked with a smirk.

"Yes sir. We're gonna head back to my hotel." I gave him the doe for the check.

I didn't want too many people to associate me with him because I was convinced he wasn't *that nigga.* Chasity had saved the day because I was really thinking twice about doing business with him at all. If Kwame wanted to fuck with Malik he could, but my instinct was telling me that I should just stick with the family business.

Finally, Chasity came out a few minutes later, we left. When valet brought her car around, to my surprise she was driving a Bentley Coupe. *What type of shit is this bitch on? She told me she was driving a rental, who the fuck rents a Bentley,* I thought to myself as the two door silver beauty pulled up.

When we got inside and peeled out, I wanted to ask her so bad was the car really a rental, but I had to let her know I was used to this type of shit.

"So, what brings you to the 'A' Juan?"

"I had some business to take care of. What brings you here Pretty Lady?"

"I come down here to get paid. I don't fuck around, and especially don't deal with no broke-ass niggas."

"Well, baby, I'm far from broke. I'm about my paper and I respect your hustle."

"Well, your night will be well worth it then. I usually charge $1,500, but since you looked out at the club, you can just give me a 'g'."

"For that type of cash you better show me that it'll be worth it."

"Oh trust me, it will be."

When we got back to the hotel, it was still packed. After

we pulled up, I paid the valet a little extra to keep her ride out front so she wouldn't have to wait when it was time to roll. All this money I was spending, if her pussy was some shit, I was definitely gonna put her ass out.

When we finally went through the glass doors, I stumbled a little bit. I knew it was reckless for me to drink as much as I did, but I figured after I fucked Chasity I could sleep it off and start over in the morning. However, I wasn't fucking with Malik. I'd already made plans to call Kwame and let him know that shit as soon as I got settled.

When we got to my room, Chasity wasted no time. She'd popped an E pill and took her clothes off before I even was out of my shoes. It was if she had another date lined up for the night and couldn't afford to spare one minute.

"Hold up baby, I gotta make a call real quick," I informed.

"Okay. I'm just gonna play with my pussy until you're ready. I'm already wired up from earlier and I need to fuck."

My eyes widened. "Damn. Alright, I'ma give you some of this good dick, just hold fast."

I went in the bedroom area of my suite and quickly called Kwame.

"Yeah Juan, wassup?" he answered.

"Man, I'm not fucking with that nigga, Malik. You told me he was a boss type dude, but he don't have no respect down here. That nigga couldn't even park his car in front of the club."

"What are you talkin' about? I know Malik got money. I guess since he ain't Columbian, then you can't fuck wit' 'em, huh?"

"What the fuck does that have to do with anything? Just let your man know that I'ma fall back."

Before he could even respond, I hung up on his ass and turned my phone off. Kwame was definitely getting beside himself. *I don't know who that nigga thinks he's talking shit to. I'm the reason why his kids even eat.*

As soon as I started getting pissed, I heard moaning from

the other room and knew it was time for me to handle my business. I was drunk as shit, but I knew it was a bitch with a phat ass in the next room who needed me to give her some of this good DC dick.

"You ready for me?" I asked, walking back into the room.

"I was born ready. But you know you gotta pay before you play," she replied.

As soon as I gave her money, Chasity pulled my dick out of my pants and started stroking it just before putting it in her mouth.

"I didn't expect all this from such a pretty boy."

"They never do? Don't let the curls fool you," I said, referring to my hair.

I fucked the shit out of her for over an hour before passing out across the bed. She did have some good pussy, but I had better. In a deep sleep, I was suddenly awakened by a loud noise in the other room. When I got up to see what it was, I was surrounded by four goons dressed in black with masks covering their faces. Chasity of course was nowhere in sight.

"Surprise DC! Time to give up that paper," a deep, voice said through the mask.

My life flashed before me as the butt of the gun smacked me in the back of my head and all I could think about was, *somebody set me up.*

Chapter Nineteen
RICH

All I could do was shake my head at the fact that Marisol and I had fucked the night before. Even though that had been my plan, a part of me still felt like shit. Back in the day when Marisol and Carlos got engaged, she caught him cheatin'. She ended up comin' to me for comfort, but instead of givin' her a shoulder to cry on, I crossed the line and gave her a dick to ride. She left town to go back to Puerto Rico for a year because she was so hurt and felt guilty. I didn't really care since she was just a fuck at that time 'til I saw how bad it hurt Los. When Marisol came back, of course her and Carlos got back together and we promised never to let that shit happen again. It was our secret and we never told a soul.

As I continued to reflect, the doorbell started ringin' out of control. "Who in the fuck could that be," I said to myself before lookin' over at Marisol's naked body. Seconds later, the doorbell rung again. Irritated, I hopped out of bed and grabbed my robe.

"Man, who is it?" I said, walkin' down the stairs.

"It's your uncle. Open the door."

My eyes immediately bulged. "Oh, hold up."

I ran back up the steps takin' two at a time and woke Marisol up. "Get up. Renzo is downstairs." I made sure to keep my voice low.

She was instantly sober. "Are you serious? Does he

know I'm here?"

Before I could respond, the doorbell rung again. It was obvious we didn't have time to go back and forth, so I gave her a look that said, 'shut up and disappear.' I watched as Marisol did an Olympic-like sprint toward Denie's room. Hopefully she was smart enough to hide in the closet or under the bed.

Runnin' back downstairs, I quickly opened the door. However, when Uncle Renzo smacked me in my face wit' his pistol it completely caught me off guard.

"Rich, do you think I'm a damn joke!" he yelled as I fell to the floor.

Grabbin' my chin in pain, I couldn't help but wonder if he knew that Marisol was upstairs.

"Get the fuck up! You're gonna give me some answers," Uncle Renzo demanded as he hit me again. This time he used his fist.

"What the fuck is your problem?" I said as blood poured from my mouth. I quickly ran my tongue across my teeth to make sure they were all accounted for.

"You know how I feel about betrayal! You're supposed to be family, Rich!"

I really didn't know how to respond, and my gun was nowhere in sight me for me to try and protect myself. *Did Marisol set me up? What the fuck is goin' on?*

"If we're supposed to be family, then why are you doin' this? I'm I supposed to sit here and take this shit?" I finally asked.

"What the fuck do you know about my son's death, Rich? And don't lie to me anymore," he said before placin' the gun in my mouth.

I'd seen my uncle do a lot of ruthless things to people, but never to me. He had no regards for anyone, not even women and children, so I didn't have a chance. At this point, I knew someone had to say somethin' in order for him to be reactin' this way. There was no soul in his eyes as he stared at me, waitin' for a response. Seconds later, he slowly removed the gun out of my mouth so I could speak.

I chose my words carefully because the last thing I wanted was for him to suspect me. Not to mention, Marisol was upstairs listenin'. It was important for me to remove any doubt from the both of them.

"Are you tryin' to say that I had somethin' to do wit' that shit? That was my brother. I'm lost out here without him. Before I even knew he wasn't my cousin, I loved him like a brother. You're not the only one mournin' his death. The same way you're comin' up blank, that's what I've been goin' through since he first disappeared. I've been doin' the leg work tryin' to figure out somethin'. Trust me, I've been focused on findin' his killer."

I thought I'd possibly hit a soft spot wit' him 'til he kneeled down and punched me again.

"That's the fucking problem! I can't trust you. I just told you not to lie!"

Yeah, he definitely knew somethin', but there was no way in hell I was about to snitch on myself. "I'm not lyin'!"

"Oh really? Then why didn't you tell me about Lisa getting raped? Why didn't you tell me that you and Carlos took care of the guy, Mike?"

I was speechless. A million thoughts about who could've told him that shit ran through my mind as he continued. "I know about Trixie. I also know that apparently one of Mike's family members may be responsible for Carlos' death," Uncle Renzo said. He paced the floor back and forth. "Why the fuck would you keep important information like this away from me?"

I let out a quick sigh while he wasn't lookin'. As long as I wasn't a suspect, it didn't matter who he thought killed Los. But that still didn't hide that fact that someone was feedin' him information.

I finally stood up. "I'm sorry, Unc'. I just didn't want you to get all worked up like you are now. Yes, that did happen to Lisa, but that was my business. Why bother you wit' somethin' that I could handle myself?"

He got up in my face. "Because that shit got my son killed!"

"We don't know that for sure, Unc'. That's just a rumor."

"So fucking what. You should've buried everyone involved!" He put the gun in my face again. "Are you trying to cover for those niggas?"

I shook my head. "No...not at all."

"Why should I believe you? Oh, and explain this...what the hell was that girl Jade talking about at the service? She blamed you and now she isn't answering Marisol's calls."

"That bitch is just delusional because I stopped fuckin' her. She would think of anything to get back at me."

"You need to come up with a better excuse than that. You mean to tell me everybody wants your dick. You're so full of yourself and it's making me sick."

"Fuck Jade! I haven't talked to that bitch in months."

At that moment, my phone started ringin', but I decided to ignore it.

"Somebody knows what the fuck is going on, and I want answers! How was someone able to call Marisol and tell her exactly where the body was? She said it was a woman. Then all of a sudden you're blamed. Then your wife is acting like a nervous wreck every time I come around with Juan feeling like he has to protect her every five minutes. There's something fishy going on and it has your name written all over it!"

"Unc', you know me. Give me one reason why I would hurt Los, just one reason."

"That's what I don't understand."

He finally turned the gun off of me and sat down on the couch. He scanned the room, looking at Marisol's clothes and panties all over the floor along wit' several champagne bottles.

"I see you had a busy night, huh. Is she still here?"

My phone rang again.

"Umm...no, but I need to get my phone because she might be callin'. Or it might even be the hospital callin' about my baby girl."

He nodded his head as I went to get my phone off of the kitchen counter. It was Juan.

"What's up son, you alright?"

"Rich, I'm in Atlanta. Somebody set me up and robbed me in my hotel room."

"What? Are you alright? Why the fuck are you in Atlanta?"

"I had some business to take care of."

"Well, who the fuck do you know down there? Who did you go wit'?" I had tons of questions.

"I came down here by myself. Kwame was supposed to come, but he backed out at the last minute."

"Are you alright?" I asked again.

"They roughed me up a bit, but I'll live."

"Get back home now. Jump on the next plane and get back here ASAP!"

"I need some money to get back. They took everything I had."

"Alright. I'll call and make you a reservation."

"Please don't tell Ma. I don't want her worrying."

"I don't talk to that bitch. I'll call you after it's done. In the meantime, get to the airport!" I said before hangin' up on his dumb-ass.

I was so fuckin' pissed wit' my son. He was so hard headed and always wanted to step out and do his own thing just to despite me.

"What's going on with Juan?" Uncle Renzo asked wit' deep concern. He'd never expressed this much interest in Juan before.

"He got caught up in some shit in Atlanta and I have to get him back home."

"What type of shit?"

"He got robbed tryin' to make moves down there by himself."

"What the fuck was he thinking?" he said just as pissed as I was.

I immediately thought back to the way the two of them were so sociable at the memorial service and then it dawned on me. *Juan called me because he probably fucked up Unc's money.*

"I gotta go," Uncle Renzo said, storming out of the door. Just when I thought the focus was off of me, he turned back around. "You need to find Mike's people and handle them before I handle you. Whoever killed my son, will die of a slow painful death. They're going to pay, even if it's through their kids. I promise you. they will feel my pain."

"I'm on it."

"No more lies," he said, before walkin' out.

After closin' the door, I went straight upstairs to get on the computer to book Juan a flight back home. Tryin' to win Marisol over wasn't a focus at this point. I had to get my son home safe. Juan was always so trustin' of people, which had always been his down fall. He always wanted to prove that he could make it without me, but I hope his ass knew now that he needed me. This was the perfect time to fix everythin' wrong between us. He needed to know that I had his back.

"What the fuck was all that about, Rich? Oh my gosh, look at you, you're bleeding," Marisol said.

"I'll be alright."

"You know Renzo is just grabbing for straws right now. He feels vulnerable and doesn't like feeling this way. He needs closure and he feels like you're the only person who can give him that."

"Fuck him! I don't wanna talk about that shit right now. My son needs me. I need to get him home."

"What happened?"

"Hold up," I said, dismissin' all of her questions as I got Juan back on the phone.

"Your flight is in an hour and a half. That should give you enough time. Call me once you're boardin'. I'll be at the airport to pick you up."

As soon as we hung up, Marisol wanted answers.

"What's going on?"

"Juan got robbed down in Atlanta, but it's no big deal."

"What? Who does he fuck with in Atlanta?"

"It doesn't matter. I just need to get my son home."

"It does matter. If Juan is in Atlanta and he got robbed that's my business. I supply Juan and that's my loss."

I looked at her in shock. "What? You supply him."

"Yes, I do. Renzo doesn't know about it, so don't say anything. I just didn't know he was trying to venture off to Atlanta. Now I need to know what they got from him. Where's my phone, I'm about to call him."

"No you can't. Do you want him or anybody else to know that you spent the night in my bed last night? Anyway was this a set up? Did you know Renzo was coming here? So, you think I killed my brother, too, huh?"

"Shut your fucking mouth right now! Do you think if I thought you killed my husband I would be here with you? Do you think I would've let you put your dick in me if I thought that shit? You would be dead. I'm not Lisa! I'm cut from a different cloth and I would have no problem killing you."

"I'm tired of you and Renzo actin' like y'all are the only ones hurt behind Los' death. He was more to me than both of you."

"Fuck you, Rich! I have his kids! Do you think I could explain fucking you to anybody if you were his killer? I'm not gonna lie, I suspected that you knew something at first, but those thoughts quickly disappeared. I know in my heart you wouldn't hurt anybody you care about. You proved that to me when I let Carlos back in my life. And all these years, you never told him about our one night. I've always respected you for that."

"Why did you leave and go back to Puerto Rico? Were you that hurt?"

"I felt guilty about us. I thought about you a lot and I didn't want to. I just needed to get away."

Marisol walked out of the room. For some reason, I

knew there was more to the story that she wasn't lettin' on, and hopefully one day I would find out. By the time she came back upstairs, she was fully dressed and in a different mood. You would've never thought that I fucked her all night from the serious look on her face. One thing I did know about Marisol, she could turn her feelings on and off like a switch and that seemed to be dangerous. That's why I knew it was goin' to be a challenge to do business wit' her. Wit' no emotion in her eyes, I could tell she was ready to handle business, which ultimately meant gettin' to the bottom of what was goin' on wit' Juan and her money.

Chapter Twenty
RICH

Tryin' to beat Marisol to the punch, as soon as she left, I called Juan immediately. He couldn't even get out the word hello, before I went in on him.

"Man, what the fuck is goin' on wit' you and Marisol?"

"What do you mean?"

"Look, keep the shit one hundred wit' me cuz I don't have time for games. Why are you fuckin' wit' her and you didn't even tell me?"

Juan was quiet…too damn quiet.

"Hello."

"Yeah, I'm here," Juan replied.

"So, are you gonna answer the question or not?"

"Look, Rich I'm not trying to get into that shit right now."

"Oh, really. Well, what about you and Renzo? Y'all got something goin' on that I need to know about, too? He was here when you called and seemed overly concerned about what happened."

"Nah, me and Unc' don't have nothing going on."

"Good, keep it that way. He'll probably just try to use you to get to me. If either of them call you, don't answer. I'll see you at the airport. We'll continue this conversation then." He was quiet once again. "Juan, just trust me for once."

When I hung up the phone I laid across my bed and

thought about how I could make all this go away. I needed to make amends wit' my son before it cost him his life. This last thing he needed was to get in knee deep wit' the Columbians. He wasn't built like that, which was why he was in this predicament now. I wanted better for him. Because of my lifestyle, I'd lost one child and was on my way to possibly losin' another.

After eatin' some of Marisol's leftovers, hoppin' in the shower, and watchin' a bit of CNN, it was time for me to make my way to the airport. It was gonna take a lot for me not to smack the shit out of Juan for gettin' caught up in Atlanta. That nigga was never careful, which pissed me off. He was so caught up in the material shit that this life brought, but was never ready for the consequences.

"I guess he's learnin' the hard way," I said to myself just before gettin' in the car.

When I pulled up to the US Airways baggage claim at National Airport, Juan was already outside waitin'. His face was fucked up. All he was missin' was a sign that said, 'I lost the fight.' But then again, who was I to judge? Lookin' in the mirror, my own lip was swollen from Uncle Renzo kickin' my ass. I couldn't speak for Juan, but there wasn't gonna be a next time for me though.

Gettin' out of the car, I immediately gave him a hug. I hadn't given my son a hug in such a long time, but something told me we both needed it. It was an emotional moment as we patted each other's backs. From the outside lookin' in, I'm sure bystanders thought we hadn't seen in each in months. If only they knew. As soon as we got in the car and pulled off, my curiosity sprung into action.

"So, tell me from the beginnin' what happened," I said calmly.

I wanted my son to know I was on his side. I also had to convince him to stop fuckin' wit Marisol and to dismiss any thoughts about Renzo. If Juan were to get caught up, there was no doubt Uncle Renzo would try and turn my son against me. The same way he'd used me and Carlos for years.

"It's a long story," Juan stated.

"So...we got time."

At that point, he started by lettin' me know about Kwame and how he kept tellin' Juan that the nigga Malik was a made dude in Atlanta. Once he was deep in the story and got to the part about the bitch, I couldn't hold back my emotions any longer. All I could think about was Trixie and how her bitch-ass man, Mike robbed me. I never wanted this for my son. The more I looked at his bruises on his face and his puffy right eye, the angrier I got.

"First off, don't ever trust a bitch. Juan! She should've never been in your room!"

"I don't think it was her."

Instantly, my fist hit the steerin' wheel. "Are you listenin' to yourself right now? How the fuck do you know that?"

Juan lowered his head. "I don't."

"Exactly. How the fuck you gon' trust a stripper? Damn right it could'a been her. You down there wit' no gun, makin' it rain in a strip club full of goons. Hell, it could'a been anybody. All them niggas down there knew you were an out of town dude wit' money. That nigga Kwame and Malik probably set your ass up."

"Are you serious?"

"Damn right I'm serious. You were a mark. Now, since you don't know much about Malik, Kwame gotta go. You can't let these muthafuckas ruin our family name in the streets. You have to make an example out of these niggas."

"Man Rich, I ain't no killer. I've been around that nigga Kwame since I was knee high."

"Fuck that nigga. You think he cared about that shit when he set you up? I bet you that nigga was in Atlanta wit' your ass the whole time. He probably still down there. Call his mother and see if she knows where he's at. You know her drunk-ass won't remember what she told you anyway. If anyone knows where he is, it would be her."

Even though Juan had a hesitant look on his face, he still

pulled out his phone. My mind started spinnin' instantly when I thought about how different Juan was from me and Los. I guess our street cred had gotten him by so long that he never had to stand up for himself. However, all that shit was about to change. My son had to break out of this bitchassness quick if he wanted to survive in this game. This shit wasn't for weak hearted muthafuckas.

Fuck that, he's gonna do this job himself, I thought as he dialed the number. I had him put the call on speaker.

"Hello," a woman answered.

"Hi Ms. Johnson this is Juan. Is Kwame around?" Juan asked.

"No baby. Him and Kyle went to see my sister Elaine in Atlanta. They've been gone for the past week. He should be home today though. You want me to tell him you called."

"No, I'll just call his phone. Thanks."

"No problem. You make sure you tell that fine-ass daddy of yours I said hi."

"I will."

When Juan hung up the phone, he looked at me wit' so much pain in his eyes. I'm sure he knew now that I was on his side and not the enemy. I needed my son to trust me and this was gonna be the glue to put our relationship back together.

"Now you see what I've been talkin' about? I'm all you got out here. Those muthafuckas used you to get bread and then threw you to the wolves. They knew they couldn't get away wit' doin' that shit here, so they baited you and took you to Atlanta so their family could do the dirty work. Now, we really have to send a message. Niggas need to know you're not to be fucked wit'. Kwame and Kyle both gotta die tonight." It was times like these that I missed Carlos. He woulda been down wit' this shit…no questions asked.

All Juan did was shake his head as I gave him a quick lecture about betrayal. Although I'm sure he didn't wanna hear it, he had to be reminded once again to stop trustin' these niggas out in the street. I didn't give a fuck how long they went back.

When it came to this game, it was the same motto every time, *trust no man*. I walked him through my experiences about killin' niggas wit' no remorse then jogged his memory about the Mike and Trixie situation. He was takin' it all in, but I could tell his mind was heavy. Now, it was time for him to get his revenge.

Juan knew the first place Kwame would go if he had the money was to his baby mother's apartment in Temple Hills. After drivin' in that direction like a maniac, we sat in the parkin' lot of the high rise for almost two and a half hours. We kept the conversation to a minimum 'til finally Kwame and Kyle pulled up in their raggedy-ass Impala.

I reached under my seat and grabbed my .45 then proceeded to the secret compartment in my glove to retrieve the .9mm. I never left out the house naked.

"You ready?" I asked handin' Juan the nine.

"Yeah."

Kwame and Kyle's first mistake was pullin' in, instead of backin' up because they never saw us comin'. As they opened their car doors and tried to get out, Juan and I both walked up on each side wit' our pistols in hand, silencers attached. I let Juan know I would handle Kyle, but Kwame was all him.

Juan put the pistol to Kwame's head, while I placed the pistol in Kyle's mouth. I didn't want to hear shit he had to say.

"Man, what the fuck are you doing. Juan?" Kwame asked.

"Nigga, shut the fuck up. Did you think you were gonna get away with robbing me? You thought I didn't know it was you, bitch!"

Surprisingly, Kwame didn't show any fear. "I see you ran back to daddy. Rich, did you know word on the street is your son a snitch?"

Both Juan and my eyes widened, but I wasn't about to listen to that shit.

"Snitch this nigga!" I said, lettin' off a shot into Kyle's mouth. He slumped over instantly.

"Kyle...Kyle!" Kwame yelled. "Fuck you, Rich! I knew

I should've killed your ass when I had the chance. You killed my Uncle Mike!" He looked over at Juan. "I never fucked with your punk-ass. Oh, by the way, your mother got some good pussy. Ask her about the warehouse. I'm sure she remembers."

It was satisfyin' to finally see my son take a nigga out as he let off two bullets in Kwame's head. As crazy as it was, I felt proud…like he'd just graduated or some shit.

Juan didn't waste time climbin' in the car and pullin' out a black duffle back from the back seat. By the time we sped out the lot and made it down Suitland Parkway, he'd already thumbed through the doe. It was a little under twenty five thousand, which wasn't all his money back, but it was a start. I couldn't believe all this time Juan had been runnin' wit' Mike's nephews. I guess they called themselves payin' me back, but in the end…they didn't succeed. Now, that chapter was over.

Chapter Twenty-One
LISA

It had been days since I'd been to the hospital to see Carlie. No matter how hard I tried, it was difficult to embrace the fact that what I thought was left of Carlos, now belonged to Rich. I'd been so distant from everyone lately. I ignored everybody's call, especially my annoying-ass mother. I didn't want to talk to the hospital staff, so I'm not sure why that bitch thought I was up to her negativity. I hadn't even spoken with Juan, which was a good thing because the privacy allowed me to indulge in my bad habits again. I couldn't help myself. My life had been such a mess that the powder was the only way I was able to escape my problems. I never understood how Marisol didn't get addicted to this shit. It was definitely a weakness for me and I couldn't stop.

Massaging my temples, I tried to get some relief from the daily headache that kicked my ass, but it never worked. At that point, I pulled myself out of bed, which had been hard to do lately and walked toward the bathroom. However, before I could even get in the shower, I had to take a seat at my vanity and do at least two lines.

When my head finally came up, I couldn't help but break down as soon as I looked into the mirror. Ashamed of what my life had become was an understatement. Hell…I didn't even know the person who was staring back at me. Not only did I look like shit, but I felt alone…I missed my father.

I would've given anything for him to come and hold me. To tell me that everything would be okay. As tears made a grand appearance, regrets of how I'd chosen Rich over my dad invaded my entire body. I hated myself for that decision.

Once I get myself together, I'm gonna call my dad. He'll be proud to know that I finally left Rich's ass.

After doing another line, all of a sudden I got the energy to get up from my vanity and go see my daughter. Even though I had mixed feelings about it, it was eating me up that I'd avoided her this long. As I turned on the shower, it didn't take long for thoughts about how much I missed Carlos start to emerge. No matter what, in my mind Carlie was his and that's what I needed to help me move on.

Minutes later, I stood in my closet trying to figure out what to wear. My shape was definitely back, so the days of squeezing into my clothes were finally over. I decided on a pair of skinny jeans with my new Dior knee-high suede, brown boots, an Ella Moss top and my Kenna T leather jacket. Grabbing my purse along with my favorite cat-eye Chanel shades, I was ready to go after giving myself one final look in the mirror. When a smile appeared, I could tell my mood was improving. I felt refreshed and in a better place.

● ● ● ● ● ● ● ● ● ● ● ● ● ●

As soon as I got to the hospital, my high was instantly blown once I walked into the NICU and saw Rich standing over Carlie. Obviously, she'd progressed since I'd last seen her because she was no longer in an incubator. Even most of the tubes were gone. I wanted so badly to walk over to where they were, but I decided to stand back and watch. I especially got heated when I listened to him speak to her with the same voice he used when talking to Denie as a baby.

"Sweetheart, I love you. I'm sorry that you have to go

through all this. I think about you all the time. I can't wait 'til you meet your big sister, Denie. You all look just like your daddy."

"He's good with her you know," Nurse Brooks said as she came up behind me. "He's been here all day." She didn't even ask where I'd been, which was surprising. She just patted me on my back, smiled and walked off.

I guess she was trying to reassure me that everything was gonna be okay, but that shit didn't work. I didn't want Rich anywhere near my child. *She didn't even bother to give me an update on Carlie's status? Did Rich tell them something about me?* Beyond pissed at this point, I walked up to him and snatched his hand off her crib.

"Why are you here?"

Rich looked around the room. "Shhh. Lower your voice Lisa, are you high?"

"Fuck you, Rich. I want you out. I don't care what the courts say, you don't have a right to be here. You didn't care about her when you were calling her a crack baby. Get out!"

At that point, several nurses looked in our direction. It was only a matter of time before one of us had to go.

"Man, I don't have time for your shit right now. You better watch yourself bitch and enjoy your time with her now. Remember the disappearin' act you just pulled. You aren't doin' nothin', but makin' shit easier for me. When Carlie leaves this hospital, trust me…it won't be wit' your coke sniffin' ass."

"Is everything okay here?" Nurse Brooks asked.

"I'm sorry if we caused any type of disturbance. I'm leavin' now," Rich said, trying to make me look like the culprit.

"Yeah, get the fuck out!"

Nurse Brooks' eyes enlarged. "Ms. Sanchez, please. That language is totally inappropriate."

I watched as Rich made his way out. "I'm sorry. It's just that he gets me so worked up."

Staring down at Carlie, I wondered why I was in denial for so long. She looked exactly like Rich...to the point where it instantly made me sick on my stomach. Now, it was evident and I knew exactly what I had to do to rid Rich out of my life for good. It was obvious that his ties to Carlie were gonna be a problem and I couldn't deal with it.

"I can understand that, but I'm gonna have to call security if this behavior continues."

Damn…what happened to the sweet woman you used to be? I thought. Carlie was about to drift back to sleep, so wanted to try and feed her.

"I'm sorry. It won't happen again. Listen, I wanna try and feed her if that's okay."

Nurse Brooks looked at her watch. "Actually, that's fine. It's been a while since your husband fed her, so I'm sure she might be hungry."

The fact that they'd allowed Rich to feed Carlie made my skin crawl.

"I'm gonna try and breast feed, so can you bring her to the private area?"

"Sure."

The fact that I hadn't nursed Carlie in days, I wasn't sure that she would even take my breasts. The drugs were definitely in my system, so I knew it wasn't a good idea to feed her, but how much more harm could I do now anyway? Since Rich had this newfound love for her, I wanted to see how he would handle what I had planned. This was my only way to cut my ties with him. It had to be done.

Once Nurse Brooks handed the baby to me and left out of the room, I placed my nipple right beneath Carlie's nose and pretended to feed her. Looking down at my innocent daughter, I suddenly felt bad, but it had to be done.

"I'm so sorry, Carlie," I whispered.

Pressing my breast firmly against her nose, it didn't take long for her to start squirming. She tried to fight for air for at least a minute, but eventually her tiny body went limp. I waited a few more seconds before lifting my body back up to make sure the task had been complete. Once I saw her face, I knew she was no longer breathing. She was gone. Staring at my baby girl one last time, I kissed her forehead then said a quick prayer.

Father God, please forgive me for taking my own daughter's life. I just decided that I would rather her be with you than him. I'm sorry. In your name I pray. Amen

As soon as I was done, the theatrics started. Instantly, I started screaming out of control. Maybe this is what I needed. I just needed to let it all out.

"Something is wrong! She's not breathing! Please help my daughter!"

Seconds later, several nurses came running in.

"Code blue!" one yelled as loud as she could.

Snatching her out of my arms, I watched as one nurse tried to resuscitate Carlie. Even a doctor came in and worked on her, but after several minutes it was obvious there was nothing that could be done.

"What's wrong? Is she gonna be okay?" I yelled.

"I'm sorry, Ms. Sanchez, she's gone," the doctor finally informed.

"Nooooooo!" I screamed.

Now, I was done with Rich for good. I put on quite a performance as all of the nurses tried to console me.

"I need to call my son," I finally said after screaming a little bit more.

"Are you gonna be okay Ms. Sanchez?" one of the nurses asked.

"I just need to call my son."

After she handed me my purse, as soon as I turned my phone on, a text message popped up from my mother.

I've been trying to reach you for days. We buried your father today.

Chapter Twenty-Two
RICH

For the past few hours, Marisol's mind seemed preoccupied. Chances were, it was due to the fact that our sex life had been very active lately and she felt guilty. When I turned over, she was starin' out into space wit' the comforter pulled up to her neck. I didn't understand the point of her sulkin' so I decided to ask her what was wrong to ease my thoughts before my mind went on a tangent.

"Umm, Miss, are you okay? What's up? Why do you seem so down?"

"What do you mean, I'm alright?"

"No you're not. Something's botherin' you. I can tell."

"Well Rich, if I ask you a question would you be honest without getting upset?"

"Yeah of course. What's up?"

"I keep getting these crazy text messages from Jade and I don't know what to think? I mean…crazy-ass messages from an unknown number." When Marisol handed me her phone, the messages were unbelievable. I was instantly pissed off.

I just wanted to say that Rich is some shit for what he did to Carlos. Don't trust him.—Jade

The second message read-

You haven't responded back, so I guess

he lied and told you he didn't have anything
to do with his death and you believed him.
Go ahead and be stupid.—Jade

Lookin' at the dates, I rubbed my hand down my face because I knew Jade couldn't have sent the messages. She was
dead! This couldn't be anyone but Lisa playin' games. She was
gonna get a royal ass whoopin' for this one. She was playin' wit'
fire and I needed to remind her I was not to be fucked wit'.

"I'm sick and tired of this shit. My brother is dead, and
just because no one knows who killed him, now it's my fault.
I'm tired of Unc' and everybody else pointin' their finger at
me." I said as I threw her phone into the mirror. Glass shattered
everywhere. I hoped like hell she would believe my performance.

"Rich, I'm sorry. That's why I didn't want to say anything. I knew you was gonna get mad."

"Damn right I'm mad. Why shouldn't I be? Do you believe that stupid shit?"

"Not really, but I can't lie. I did wonder why Jade made
those accusations at the memorial service. And now by her tex-
ting me all these crazy messages, I didn't know what to think."

"Fuck Jade! Don't you get it? She's just mad because I
don't fuck wit' her dumb-ass any more. I can't believe you're
questionin' me about this. Who was there for you when your
daughter was sick? It was me, Marisol. Not Jade! So, don't
come at me wit' this nonsense."

"First of all, I didn't accuse you of shit yet, so you need
to calm the fuck down!" Marisol got up out of the bed to get her
phone off of the floor exposin' her naked body. At that point, I
was no longer upset. She looked so damn sexy. I needed to fuck
her again so she remembered who was boss. One thing I knew
about Marisol was if I consistently fucked her, I could definitely
get into her head. She was smart and didn't go for shit, but she
was weak for good dick.

"You broke it asshole!" she said, holdin' the damaged
phone into the air.

"Fuck that phone!"

Standin' up, I grabbed her by the hair and threw my tongue straight down her throat. Kissin' wasn't really my thing, but I had to do somethin' to calm her down. When I finally pulled back, she had a huge grin on her face.

"You alright now?" I asked.

She nodded her head. "Yeah, I'm straight."

"Good," I said, smakin' her on the ass. "Delete them stupid-ass text messages then."

Walkin' toward the bathroom, I didn't even look to see what type of expression she had on her face before I grabbed my towel and hopped in the shower. Moments later, I came back clean and refreshed, and watched as Marisol flicked through the T.V. channels. She was still in her birthday suit.

I smiled. "You plan on puttin' some clothes on today?"

"Maybe."

When Marisol saw me put on some boxers and a white t-shirt, she gave me a disappointed gaze. "Where are you going? I thought we were gonna start on round two? Oh…wait, round two was last night. I meant round three."

"I gotta meet up wit' somebody. You know…handle some business."

I wanted her to think that I didn't need her help, but it was all a part of my plan to make her feel guilty. Even though we'd been fuckin' almost every day, she still hadn't offered to bring me into the business. I had no idea what her ass was waitin' on, but she needed to get at me soon."

"Who are you going to meet?"

"It's no one you know," I responded. "Stay in your lane."

She sucked her teeth. "Forget you, Rich."

Juan had hooked me up wit' one of his connects before he went to Atlanta, but I didn't get a chance to holla at him since that shit wit' Juan went down. Now, it was time to see what type of numbers he was talkin' about. I only dealt wit' coke, so I was gonna be pissed if this dude fucked wit' heroin. I slipped on my Madness Sweatsuit, some Nike boots, and a ski vest before kissin' Marisol on the cheek."

"I'll be back, sexy," I said, before makin' my way to the car.

Grabbin' my phone, I punched in Juan's number to make sure this dude was a coke connect and not a waste of my damn time.

"Hello."

"What's up son? Look, the dude that you told me about, I'm on my way to meet him and…"

"Hold up, where you at?"

"Pullin' out of my driveway, why what's up?"

"Stay right there. I'm less than ten minutes away from your house. I need to talk to you about something," Juan said.

"Alright, cool."

As I sat and waited on Juan to pull up, I wondered what was going on. He sounded frantic. Seconds later, my phone rang. It was the hospital.

"Mr. Sanchez speakin'."

"Hello, this is Mr. Smythe calling from Holy Cross Hospital. I'm the hospital's administrator. Is this Carlie Sanchez's father that I'm speaking with?"

"Yes it is. Is everything okay?"

"Oh my, you don't know, huh?"

"Know what?"

"Well, Mr. Sanchez I'm afraid I have some bad news. I regret to inform you that your daughter passed away yesterday of SIDS."

My eyes widened. "What? I just saw her yesterday. This has to be a mistake." My first instinct was to peel out of the driveway and head straight to the hospital. I needed to get to her as soon as possible.

"Well, your wife…"

"Ex-wife," I quickly corrected.

"I'm sorry your ex-wife, Lisa was here when she passed away. I thought you would've known by now."

"That bitch!"

"Excuse me sir."

"Her mother didn't tell me anything. What the hell is SIDS?"

"It stands for Sudden Infant Death Syndrome. It's the unexpected death of infants. Although there are several different types of theories, no one really knows the cause of it. However, I can say that it's very common in newborn babies who've been exposed to drugs that suffer from this."

"Where is she? Where the hell is Lisa?" I yelled.

"Mr. Sanchez, that's my purpose for calling you. Ms. Sanchez was very distraught yesterday and hasn't been back to the hospital. We've been calling her nonstop, but haven't been able to reach her. There's some important paperwork that she needs to fill out before we can release your daughter's body to a funeral home."

"Mr. Smythe, I'll be there to fill everything out. Thanks for callin'."

I hung up and headed straight to Lisa's house. There was no way I could let this bitch breathe another moment after this. Without even askin', I knew she was responsible for my daughter's death. If that dumb bitch would've just chilled off of that shit, then my daughter would still be alive. My mind raced as I thought about how I was gonna fuck Lisa up. Turnin' on my Jay-Z American Gangsta CD, I rode in silence as thoughts continued to bounce around in my head. Just before I pulled up to Lisa's house, Juan called.

"Yeah!"

"Where did you go? I told you I was on my way."

"I just pulled up to your dope sniffin' mother's house."
CLICK

I didn't even need a response from him. Besides, there was nothin' he could've said to make me change my mind anyway. Gettin' out the car, I picked up a huge rock that was layin' on the side of the house before I went to ring the doorbell. When she didn't come right out, I rang the doorbell repeatedly.

"Who the fuck is it?"

"It's Rich."

"Go away!"

"Lisa, open this fuckin' door now!" I yelled. "If you don't open it, I'ma bust the damn window. I'm not goin' away!"

"What do you want?"

As soon as she opened the door, I dropped the rock and hit that bitch across her face wit my fist. She fell to the floor instantly.

"Oh my God! Get out of my house!" Lisa screamed before holdin' her mouth.

I tried to beat the shit out of her right there in the foyer. After hittin' her in the face again, I banged her head against the marble floor as she tried to fight back. She managed to scratch my face a few times, but that shit didn't faze me.

"You stupid bitch, you killed my daughter!"

"Rich, stop! Stop! I'm gonna call the police!" she said between screams.

"Fuck that. I'ma kill you. First, you text Marisol that shit about me killin' Carlos and now you couldn't even tell me that my child died!" I punched her in her face repeatedly. My intentions were to try to beat Lisa to her grave.

She was damn near unconscious when Juan walked in.

"Rich, what the fuck are you doing? Get away from her!" He immediately ran over to her and pushed me away.

"Don't baby her. She deserved it this time, Juan! She killed your sister. Carlie is dead because of this bitch and her drug habits!" I roared.

"Oh my God! Did you kill her? Rich, what have you done?" Juan said, not even listening to me. His focus was Lisa…as usual.

"Your sister died yesterday because of her and she didn't even tell me."

"Juan, please help me," Lisa managed to say in a soft voice. It seemed as if she was on her last breath.

Juan wiped the blood off her face wit' his shirt. "Is it true? Did Carlie die, Ma?"

"Yeah. Help me Juan, I can't breathe," Lisa replied.

As Juan ran to the bathroom, I looked down at that bitch, cleared my throat and spit right in her face. "Drink that bitch!" I left her there gaspin' for air.

Just when Juan and I were gettin' to a better place that bitch fucked it all up, I thought as I got in my car and raced down the driveway. *I hope he understands why I fucked her up.* As I made a left turn, I felt like I was movin' in slow motion. I didn't know how to react. I'd just met Carlie and now she was gone. She reminded me so much of Denie which is ultimately what hurt the most. I felt as if I lost another daughter all over again because of Lisa's reckless behavior.

When I got to the hospital, I met wit' Mr. Smythe and I filled out all the paperwork. He asked me what our plans were for Carlie's arrangements and I let him know we wanted to have her cremated. I didn't have the energy to deal wit' another funeral. I'd lost my mother, brother, and now my daughter all within a year and just wanted it all to be over. After Mr. Smythe provided me wit' Carlie' footprints as well as a satin pouch wit' a lock of her hair, he asked if I wanted to see her.

"No, that's okay. That won't be necessary. I don't wanna remember her that way," I replied, before leavin' out of his office.

After the fucked up day I'd encountered, I wasn't in the mood to meet up wit' any type of connect, so I headed back home. No sooner than I got on the beltway, Juan called me back.

"Yeah, wassup?"

"I need to holla at you," Juan stated.

"Look, I don't wanna hear shit about your mother!"

"It's not about her and to be honest I don't blame you for being upset. But don't get it twisted, you beating on her is unacceptable. She really needs help. Did you know her father died?"

"No, and I don't care. She's the reason why me and Denie are fucked up. And on top of that, she's been sendin' Marisol text messages about me killin' Carlos. She put Jade's name like I couldn't figure that shit out. She don't need help, she needs to be fuckin' dead. She killed a baby. Juan. The doctor said that SIDS shit was from the drug use!"

"Look, I just dropped her off at the emergency room. She kept saying that she couldn't breathe."

"So fuckin' what. Is she at Holy Cross because I just left. I'll turn this car around if she even think about turnin' me in."

"No…she insisted that we go to Georgetown. Besides, I told her not to cause more trouble," Juan informed. "Listen, I told her I would be right back when I left, so I don't have much time. If you're on your way home, I need to come see you. It's important."

I started to tell my son to fuck off, but couldn't ignore the desperation in his voice. He didn't even seem pissed off that I'd fucked Lisa up, which was strange. "Alright, I'll meet you there."

When I finally got home, Marisol was still there. I was glad because I needed her at this moment. When I got upstairs, she'd cleaned up the glass that I broke earlier and finally had on some clothes.

"What the hell happened to you?" she stared at the scratches on my face.

"Me and Lisa got into a fight."

"Why? What happened now?"

"The baby died yesterday and that bitch didn't even tell me."

"Are you serious? So how did you find out? Oh my goodness, Rich. I'm so sorry."

"The doctor called because this bitch wasn't answerin' their calls."

"What the fuck has gotten into Lisa? What made her snap like this? She's always been a good mother. That's the one thing about her I always respected."

"Fuck that bitch. For real Marisol, if Juan hadn't walked in, I would've definitely killed her. Speaking of Juan, he's comin' to see me in a bit so just make sure you don't come downstairs."

"Okay. Is there anything I can do for you?"

"I'm cool babe."

"Well, I know what I can do to relieve a little stress before Juan get's here."

Before I could even protest, Marisol got on her knees, worked my sweatpants down my legs and pulled my dick right out of my boxers. She immediately went to work. As she moved her head back and forth and let out a loud suckin' sound, my eyes instantly rolled to the back of my head. Her warm and wet mouth felt so good, I tried to hold back, but couldn't help it. I needed to release.

"Aww shit, I'm cummin'."

"That's right. Cum for me daddy. Right in my mouth," she said between slurps.

As soon as I started to bust, the doorbell rung. "I'm coming Juan," I said like he could hear me.

"Literally," Marisol added wit' a mouth full of sperm.

I ran to the bathroom and quickly got myself together before runnin' downstairs to open the door. By then, the doorbell had rung two more times.

"Damn, what were you doing?" Juan asked as he came through the door.

"I got company."

"Oh, she made it over here quick didn't she?" Juan responded. "Anyway, I won't stay long. I just didn't want to be talking reckless over the phone."

I turned around, then looked back at him. "Ssshh. Keep your voice down. I don't want the chick upstairs to hear me discuss business."

"Right. Well, I just wanted to tell you that I don't trust the connect I hooked you up with. After the shit that happened in Atlanta, I don't wanna fuck with nobody outside of the Columbians, so just don't meet up with him."

"Damn, I wasn't feelin' right about that shit either. Since we're on the same page wit' that, I'ma trust my first instinct. Thanks, son."

"No problem. I got your back now, since you proved to me that you got mine."

"Cool. Hey, listen I do have to ask you a serious question though."

"What's up?"

"Is there any truth to what Kwame said that night? You know…the snitchin' accusation?"

Juan gave me a crazy look. "Come on…pops. You know me better than that. I know the code of honor."

When he called me pops that shit made me feel like I was ridin' on a cloud. Wit' my day bein' such a wreck, I was glad that our relationship was finally a priority to the both of us.

Chapter Twenty-Three
LISA

Rich was out of fucking control and needed to be put in prison. Even though I'd killed my daughter, he didn't know that for sure. For him to beat me the way that he did was inexcusable. Two weeks had gone by and my face was still a wreck. Along with a puffy right eye, he'd even given me a fractured jaw, which prevented me from opening my mouth widely. I couldn't even eat certain types of foods. Every time I looked in the mirror, I wanted to scream. I couldn't believe I'd let Juan talk me out of pressing charges. What kind of message was I sending for allowing Rich to get away with that? I hated the person that I'd become and wanted all of my problems to just disappear. With so much on my mind, my head started to pound.

Not only had I become a punching bag, but my heart ached every time I thought about my father. The only other man who ever loved me unconditionally was gone and I'd turned my back on him for Rich. My father was my world and because of all the drama in my life, I wasn't even able to say goodbye. I didn't even know he was sick. My regrets were overwhelming. *How did I allow Rich to make me cut my father and the rest of my family out of my life?* He made me choose and now I hated him more than ever. Since my life was such a wreck, I debated if I needed to be on this earth anymore. If it wasn't for Juan, I would've probably taken my life a long time ago. I felt so alone.

Rubbing my temples, I listened as my phone began to ring…again. Within an hour, it had rung at least five times with no signs of stopping. I knew it was probably Cornell because he'd left a numerous amount of messages over the past week. Most were about the baby. Even though I didn't feel like talking, I went to go grab my phone. And just like I thought, it was Cornell. This time I decided to answer.

"Hello."

"Hey, Lisa, are you alright? I've been trying to call you."

"I'm okay."

"Why do you sound like that? Is something in your mouth?"

"Umm…no. It's a long story."

"I've been worried about you. I'm so sorry to hear about your daughter. I was thankful that Juan told me."

"Thanks. My father passed away too, so I'm a mess."

"Damn, I didn't know all that."

I'm sure he thought everybody around me died at some point. "It's cool."

"Baby, you need a vacation. I'm in Miami for a couple of days because we play the Heat. What if I flew you down here? You know...to help you unwind and get some things off of your mind."

"No, I think I just need some time alone." I didn't want him to see me this way.

"Lisa, that's the last thing you need. I'm not taking no for an answer. Get some rest tonight. I'm booking you a morning flight. The sooner you get out of DC the better."

I finally gave in. "Okay, Cornell. I'll come down there. Maybe I do need to get away before I lose my mind."

"I'm about to call my travel agent right now. Thanks for allowing me to be there for you. I'll see you in the morning."

"Thanks for caring. Goodnight."

Something about Cornell's voice felt soothing. He made me feel a little better, and it seemed as though he'd called at the right time. Maybe I didn't realize that I just needed to hear that someone cared. Closing my eyes, I fell asleep laying across the bed and drifted to another place. However, it wasn't long before I woke up from a nightmare about Denie coming into my room with a knife and trying to kill me. No matter how much I tried to escape the problems that surrounded me, the devil was always working.

●●●●●●●●●●●●●●

By the time I woke up the next morning, Cornell had already sent my itinerary. A part of me had second thoughts about going, but after I talked to Juan I figured I would go and get away. Since I didn't know what Cornell had planned for us, I packed my small Louis Vuitton roller bag with just a jacket, two outfits, and a swimsuit. Hopefully when I got there, he would be a real gentleman and take me shopping at Bal Harbour anyway.

Juan called me once he was outside and met me at the door to carry my luggage. Once we got on the road, he wanted to know how I was holding up. I knew that was just his slick way of asking, *if I was still using*. Like I was going to admit that shit to him. But little did he know, I had a little stash hiding in my bra.

"Juan I've been chilling out. Even though I got a lot on my mind, I'm trying to keep my head above water."

"I'm happy to hear that. I see your eye has cleared up."

"No, you're wrong. It's called make-up," I said, in a sarcastic tone.

"Well shit, I didn't know. Anyway, have you talked to Rich?"

"For what?"

"Well, he had the baby cremated, so I thought you all would've at least spoken about that."

"I told that asshole I didn't want any parts of whatever he did with Carlie."

"Damn Ma, that was rude. What has gotten into you?

You don't care about what happened to the baby?"

"I do care Juan, but I just didn't feel like going back and forth with Rich, I'm tired of dealing with his bullshit. It's just best that we don't communicate. Speaking of him, why do you all seem so damn buddy-buddy lately? Like you all have this newfound bond. You didn't even want me to press charges. Is there something I need to know?"

He looked like I'd struck a nerve "No, Ma. Let's just drop it."

Juan was quiet for the rest of the ride to the airport. I didn't want to leave with him being upset with me, but I also didn't want to hear anything else about Rich or Carlie. I wanted to be done with that entire situation. He might've even thought I was being inhumane, but it wasn't that. I just didn't care anymore.

When we pulled up to the departure gate for United Airlines, I knew I had to break the silence. Turning to my son, I grabbed his face and told him to look at me.

"Juan, I just want you to know that I'm going through a lot right now and I need you by my side more than ever. With my father passing, it has taken all the fight that I had. I wasn't even able to say goodbye and it hurts. The reason why I'm going to Miami to see Cornell is to escape all of my problems and get a clear head. I need that right now."

"I'll always be by your side, Ma. I just don't ever want you going back to your old selfish ways. It hurts me to see you destroy your life that way. I just want my mother back. You haven't been the same since you got mixed up with Carlos. You are a drug addict, Ma!"

"Is that what you think of me? You know what…you don't have to worry about me anymore." When I got out of the car and slammed the door, Juan got out and tried to help me with my luggage.

"I don't need your help. Fuck it, I don't need you!"

"Ma, you can't get mad and blame me for your faults. I'm only trying to help. The fact that you don't even care how Carlie was put to rest is crazy. Why wouldn't you be concerned about that? Maybe you're gone more than I thought. It might be hurtful to hear me say that, but it's the truth!"

His words stung. "Fuck you, Juan! Now that you're all up Rich's ass, it's fuck me, huh? Well, remember who has always been there for you!"

I stormed off into the airport. This was the first time my son and I had ever had a fight where there were words thrown that hurt. My boarding pass was already printed so I went straight to security. The closer I got to placing my belongings on the belt, the more nervous I became. Remembering my stash was in my bra, I suddenly got nervous. I made sure every piece of jewelry was removed because I didn't want to give them a reason to have to search me. Right before I walked up to the metal detector, the butch looking TSA agent eyed me up and down, making me even more worried. I just knew she was looking for a reason to frisk me. As soon as I walked through, the alarm beeped. My heart dropped instantly.

"Ma'am you need to take your sunglasses off your head. Are you wearing a belt?" the agent asked.

"Oh, thank you, yes I am wearing a belt, I forgot."

Taking them both off, I went through a second time with no problem. Now more than ever, I was ready to be the hell out of DC.

• • • • • • • • • • • • • •

When we landed two and a half hours later, I didn't waste any time calling Cornell.

"Hello."

"Are you at the airport? I just landed," I said in an excited tone.

"No, I had something to do. But I have a driver there for you. He'll have a sign with your name on it."

"Alright, I'll see you soon."

"I can't wait."

I was a little disappointed that Cornell wasn't picking me up since I really needed a hug right now. As bad as I wanted to call Juan to let him know I'd made it, I was sticking to my guns. He needed to know that his disrespect wouldn't be tolerated.

Putting my Bvlgari sunglasses on, I made my way through the crowd until I finally saw a Hispanic gentleman holding my name up on a sign.

"Hello sir, I'm Lisa Sanchez."

"Good afternoon, Ms. Sanchez. I'm Roberto and I'll be your driver. How was your flight?" he asked, taking my carry-on luggage.

"It wasn't too bad."

"That's great. Follow me. We're right here in the garage."

When we got to the car, it was more than I expected. A Hummer limo. I was wowed. Before he put my luggage in the truck, Roberto stopped and leaned on the door.

"Ma'am, I've been given instructions by Mr. Willis that you have to put on this blindfold before entering the limo."

"What? I'm not wearing a blindfold. I don't even know you."

"Ma'am, you don't want to ruin his surprise, do you?"

I hesitated for a few seconds. "Okay, but as soon as I feel uncomfortable it's coming off."

I didn't want to seem confrontational so I thought it was best to comply with what Cornell wanted. After Roberto blindfolded then helped me into the car, the smell of fresh flowers invaded my nose. I didn't even have a chance to get excited because as soon as the car pulled off, all of a sudden I felt somebody kissing me on my neck.

I let out a bashful smile. "Cornell, this better be you."

When I removed the blindfold, Cornell was sitting beside me along with several dozen of white and pink roses.

"Oh my goodness Cornell, I can't believe you did this."

"Do you know the symbolic meaning of white and pink roses?"

"No. What are they?"

"White roses are a symbol of purity and pink roses are a symbol of admiration. I admire your courage as a woman and from this day forward I want you to be pure for me. In my line of work it's hard for me to trust a woman, but there's somethin' about you that always had me comin' back. No matter how much you tried to push me away, it was something about you that made me feel like I wanted to be a part of your life. You need to be loved and I wanna do that for you."

"Cornell, no one has ever done anything like this for me. I have a hard time trusting anyone, so you have to be patient with me. I can't promise you anything. All I can do is be myself and see where this goes."

"All I ask is for you to let me be there for you."

"I can do that," I said, kissing him on his cheek. He kissed me back but I pulled away. "I'm sorry, Cornell." I didn't get a chance to move my stash from my bra, so I didn't want to get something started and he found out about my habit.

"It's okay. I'm just happy you were able to make it."

"What time is your game?"

"The game isn't until tomorrow. We have practice today in a couple of hours then I figured we could go out afterwards to dinner at Prime 112. For now we're gonna do a little shopping. How would you like that?"

"I love that!" I said, giving him a huge hug.

The feeling I had at that moment was something I hadn't felt since Carlos, but for some reason it was still different. I knew I was vulnerable right now which is what caused me to fall for Carlos, but with Cornell it was different. We had never slept together, so it wasn't about how he made me feel sexually. It was about how he made me feel emotionally. My motive in the beginning was getting what I could from him during the divorce, but now it was about having a friend. Someone I could count on.

Bal Harbour was still the same fabulous place since the last time I was in Miami. We went to the Louis Vuitton boutique first to get me a couple of new bags from the cruise line that just launched. I picked up a couple of shoes and boots from Neiman's as well. Cornell even had all the packages shipped to my house so I didn't have to worry about lugging it on the plane. This was the life I could get used to minus being stopped every five minutes with people asking for an autograph or girls flirting.

Once we got to the Chanel boutique, I was reminded very quickly that I was dating a high profile basketball star. As soon as we walked in, some girl let out a loud laugh before whispering to her friend. It took all my patience to keep it together, but she was the poster child of a groupie bitch. She was a cute girl, long weave, brand clothes from head to toe, but still had a whorish twist to her style. When she and Cornell finally made eye contact, I could tell how he all of a sudden got uncomfortable. It was obvious that he knew her, but I didn't know to what degree. Trying my best to block the chick out, I walked around the store and was immediately drawn to the ice pearl colored bag behind the glass.

"Oh my goodness. I love this one," I gloated.

The girl must've heard me because she immediately sashayed her groupie-ass over and asked to see it.

"Good choice," her sales lady stated. "There are only three of these in the United States."

The bitch cut her eye at me before saying, "I'll take it."

I was pissed. And to add salt to my wound, she finally decided to walk over and say something to Cornell when the sales lady went to ring it up.

"Cornell, you weren't gonna speak to me?"

"What's up Raven?"he replied dryly.

"Aren't you gonna introduce me? Is this your mom?" she asked with a smirk.

"No bitch, I'm his girl," I said in a calm, but stern tone.

"Oh, I'm sorry. You just look a little older than what I'm used to seeing him with. You do look familiar though."

"I bet."

"So, you're the woman who was on Mediatakeout.com. Cornell, remember when I called and asked you who the woman was on the internet with you. Remember you said that you didn't fuck with her like that. You said it was your man's mom…right?"

"Raven, why you always like starting shit? This is *my girl*. Please leave us alone so we can enjoy the rest of our day together," Cornell blurted out.

"Sure, no problem, and thanks for the bag. I put it on your tab like I always do. Now, I see why you had something to do today. You could've just told me you flew somebody else in, too," Raven informed.

Cornell shook his head. "Man, whatever."

"I hope you'll get a moment to make it to my room before practice." As if she had the shit timed, as soon as Raven walked away the sales lady came back out with a shopping bag and a receipt. "Bye, Mr. Three," Raven taunted, before she and her friend laughed and walked out.

I was furious and embarrassed. My age showed because I wasn't in the loop of what was going on with internet gossip, but as soon as I could I was going to pull up that website she was talking about.

"I'm ready to go," I said with an attitude.

I didn't even wait for his response before I walked out the store and back to the car. Not knowing what was taking him so long, Cornell finally made his way back a few minutes later with a defeated look on his face.

"So, you're gonna let what that groupie bitch said bother you and fuck up our day?"

"Cornell, I knew this was a bad idea. Maybe I shouldn't have come. This is what y'all athletes do, but I guess I thought you were different."

"I am different."

"I can't tell. Why should I feel special? This is routine, this is what you do."

"This is not what I do. But this is what I'm gonna do. I'm

gonna send you to the spa while I go to practice and then we're gonna meet back up and have dinner tonight. We can talk about this later. I'll meet you around seven. Does that work?"

I rolled my eyes. "Whatever."

We both rode in silence until the limo pulled up to the Viceroy Hotel. Cornell stayed inside the car while a representative from the hotel whisked me away to the spa for a full day of relaxation. No matter how disappointed I was with him, I needed that spa treatment. Once I got back to the room a few hours later, there was a teddy bear on the bed surrounded by more white roses, a Chanel shopping bag and a card. I opened the card first.

Lisa,

I'm sorry that I made an ass of myself today. However, I'm not sorry that I made the choice to be with you. You make me happy and making you upset was never my intentions. Can we please leave the past in the past and work on the future?

Cornell

Opening the box that was inside the shopping bag, my eyes almost popped out of my head. I had never seen a Chanel bag like this before. It was pearl in color with double C's all over it encrusted with crystals. It was absolutely stunning.

Regardless of how amazing the bag was, my excitement quickly faded as thoughts about what Raven said earlier entered my mind. Desperate to see if she was telling the truth, I grabbed my phone and went directly to the website. I didn't even have to scroll down that far before the embarrassing headline *Cornell Willis' Cheap Date* appeared. After clicking the link, the small article went on to say that Cornell Willis loved cougars because they didn't want much more than a dinner at Chipotle. After scrolling down a little more, there I was walking out of the restaurant with Cornell. I was completely humiliated.

Pulling out the stash that I'd transferred to my purse, I needed a quick fix to get my mind off of things. I needed instant relief. After opening up the small package, I laid the powder out on my compact and began to sniff away. I was so focused on getting high that I didn't even realize that Cornell had walked into the room.

"What the hell are you doing, Lisa?"

When I looked up, I still had a small amount of powder on my nose. "I didn't hear you come in. Umm."

"Umm, what? So, you're a dope head? Oh hell no...you gotta go. I can't fuck with you like that! I thought I could help you and be there for you, but I didn't sign up for this shit."

"Wait Cornell, just listen..."

"Man, get the fuck out. You can't stay here. I can't fuck up my career messing with you."

Snatching my suitcase off the bed, he opened the door and threw it out before grabbing my arm.

"Let me go!" I said, just before he shoved me out and slammed the door in the face.

Instantly, I screamed and dropped to the floor before crying my eyes out. I was this close to a new life and had thrown it all away that fast.

Chapter Twenty-Four
JUAN

In all of my twenty-three years, I never thought I would say that I was thankful for Rich being there for me. So much that I felt an obligation to somehow fix what I'd started with the Feds. They were definitely on his heels, so it was crucial that my plan to get him off the hook worked. On my way to meet Agent Patterson, I constantly thought about the fight that I'd had with my mother. I really hadn't been in the mood to talk to her since she left for Miami, and obviously she felt the same way. I didn't even know when she was due to come home, and to alleviate any further drama I'd been staying at the Gaylord Hotel. Even though I felt bad about the fight, a part of me knew I'd been too much of a crutch for her. It took a lot for me to speak my mind, but she needed to hear it. As I made my way into Virginia, my phone rang. It was Marisol.

"Hello."

"Hey, nephew, you good? I haven't heard from you in about a week."

"Yeah, I'm actually in the middle of something right now."

"What do you have planned this weekend?" she inquired.

"Nothing much. Why…what's up?"

"Well, Renzo called. He wanted me to tell you that he needs you to fly out this afternoon so he can brief you on some things that need to be taken care of."

I couldn't be happier. Finally, Uncle Renzo had decided to let me in. Things were definitely falling into place. "Really? Yeah, that sounds good," I replied. "Hold up...but it's already one o'clock. What time does he expect me?"

"Can you be on a three o'clock flight to LAX leaving from National?"

"I don't even have any luggage packed."

"You can get clothes when you get there. It sounded urgent."

"Okay, I'll make it happen."

"I'm calling him now so he can book your flight."

"Bet."

A free trip to the west coast any other time would've been right up my alley...especially if partying was involved. But this time it had to be strictly business.

When I finally pulled into the Potomac Yard shopping center, it didn't take long for me to spot Agent Patterson's car. Luckily he was parked near the Vitamin Shoppe because I didn't know anybody who went in white-ass stores like that.

Getting out of my car, I still made sure no one was around before I hopped into his. Hopefully, this dude wasn't long winded since I now had a plane to catch. I wasn't prepared for this meeting or in the mood. As soon as I closed the door, I noticed another gentleman in the passenger seat.

"Hey, Juan, how are you?"

"Wassup Patterson. How are things going?"

"They would be going much better if you came to bear some good news."

"Well, I still don't have anything. Rich has been clean."

"You know what Juan, I'm tired of this bullshit," he said, hitting the steering wheel. His patience had obviously run out. "I wanna know what the fuck happened to the meeting between Rich and the undercover agent? It was a sure meeting and then all of a sudden, he didn't show up. I'm starting to think that you tipped him off. Do you realize that you're on borrowed time?

This is the last empty meeting we're going to have."

"My baby sister died, that's what happened! That's why the meeting didn't go through. Rich got a phone call from the hospital that same day."

"Look, I'm sorry about your loss, but we have a job to do. Every time I go back to my superiors with no information, it looks like I'm not doing my job. They want to throw your ass back in jail. Now, is that what you want?"

"Fuck no. Who would want to go back to jail?"

"Well, your actions are showing otherwise. As a matter of fact, this nice gentleman sitting here is actually here to take you back to jail. Juan, I want you to meet Officer Riley."

I couldn't believe that he'd brought some punk-ass officer to lock me up. "Oh, hell no. I'm not going back to jail!"

"Oh yes, you are. Not unless you have any other ideas for us Mr. Sanchez, because this is clearly not working," Agent Patterson stated.

Now, it was finally time to let them in on my plan. "Actually, I do have another idea. But as soon as I got in the car, you started attacking me and I couldn't even think straight."

"Okay, so what do you have?"

"Look, my Uncle Lorenzo is a huge druglord so..."

"Yeah, I heard of him," Agent Patterson interrupted. "I heard that no one has been able to get to him though."

"Well, he finally wants me to be a part of his business. I'm actually flying out to meet him in L.A. as soon as I leave here. Once I find out the ins and outs of his operation, it's a wrap."

"So, you've been holding back this information all of this time?'

I shook my head. "No, I swear to you, I just got the call."

"This is good...this is better than good." Agent Patterson lit up like a Christmas tree.

"Yeah, getting him is much better than Rich any day," I agreed.

"Oh, we still want Rich. But if you can get Lorenzo, I'll definitely take him for now."

Shit. I needed to clear Rich's name. "You gotta trust me on this one. Since my baby sister died, Rich is trying to turn over a new leaf. He just told me the other day that he's getting out the game." Hopefully my lies were believable.

"We'll see about that," Agent Patterson replied with a smirk.

"Alright, so when I get out there I'll give you a call and let you know what's up."

"Oh no, young man. Your way hasn't worked thus far so now we're gonna do things my way. Me and my team are flying out with you and this time, you're wearing a wire."

My eyes grew larger. "A wire! Are you trying to get me killed?"

"No, I'm trying to get this case solved. I can't afford to waste anymore time. If you can't get me Rich, then I need Lorenzo. I need him talking about the operation *on tape!*"

"Well, I fly out in an hour and a half. How is that gonna work?"

"Don't worry. We're the FBI. We can make anything happen. As soon as you get to L.A., my team and I will have you set up before you even see Lorenzo."

Even though I wasn't thrilled about being wired up, I knew it was something that had to be done in order for me to buy Rich more time. Hopefully, after Uncle Renzo got locked up, I really could Rich him into retiring. Maybe we both could.

Before I got back into my car, Agent Patterson gave me instructions of what to do as soon as I landed. As I pulled out the lot, he gave me a wink and rolled down his window.

"See you on the west side," he said, putting up a W with his fingers. I was instantly annoyed.

Chapter Twenty-Five
JUAN

My mind was so heavy when I got to L.A. that I almost forgot the location of the Admirals Club where Agent Patterson instructed us to meet. I still couldn't believe what was about to go down. If Uncle Renzo ever found out I was an informant he would kill me for sure, nephew or not. However, I had to go through with it. Snitching was a risky job, and since I'd signed up for the gig, I had to man up.

As soon as I found the right gate and walked into the private lounge area, a tall white guy with dark glasses stopped me. "Is he confirmed?" the guy said with his hand pressed against my chest.

I didn't know who he was talking to until I saw a small microphone attached on his shirt.

Moments later, the guy moved to the side then locked the door behind me. "You can proceed," he said in a serious tone.

I was just about to ask him what to do when Agent Patterson suddenly appeared. "Juan, how was your flight?" he asked.

Damn I guess he wasn't lying about being here by the time I landed, I thought. "It was cool."

"Good. So, are you ready?" He had a smile on his face like I was about to get married or some shit.

"Not really, but let's get it over with." I didn't want to prolong the conversation any longer.

"Okay, do you see how small this microphone is?" Agent Patterson pointed to the tall guy's shirt. "Well, we left that out so you could see it. We didn't want you think it was gonna be this massive thing attached to you. It's small enough so no one will detect it."

"If you say so."

"No worries, Mr. Sanchez. Things will work out," Patterson tried to convince.

"Hmph…that's easy for you to say."

Within fifteen minutes, Agent Patterson and another man had securely placed one part of the device to my thigh while the microphone part was tapped to my chest. After testing at least three times, they finally let me go.

I felt like the whole word was watching me as I made my way outside the terminal. It wasn't even that hot and I was sweating like a whore in church. When Uncle Renzo called to let me know one of his guards was there to pick me up, the sweat increased. I knew he probably had no idea what was going on, but my guilty conscious had completely taken over.

As soon as I pulled up to Uncle Renzo's gated house thirty minutes later, I immediately got flashbacks of me and Denie coming here when we were young. Those were the times when problems didn't seem to exist. When our family appeared to be happy and most of all…sane. As fucked up as our family was now, I would've given anything to get those moments back.

I snapped out of my daze when Uncle Renzo came out to greet me.

"Hello, nephew. I'm glad you made it safely. Let's go inside. We have a lot to discuss," he said, giving me a hug.

I tried my best to keep a small distance between us so he wouldn't feel anything. "Thanks for inviting me."

I followed him to a part of the house that I'd never been to before…the basement. When we walked into the room, five other men were sitting at a huge cherry wood table in the middle of the room. The only one I recognized was Armondo.

"I want you guys to meet my nephew, Juan. He'll be rep-

resenting the East Coast today," Uncle Renzo announced before
sitting at the head of the table. They all nodded, but didn't say
anything. "Take a seat, Juan," he instructed.

"The reason I'm calling this meeting is because of the
death of my son and with Rich no longer being a part of the
business, our numbers have dropped tremendously.
Now…"Uncle Renzo said.

"You never did tell us what happened with Rich. Why
can't we bring him back? He was a good earner," one guy said.

"Vito, don't fucking cut me off again," Uncle Renzo
snapped. "Besides, I don't care to get into that. Now, our ene-
mies are starting to move into some of our areas and are supplying our men. We're losing credibility because the streets see a
rift in the family business and are taking advantage. Juan, right
now Marisol was entirely responsible for supplying the territories in DC, but now I'm ready to give you some responsibility.
You cool with that?"

"Most definitely," I said, trying to hold back my excitement. I couldn't believe he was talking like this on the first
meeting. It was a matter of time before he would be going down
thanks to me.

Uncle Renzo went on to talk about business and pretty
much let me know I would be handling not only Maryland, DC,
and Virginia, but also New Jersey, New York, Miami, and a couple of cities in North Carolina. Even though I knew what my
real intentions were, it hurt to know that all the money I
could've made was never gonna happen. My biggest dreams
were slowly going down the drain. This was all I ever wanted.
Now, I was having regrets.

"Juan, did you hear me?" Uncle Renzo asked.

"No. I'm sorry I didn't hear the last part you said."

"To celebrate your new responsibilities, I'm gonna have
some of the guys take you out tonight to celebrate. Then you
will have a little night cap with Mandy."

The room was filled with a lot of oohs. Mandy must've
been a hot chick.

"Can I go?" one of the guys yelled out.

The room erupted in laughter.

"No…Mandy is just for Juan tonight. I've already set everything up. The hotel room is already reserved," Uncle Renzo replied.

After wrapping up the meeting, Uncle Renzo insisted that I borrow his 2010 black Grancabrio Maserati to go shopping for something to wear for the night. Driving a Maserati in L.A. wasn't a big deal, but back in DC I would've been the shit, so I didn't decline the offer. Before he could change his mind, I hopped in the car and headed straight for Rodeo Drive. I didn't even know what time the stores closed, but if that plan failed, my next stop was the Beverly Center.

As I drove toward the first Armani store, I felt like a million bucks. Especially when Uncle Renzo's friend Joe, called to let me know where my hotel was and that he would meet me there in a few hours. He even asked if he could ride with me to the club, which definitely wasn't a problem. The longer I had with the beautiful car, the better. As soon as I turned the music back up, my phone rang again. It was Agent Patterson. My mood automatically went south.

"Yeah," I answered.

"Enjoying L.A. I see. Nice car."

"Damn, are y'all following me, too? The wire wasn't enough."

"The more surveillance we get, the better. And I have to be honest Juan, you've given us some great stuff to start with. That meeting was excellent info. My superiors are going to be quite pleased with you."

"Look, I just want this to be over with. What else do you need him to say before I can take this shit off? I wanna go on with my life."

"We'll be in touch."

CLICK

• • • • • • • • • • • • • •

When I pulled up to my hotel two and a half hours later, I asked valet to keep the car out front while I got dressed really quick. Once I checked in, I went straight to my room and turned on the shower. Before I took off the wire, I called in to let the Feds know what I was about to do since they had to know my every move. Ultimately, I was only given ten minutes which was annoying.

After basically taking a quick bird bath, I slipped on my Armani t-shirt and jeans before putting on my hoodie since the weather had dropped. When I got down stairs, Joe was already out front. He seemed like a really cool dude. We even had a decent conversation as we drove to a club in downtown L.A.

However, as soon as we pulled up, I didn't even get a chance to make it inside before Joe pointed Mandy out. She had to be one of the finest woman I'd ever seen in my life. With flawless brown skin like Gabrielle Union, long black hair, big breast, and a phat ass, I couldn't wait to hit.

"Hey, Mandy. Come on over here," Joe called out.

I stared at her shapely legs as she made her way toward us. "Hey, Joe," she greeted.

"You looking good as always, my love," Joe said, eyeing her up and down. "Mandy…this is Juan. Renzo's nephew."

"Oh…nice to meet you Juan. I hear that I'm supposed to be riding back with you once the club closes," she informed. It's funny how she put a big emphasis on the word riding.

"Shit, we can roll now." I looked over at one of the valet dudes. "Hey…hold up. Don't park my car yet!"

She smiled. "I see you don't waste any time."

"Not if I see what I want."

After grabbing her hand, I nodded to Joe letting him know I was leaving. Being a true gentleman, I helped Mandy in the passenger seat before jumping behind the wheel. After putting the hotel's address in the navigation, we were on our way.

"So, how do you know my uncle?"

"Well, I do work for him from time to time," Mandy replied as she licked her glossed lips.

"I guess you know my father, Rich, too huh?"

"Do I ever? I love me some Rich. How's he doing?"

I had to smile. "He's cool." It wasn't surprising at all that my father had tapped that ass.

When we pulled up to the hotel room, a few minutes later and made our way to my room, it seemed like the door hadn't even been closed before Mandy's little black dress was on the floor. She was obviously ready for business. I had to get to the bathroom to take off the wire…fast

"Hold on baby, let me take a shower before we get started. I feel sweaty."

"This is what I do. I don't care if your balls are sweaty. I just want to make you feel good so I can get paid."

"I promise, it won't take long."

Pulling her hands off of my waist, I made my way to the bathroom. Turning on the shower so that Mandy couldn't hear me checking in, I let the Fed's know I was about to have some fun. I knew they would be pissed once all they heard was the shower continuously running, but there was no way, I was about to miss out on some ass. After placing the device on the marble counter, I told myself I was about to knock her back out just before there was a knock on the door.

"Wait a minute, Mandy. I'm coming."

Taking off my clothes, I kept my boxers on and then looked at myself one last time in the mirror. Nevertheless, when I finally opened the door Mandy was gone. But to my surprise, Uncle Renzo and Armondo were sitting on the bed while another guy who was at least three hundred pounds stood by the desk.

"What's up Unc'?" I said nervously. "Where did Mandy go?"

"Son, I want to explain something to you. I've been in

this game for quite some time. I know that you don't get locked up for a gun and some heroin and just do a couple of months. No probation, no programs...nothing. When we sat in your mother's living room and Armondo asked about your charges, somehow you escaped that question. I should've known then."

I felt like I wanted to throw up. "What are you talking about?" I said, nervous as hell. It felt as if my life had just flashed before my eyes. There was nothing I could do. He knew.

Uncle Renzo shook his head like he was disappointed. "Juan, I wanted to trust you. I wanted to have another Sanchez man, take over where my son left off. I put all of my doubts aside and still tried to have faith in you. You let me down!"

"It's not what you think."

"No man makes pussy wait. While you were in the car I gave Mandy specific instructions. If you rushed to the bathroom and closed the door she was to call me. You see...I've been downstairs waiting on that call since I watched you two pull up. Now, if I go in this bathroom and there's a wire in there, you're a dead man."

Trying to make a run for the door, Armondo immediately hit me in my forehead with the butt of his gun. As I felt the blood gush from my head, Uncle Renzo came out of the bathroom with the wire in his hand.

"You're a fucking informant, Juan!" he shouted. "Armondo where's the plastic?"

"No...wait, please," I begged.

Ignoring my pleas, Armondo laid the plastic out on the floor as Uncle Renzo filled the sink with water and dropped the wire inside. Seconds later, Armondo pulled out a huge dildo from Mandy's bag along with a pair of handcuffs.

"Damn...if you hadn't fucked up, Mandy was really gonna put on a show," Armondo finally said, before putting his knee in my chest and handcuffing me to the bottom of the bed.

"Do you know what they do to snitches in prison, Juan?" Uncle Renzo asked. "See, you have a choice here. Either you can get fucked with the dildo or I can have my man Pablo here fuck you. So, which one is it gonna be?"

There was no way I was about to be fucked *at all*. "Just kill me," I responded.

"I didn't give you that option yet," Uncle Renzo responded.

"I want some of that sweet ass," Pablo chimed in. He barely knew how to speak English.

"No! Don't do this!" I yelled right before my boxers were ripped off.

Before I could say another word, Pablo rammed his dick in my ass so hard, I was ready to die instantly. I yelled as loud as I could, hoping someone would hear me as Pablo fucked me like a virgin. I felt completely violated.

Moments later, Uncle Renzo put the gun to my head with the silencer attached and asked, "Any last words son?"

"Fuck you, nigga. In a matter of seconds the FBI will be up here and your ass is going down regardless, if I'm dead or alive."

"Well, how about I take that chance," he responded just before the room went dark.

Chapter Twenty-Six
LISA

My life was a complete mess. I just didn't know what to do at this point to get back on track. I'd been calling Cornell since Miami, and each time he sent me straight to voicemail. With me and Juan still not speaking, now I really didn't have anyone to talk to. Hopefully the appointment with my stylist Jermaine would lift my spirits.

When I walked into the shop, it was eleven o'clock and the salon was already busy. Looking around, I noticed that his assistant Kelli, washing somebody's hair, but Jermaine was nowhere in sight.

"Kelli, where's Jermaine?" I inquired.

"Girl, he's on his way. How have you been? I haven't seen you around in a while."

"I've been okay. How long is he gonna be because I rushed up here so I wouldn't have to hear his mouth."

"He should be here…"

Before she could even finish, Jermaine walked in and greeted everyone looking fabulous as usual. I always loved his creative style of dressing.

"You know you were about to get it," I said as he walked up to me and looked at his watch.

"Wow, Miss Lisa. It's 11:05. You're on time for a change."

I gave him a playful push. "Shut up."

"Come on, girl. Let me see what we need to do with this hair," Jermaine replied.

"As long as it's not a weave, you can do whatever. The last time I got that, all types of shit happened in my life."

Jermaine smiled and ran his fingers through my hair. "Well, you're definitely gonna need a trim. Let's go to my private room because you look like you need to talk."

When we went to the back of the salon where he did several celebrity's hair, he got right to work.

"So, what's going on sista?" Jermaine asked, before he pulled out his shears.

"Jermaine, my life is a mess. Where should I begin?"

I was usually a private person, but for some reason I trusted Jermaine. I knew that I could tell him anything without it being repeated and more importantly without being judged. It didn't take long before I laid it all out for him. From the death of Carlie, to the divorce, my fight with Juan, and the situation between me and Cornell, I was an open book. As usual, Jermaine was a true friend and just listened.

"Lisa, this is what you have to remember. God don't make no mistakes. You have to remember prayer cures all."

"I know, but I've been feeling like I just want to give up."

"You can't. Look at all I've been through in my life. Do you see me giving up? No, I keep pushing."

"You always know how to make me feel better."

"That's what friends are for," he sung in his best Dionne Warrick impression. "You need to call Juan. That situation has gone on long enough. Someone has to be the bigger person."

"I don't know. That fight was pretty bad."

"Lisa stop being so damn stubborn and call him."

"I'll call."

"You're not leaving this shop until you call him. That's your son."

"Okay, Jermaine, damn."

As I reached down in my purse to get my phone, I had to admit…Jermaine was right. The situation had gone on long enough. Besides, I missed hearing Juan's voice anyway.

Scrolling through my I-phone, I stopped on Juan's name then touched it. As the phone started ringing, I made a promise to myself that I would never go this long without speaking to my son again. When the call went to voicemail, I called back a second time and that's when a strange voice answered.

"Hello."

"Umm, may I speak to Juan?"

"May I ask whom I'm speaking with?"

"This is his mother. Who is this?"

"Ma'am this is Agent Patterson. We were hoping that someone would call his phone."

"Why, what's wrong? Is my son in jail? What's going on and why do you have his phone?"

"Well ma'am we hate to inform you, but Juan was murdered early this morning at a hotel in Los Angeles."

Instantly, I felt flushed. "No, you must have the wrong person. Juan didn't go to Los Angeles."

"I'm afraid he did, Mrs. Sanchez. Juan was working as an informant for our office and unfortunately things went wrong. We weren't able to get to him in time because he took off his wire. Now, I actually just landed back in DC right before you called. I would love to stop by your house to give you more…"

I cut him off. "Sir, you must be mistaken. My son isn't a snitch. Please stop playing games."

"Ma'am we have Lorenzo Sanchez, Pablo Galan, and Armondo Galan in custody right now in connection with his death."

It felt like my heart stopped. At that moment, something told me that this man wasn't lying. I covered my mouth with my hands as tears welled up in my eyes. "Oh my, no, please no. Don't tell me this." I dropped my phone, fell to the floor and screamed to the top of my lungs.

"What's wrong?" Jermaine asked as he tried to console me.

"Oh my God! Noooooo!" I continued to scream. By now, Kelli had made her way into the room.

"What's wrong?" she said.

"I don't know," Jermaine replied. "Lisa, tell me what happened. Is it Juan?"

"Jermaine call Rich right now," I managed to say.

I couldn't fix my mouth to say the words. My son was all I had, all I ever had and there was no way I could live with him being dead. No matter what my son did, there was no reason for Lorenzo to kill him. After Jermaine called Rich, he took off my cape then walked me outside and sat with me until Rich got there.

"Lisa…please tell me what happened."

I shook my head back and forth. "I can't believe this."

Jermaine continued to pry until Rich arrived, about twenty minutes later.

"What's goin' on Lisa?" Rich questioned as he jumped out of the car. "This shit better be good. You know I don't fuck wit' you like that anymore. I started to not even come."

"Rich! Oh my God!" I cried out as I held his chest.

"Man, what the fuck is wrong wit' her, Jermaine? Is she high?"

"No, she's not high? She was on the phone and got some bad news about your son."

Rich turned to me. "Lisa, talk to me. What happened to Juan?"

"Juan is dead Rich, he's dead!"

Both Rich and Jermaine's eyes lit up.

"What the fuck do you mean he's dead?" Rich questioned.

"Renzo killed him."

"What?" Rich yelled.

"When I called Juan's phone, some FBI agent answered and said that Juan was an informant. He said that Renzo killed him before he could get there."

I could see the pain in Rich's eyes as he told me to get in the car so he could drive me home. I'm sure he didn't want to get emotional in front of me, but he probably thought Jermaine had heard enough of our family business. However, that's far from the way I felt. I sobbed uncontrollably as Rich made his way to my house. With Juan gone I had nothing else to live for. Everyone who I ever cared for was now dead, so what the fuck was the point in living anymore?

"Who the fuck is this?" Rich asked out loud when he pulled up in the driveway.

He hadn't even turned off the car good before a strange white man with freckles, made his way toward us.

"Mr. and Mrs. Sanchez, I'm Agent Patterson. Mrs. Sanchez, I'm the one who you just spoke with."

As Rich and I got out the car, Rich didn't waste any time going off.

"Where the fuck is my son's phone?"

Agent Patterson stared at Rich a few seconds. "I'm afraid I'm gonna have to keep it for a few days before I give it back. Just in case Juan had any correspondence with Lorenzo, I'll need that for evidence."

"So, what do you want?" Rich asked in an irritated tone.

"First off, I would like to say that I'm sorry for your loss," Agent Patterson stated.

"You don't have to apologize for my son being dead because if you gave a fuck he would be here right now. All the fuck you pigs ever care about is solvin' your case!" Rich yelled.

"Now, Mr. Sanchez, your son has been an informant since he was released from prison last year. It was his choice to try and take Lorenzo Sanchez down. The good thing is, now Lorenzo is off the streets and can't hurt any of you."

Agent Patterson looked at me like he wanted a reply, but I was too distraught to say anything.

"Is that your way of sayin' you're sorry? That's your way of apologizin' for my son's death? Was my son's life worth your deal? You know what…get the fuck off my property!" Rich shouted.

"As you wish, Mr. Sanchez. But before I go, I think you should know that your son spared you for your Uncle. If that makes you feel any better."

Rich looked like he wanted to hit the agent so bad, it hurt. "Get the fuck off my property, now!"

As I watched Agent Patterson make his way back to the car, I still couldn't believe that my son was gone. Life was not only unfair…it was fucked up.

Chapter Twenty-Seven
RICH

Why now? Now that I'd repaired years of damage to me and my son's relationship, he was gone. I felt guilty. I knew I should've been there to protect him. I knew it was my fault that he'd gotten into drugs in the first place. None of this would've happened if I hadn't been such a fucked up father. Now, it was too late to tell him that I loved him. To tell him how proud I was of the man he'd become. It hurt like hell to know that Juan had turned out to be an informant, but I had to look on the bright side. At least Uncle Renzo was locked up and not me.

The love I had for Lisa had vanished some time ago, but I never could've left her in the state she was in. I put our differences aside and watched as she cried nonstop for hours. Even though I had to get to Marisol to see what her involvement was, I couldn't leave Lisa by herself. She was so fragile that I was almost positive that she would hurt herself. After debatin' what I should do, I decided to give her a couple of sleepin' pills so she could rest until I made it back.

When she finally fell asleep, the rage instantly took over my body. If I couldn't make Uncle Renzo pay, then I would get him where it would surely hurt…through Marisol. I knew I'd fucked up by not killin' that nigga when I had the chance.

Once I left Lisa's house, I got in my truck, but strangely couldn't pull off. My emotions obviously had finally gotten the best of me and I couldn't pull off without lettin' out a huge scream. Tears ran down my face as I banged on the steering wheel several times. Holdin' my head in my hands, I thought hard. How could my son be an informant? Then it dawned on me. When he was in jail, Lisa went through a lot so Juan probably felt that he needed to be home wit' her. He hated me that much that he was willin' to send me to jail in exchange for his freedom. But why didn't he? He could've told on me about Carlos, and about me killin' Jade, but never did. I couldn't help but wonder why.

So, how did he spare me, I thought. *Why did the Agent say that?*

I had so many questions for Juan, but he was no longer here to answer them. Then a light bulb went off. *Hold up, that connect. He was adamant about me not meetin' up wit' him that day. Maybe he was a Fed. Maybe Juan felt as if he owed me for that whole Kwame and Kyle situation.*

I reached in my glove compartment and pulled out some tissues to wipe my tears. My pain had turned back into rage as I thought about Uncle Renzo and Marisol. She had to know about Juan because any other time she would've called my phone a million times by now. After finally pullin' off, I headed straight to Potomac, Maryland. I was ready to get to the bottom of all of this. Even if it meant lettin' Marisol meet her maker.

Ridin' on the beltway, I turned on my radio and put my Sade CD in. I needed somethin' smooth to listen to, so I could calm my nerves. Although my anger was out of control, I still had to be smart wit' my actions. Wit' Juan bein' an informant, the FBI still could've been after me or maybe even watchin'. I'm sure they knew by now her connection wit' Uncle Renzo. I had to make sure I was smart wit' how I approached the situation. I wasn't tryin' to give those pigs a reason to come and pick me up.

Finally arrivin' at Marisol's house fifteen minutes later, I pulled up to the gate and punched in the code. *The dumb bitch hasn't changed the code yet,* I thought to myself. As I drove up to the house, I collected my thoughts to make sure I didn't do somethin' stupid. Especially if I got the feelin' that the bitch was lyin'. After placin' my gun in my waist, I used the spare key Marisol had recently given me to go inside. As soon as I walked in, Marisol's daughter, Carmen ran up and hugged me.

"Uncle Ritchie! Uncle Ritchie!" the six year old yelled. She was so excited.

Ever since me and Marisol started sleepin' together, I'd seen more and more of the kids. I picked her up and gave her a kiss on the cheek.

"Where's your mom?"

"She's in Mia's room giving her medicine."

When I walked in the room, Marisol looked up at me wit' surprise. Her eyes were red and puffy like she'd been cryin'. As she administered Mia's medication, my heart sank. She looked so weak.

"We went to the doctor yesterday. They think Mia's leukemia is back," Marisol informed. "They're running more tests, but they seem certain."

Even though I felt her pain, I couldn't let that interfere wit' what I was there for. At least she still had her daughter. My son was dead.

"So, you don't know," I said in a dry tone.

"Know what?"

"Are you gonna play stupid wit' me or are you gonna be a woman and tell me what your involvement was? You always act like you this go hard bitch. Now, you gonna act like you don't know what the fuck is goin' on."

Marisol looked at me like I was insane. "Are you gonna be that disrespectful and speak to me like that in front of my daughters? How dare you?"

Even though Carmen was on the floor playin' wit' her doll, I'm sure she was still listenin'.

"Well, get your nanny up here right now because we got some real shit to discuss!"

I walked out of the room and went back downstairs. A

few minutes later, Marisol ran down like she had a bone to pick. We ended up in the foyer by the front door.

"Rich, what the fuck is your problem?" She had her hands on her hips.

"No bitch, what the fuck is your problem?" I shot back.

"Is this a conversation that needs to happen outside? I don't like the way you're disrespecting me in my own house."

"Did you give a fuck about my son? You set him up! I can see it in your eyes."

"What the fuck are you talking about? Spill it out because I don't have the patience for this back and forth bullshit, I have a sick child upstairs that needs my attention."

"Juan is dead, and you killed him! Bitch you fed my son to the wolves."

Marisol paused for a few seconds. "What? I just talked to him yesterday. What do you mean he's dead?"

"You let Uncle Renzo talk you in to sendin' him to California so they could kill him! Were you just fuckin' me so I could let my guard down and trust you?" I felt like a fool. Here I was tryin' to play her and she was playin' me all along.

She sat on the bottom step in complete shock. "Oh my God. He used me. Lorenzo used me. Is that what you're telling me?"

"Oh, you're good. Now, you're gonna fake as if you didn't have any idea about what was goin' on." I walked up to her. "I should fuck you up right here."

Marisol jumped up. "Why would I want Juan dead? That's stupid. Hell...what did he do to make Lorenzo want to kill him?"

"Bitch, stop actin' dumb!"

At that moment, my anger could no longer be controlled and I smacked the shit out of her. I couldn't stop beatin' her after that. As I kicked and stomped her, the nanny ran downstairs to let me know that she would call the police if I didn't leave.

Marisol managed to wave her hands. "No, Audrey. Go back upstairs. Go be with Mia."

"But…" Audrey tried to say.

"Go!" Marisol replied, before the nanny did as she was told.

She looked defeated and that was somethin' I'd never seen before. She had a look of guilt about somethin' else that had nothin' to do wit' Juan, to allow me to beat her that way. Honestly, in a way I believed that she didn't know anything about Juan's death, but I needed to take his passin' out on somebody. If Uncle Renzo wanted Juan dead, it would've been done regardless if she knew or not. I just felt betrayed and at that point Marisol was the closest to Uncle Renzo I could get.

"Rich, I would never hurt you. I always loved you when I couldn't have you," Marisol said crawlin' on the floor. She held onto her side. "Do you know what I sacrificed for you in my life? I always loved Carlos, but there was something about you that I always wanted. I always saw a side of you that no one else saw…"

"And you took me for granted. You knew how I felt about you and you used it to get what you wanted!"

"To get what I wanted! What was that Rich? I've never wanted for anything. My life has always been great. There was only one thing I was missing. You were my first, my first experience. Why did you think Carlos was cheating on me? I wouldn't fuck him…that's why. It was that easy for you to console me and just that quick you fucked me. I was embarrassed. You and Carlos were the only men I'd ever been with in my life and all these years I'd been living a lie."

As Marisol poured out her heart, I wasn't listenin' to anything she had to say. I needed my son. Deep down inside, I knew Marisol might not have personally killed him, but if Juan hadn't been caught up in their business, he would still be here. All of a sudden, my mind thought about Lisa. I wanted to get back to make sure she was okay.

Marisol continued to talk as I made my way toward the door.

"Rich, where are you going? I have something to tell

you!"

I closed the door behind me as she yelled out my name several times. There was nothin' she could say that I wanted to hear.

Chapter Twenty-Eight
LISA

Now, I understood the meaning behind the quote, *life is too short*. I couldn't believe that I had to go through life knowing that my son and I were at odds before he died. Now, he was gone and I couldn't tell him how sorry I was for being so stubborn. I knew that Juan would've wanted me to be strong for him, but he was my rock, and without him I was nothing. I had no problem admitting that. Maybe if I'd realized that before, things would've turned out different.

Rich had given me some sleeping pills before he left, which only worked for about an hour. Since I'd been so addicted to them in the past, they didn't really affect me anymore. Waiting for him to come back, I turned on my television to try and get my mind on something else, but I soon realized that wasn't going to work either. I needed an escape. I needed a fix. I'd been meaning to go see Black Moe after I left the hairdresser earlier, but once I heard the news about Juan, my mind went somewhere else.

Hopping off the bed, I walked over to my vanity and looked in my drawer to see if there were at least some crumbs left in one of my little baggies. After pushing aside a few tubes of lip gloss, to my surprise, there was a package sitting right in my face. I had no idea where it had come from, but at that point I didn't care. I just needed to feel better.

Thank goodness for stash spots, I thought before placing the powder on the table. After making three lines, I took several huge sniffs then sat down on the stool. Almost instantly, I started to feel weird. Maybe I was sniffing too much at a time because my head started pounding. It started to feel like I was having an anxiety attack. *Maybe it's a combination of the sleeping pills,* I thought. I hoped like hell this side effect wouldn't prevent me from moving forward.

Suddenly, I heard someone coming through the door and up the stairs.

"Rich, is that you? Give me a minute!" I hurried and tried to hide the powder so he wouldn't snap on me. Besides, I didn't want him to take it. I needed it for later.

"Sorry, it's not Rich."

When I turned around, Denie was standing in the doorway looking completely deranged. She'd cut all of her beautiful hair off, and had on a soiled white sweat shirt. It looked like she'd been through a lot over the past year. Like she'd let herself go. The only thing she still had going for her were the deep dimples.

"Denie, what are you doing here?" I asked in shock.

Hey, Lisa it's been a while. How the hell are you?"

I hadn't seen her since our encounter in the warehouse so I didn't know what to expect. I had no idea what she was up to.

She walked toward me. "Some things just never change. Wow, still a dopefiend, huh?"

"Look, I don't have time for your insults. You need to get the fuck out of my house!"

"It's so sad how predictable you are. I told you I would get you back, now didn't I?"

It felt like I could barely breathe. "Denie, there's nothing you can do to hurt me more than I'm already hurting, so take your best shot," I said in between short breaths.

"It's no fun putting someone out of their misery. I mean that shit was so easy. I'm gonna just sit here and watch you die slowly from an overdose of poison that I planted in your vanity drawer. I didn't think it would work at first, but I see that you're so far gone that you couldn't recognize the difference between heroin and boric acid. The little conniving bitch that you are, I felt that the boric acid would suit you just fine."

"You bitch," I said between breaths. "What have you done?"

"Well, where should I begin?" she asked with a crazy expression. She got up real close in my face. "I've been doing all types of shit."

I felt damn near paralyzed as I held my chest. "You're crazy."

"No, you're fucking crazy! Do you remember what you did to me? Do you?" Denie screamed. "I shouldn't have waited this long to kill you!"

All of a sudden, I heard someone running up the stairs. I hopped it was Rich.

"Rich, help me!" I tried to yell.

It didn't take long for Denie to jump behind me, pull some type of pocket knife out of her jeans, and place it to my throat. I was too weak to fight back. When Rich finally walked into the room with his gun drawn, you could tell by the look on his face that he had no idea he'd be going to war against his daughter.

"Hello, father. I'm glad that you're here so I can kill two birds with one stone."

Rich lowered the gun slightly. "Denie, what are you doing? Where have you been?"

"I've been busy. You would've been proud of me operating like a true Sanchez. If you don't plan on shooting me, I need you to put that gun away."

As Rich put the gun down easy, his facial expression showed that he was in shock. "Denie, you don't have to do this. Lisa has been through enough."

"So, after what this bitch did to me, you still want to defend her?" Denie asked. She pressed the knife up against my throat a little harder.

"Denie, your brother is dead. No one else needs to suffer," Rich pleaded.

"See what I'm having a hard time understanding is why you're telling me that shit, like I should really give a fuck about any of you? Do you know how long I lived for this moment? Since I was in recovery I thought about how I could get Lisa back. I really didn't think you would care as much about Juan dying so I made sure that I planted that seed, and he made it easy. Hell…you all made it easy. You see, Juan was my trump card. I knew that he was the only thing you cared about Lisa. I knew that's where I could really get to you."

"Uncle Renzo killed Juan, Denie. What are you talking about?" Rich asked. He was still as puzzled as I was.

The knife was digging deeper into my skin as I fought for air. Rich was so in tune with what Denie was saying, I could tell that I was no longer a priority.

"Well, let me see how can I best explain to you slow people about how good I am. Where should I begin? For starters, it wouldn't take a rocket scientist to figure out how the hell Juan got out of jail. You see, the same man that you hated so much Rich, my boyfriend Nelson, the Feds approached him first about taking you down, but he declined. Yeah, see that's what real niggas do…they don't snitch. They would harass and pick him up for stupid shit, but all of a sudden it stopped when Juan was released. We figured out how Juan got out and it was obvious that he was offered a deal. I knew he was gonna take you down."

"You knew this while I took care of you and didn't tell me!" Rich yelled.

"For what? I had plans for you myself. All of the the text messages to Marisol…it was all me. Even that high speed chase through DC that day. It was all my plan. I had people following you from time to time and that day, I gave them orders to fuck with you a little bit," Denie bragged.

Rich looked like he'd lost his best friend as she continued.

"I started to get a little desperate because Uncle Renzo

wasn't reacting fast enough. I was hoping that Marisol would tell him about the text and he would kill Lisa to get back at you, Rich. But once you showed you didn't give a fuck about her anymore, I had to use my trump card."

"Denie, I loved you! How could you hurt me like this?" Rich asked.

"I don't wanna hear that shit. You let this bitch torture me. You let her shoot me and still allowed her to live. You chose Lisa over me. So that's why I used my trump card, Juan. And that last text message did it. When I texted Uncle Renzo and said Juan was hot, I knew he wouldn't let that go. See when Marisol got the text messages about Carlos, I'm sure you were so convincing that she ended up thinking you would never kill your own brother. However, one thing I knew for sure, Uncle Renzo wasn't going to allow a snake to live in his organization, nephew or not." Denie smiled.

"You crazy bitch. That was your brother," I said. Seconds later, I started to vomit, but she still didn't let go of me.

"So, how does it feel Lisa? Your boy is gone and now you have no one. You miserable bitch!" Denie responded.

At that moment, we heard someone coming up the steps. I prayed that it was Agent Patterson coming back. I prayed that the Feds had bugged the house for some reason and could hear what was happening. Once I saw that it was Marisol, I knew it was a matter of time before I joined my son.

"Denie, what are you doing? It's not worth it. She's still your mother," Marisol said.

"I don't have a mother, Marisol! I guess they didn't fill you in on how this bitch tortured me and made me feel like I was some kind of charity case that was left on her doorstep! My father was a whore and fucked so many bitches that he didn't even know who my mother was. Lisa, lied to me all my life and said she was my mother. But she never loved me the way she loved Juan! The whole time I've been gone, nobody cared!" Finally, Denie was showing some type of emotion.

"I did care Denie. I love you. You're always gonna be

my daughter!" Rich yelled.

"Who knows if I'm even your daughter, Rich. I have no identity!" Denie shouted.

As Denie cried, she finally loosened her grip on me. She was so emotional, that she just sat there and held the knife as if she didn't know what to do next. By that time, Rich was able to get me out of Denie's reach. Like the fake bitch she is, Marisol walked over to Denie and held her as she cried.

"What have I done, Denie? What have I done?" Marisol said as she cried, too.

"I hate them! I want both of them dead. They ruined my life!" Denie screamed as she hugged Marisol.

"Denie sweetheart, don't blame them, blame me. Lisa and Rich both did all they could when I couldn't. It's not their fault. I caused all of this chaos. Please forgive me Denie, you do have an identity. I'm your mother," Marisol admitted.

TO BE CONTINUED...

THE DIRTY DIVORCE PART 3 (The Final Chapter) COMING SOON

LCB BOOK TITLES

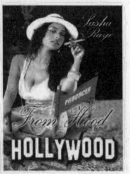

In Stores Now

Coming Soon

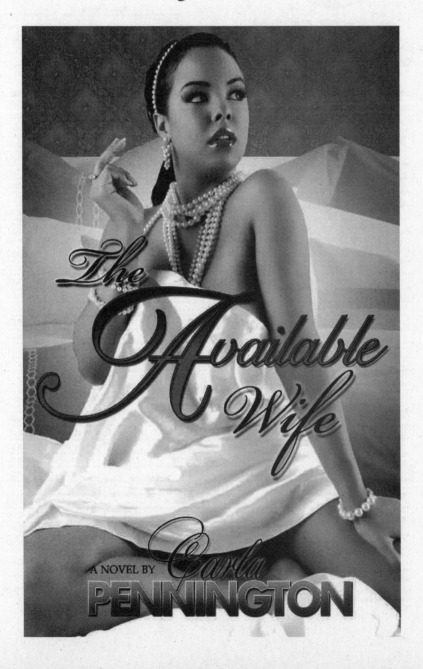

The Available Wife

A NOVEL BY Carla PENNINGTON

MAIL TO:
PO Box 423
Brandywine, MD 20613
301-362-6508

FAX TO:
301-579-9913

ORDER FORM

Ship to:	
Address:	

Date:	Phone:
Email:	

City & State:	Zip:

Make all money orders and cashiers checks payable to: **Life Changing Books**

Qty.	ISBN	Title	Release Date	Price
	0-9741394-2-4	Bruised by Azarel	Jul-05	$ 15.00
	0-9741394-7-5	Bruised 2: The Ultimate Revenge by Azarel	Oct-06	$ 15.00
	0-9741394-3-2	Secrets of a Housewife by J. Tremble	Feb-06	$ 15.00
	0-9724003-5-4	I Shoulda Seen It Comin by Danette Majette	Jan-06	$ 15.00
	0-9741394-6-7	The Millionaire Mistress by Tiphani	Nov-06	$ 15.00
	1-934230-99-5	More Secrets More Lies by J. Tremble	Feb-07	$ 15.00
	1-934230-98-7	Young Assassin by Mike G.	Mar-07	$ 15.00
	1-934230-95-2	A Private Affair by Mike Warren	May-07	$ 15.00
	1-934230-94-4	All That Glitters by Ericka M. Williams	Jul-07	$ 15.00
	1-934230-93-6	Deep by Danette Majette	Jul-07	$ 15.00
	1-934230-96-0	Flexin & Sexin Volume 1	Jun-07	$ 15.00
	1-934230-92-8	Talk of the Town by Tonya Ridley	Jul-07	$ 15.00
	1-934230-89-8	Still a Mistress by Tiphani	Nov-07	$ 15.00
	1-934230-91-X	Daddy's House by Azarel	Nov-07	$ 15.00
	1-934230-88-X	Naughty Little Angel by J. Tremble	Feb-08	$ 15.00
	1-934230847	In Those Jeans by Chantel Jolie	Jun-08	$ 15.00
	1-934230855	Marked by Capone (SOLD OUT)	Jul-08	$ 15.00
	1-934230820	Rich Girls by Kendall Banks	Oct-08	$ 15.00
	1-934230839	Expensive Taste by Tiphani (SOLD OUT)	Nov-08	$ 15.00
	1-934230782	Brooklyn Brothel by C. Stecko	Jan-09	$ 15.00
	1-934230669	Good Girl Gone bad by Danette Majette	Mar-09	$ 15.00
	1-934230804	From Hood to Hollywood by Sasha Raye	Mar-09	$ 15.00
	1-934230707	Sweet Swagger by Mike Warren	Jun-09	$ 15.00
	1-934230677	Carbon Copy by Azarel	Jul-09	$ 15.00
	1-934230723	Millionaire Mistress 3 by Tiphani	Nov-09	$ 15.00
	1-934230715	A Woman Scorned by Ericka Williams	Nov-09	$ 15.00
	1-934230685	My Man Her Son by J. Tremble	Feb-10	$ 15.00
	1-924230731	Love Heist by Jackie D.	Mar-10	$ 15.00
	1-934230812	Flexin & Sexin Volume 2	Apr-10	$ 15.00
	1-934230748	The Dirty Divorce by Miss KP	May-10	$ 15.00
	1-934230758	Chedda Boyz by CJ Hudson	Jul-10	$ 15.00
	1-934230766	Snitch by VegasClarke	Oct-10	$ 15.00
	1-934230693	Money Maker by Tonya Ridley	Oct-10	$ 15.00
			Total for Books	$

Shipping Charges (add $4.95 for 1-4 books*)	$
Total Enclosed (add lines)	$

*Shipping and Handling of 5-10 books is $6.95, please contact us if your order is more than 10 books. (301)362-6508